FUGITIVES

STARS EDGE: NEL BENTLY BOOK 5

V. S. HOLMES

FUGITIVES

Amphibian Press

13820 NE Airport Way
Suite #K471902
Portland, OR
97251-1158
United States

www.amphibianpress.online
www.vsholmes.com
ISBN : 978-1-949693-62-1

OTHER BOOKS BY
V. S. HOLMES

NEL BENTLY BOOKS
Travelers
Drifters
Strangers
Heretics
Fugitives
*Emissaries**

BLOOD OF TITANS WORLD
Smoke and Rain
Lightning and Flames
Madness and Gods
Blood and Mercy

SHORT FICTION
"Nowhere Fast" (We Came to Dance)*
"Starfall" *(Vitality Magazine)*
"The Tempest" *(Out of the Darkness)*
"Disciples" *(Beamed Up)*
"Familiar Waters" *(Love and Bubbles)*
"Mere Primordium" *(poem, Mystic Blue Review)*

**Forthcoming*

In memory of Dome

Without your kindness and faith,
and the entire Sci Fi Saturday Night
crew, this series would not exist.

AUTHOR'S NOTE

This series combines archaeology with science fiction. This book is a work of fiction, and something to be enjoyed as entertainment. I wholeheartedly believe we are far from alone in the universe.

That being said, I am an archaeologist by trade, and I know humans are ingenious and resourceful enough to build pyramids and other architectural wonders all on their own. I strive to turn the stereotypes of "ancient aliens" on their heads—and portray a world as complex and nuanced as the humans that forge our future.

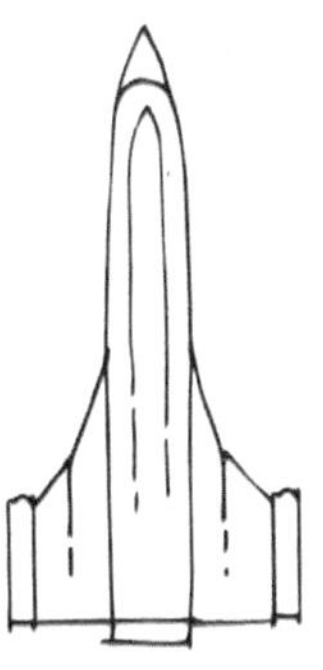

ONE

"PROXIMITY ALERT!"

Nel dismissed the warning from her screen with a snarl before tossing over to face the window. Outside space was black. Before, *Odyssey*'s soft phosphorescent ambiance had allowed her to see billions of stars scattered across the black. Here it was different. The narrow infirmary room held a single porthole at chest-height. *Chest-height if I could still stand.* The alert had been sounding for the last two days. If collision was imminent, surely they would have plowed into something by now.

The alert clicked off, only to be replaced by her door chime. Ignoring that too, she pulled herself out of bed, balancing on her left leg enough to lean against the slim porthole's sill. Her head rested on the cold acrylic wall. A massive asteroid appeared through her window. Its pocked surface loomed just outside inches of reinforced glass, seeming close enough to graze the ship's side.

Realistically, it was probably several thousand meters away. It would have been thrilling if Nel cared about asteroids. The entire journey would have been thrilling if Nel cared about anything at all.

Another asteroid drifted behind this one, and another and another, dotting the sky above their ship for miles—probably more. Nel's Earth-born depth perception was utterly useless in a place where distances were measured based on the speed of light. "Where the fuck are we?" she muttered.

The door dinged again and she jabbed a finger at the comm button. "I can't make it to PT today, sorry."

"I'm not PT," came the answering drawl.

Nel grimaced. There was only one person she wanted to see less than the hideously chipper PT tech, and it was Komodor Muda Dar Nalawangsa. "What do you want?"

"Open up and I'll tell you."

"If it was important, it'd be one of the hundred fucking notices pinging around my computer screen. I'm not interested and really don't want to talk to anyone."

"As evidenced by your treatment of those who still attempt to visit." He quipped. "Just open the door."

"I can't reach it," she lied.

"I can bypass the security of your room and set off every single med alarm. The whole team would come rushing in there to see what's wrong and probably jab you with needles."

Oh fuck right off, you pompous asshole. Still, his clever threat was not Nel's idea of a good time. She hopped over to her chair. A glance at the brakes told her it wasn't going to roll away the second she put her weight in it like the first two times she'd transferred herself unsupervised. Seated, she shoved herself over to the door and slammed her hand onto the panel. There was a pause, then the door hissed open.

Dar leaned on the wall across the hall from her. Immaculate, of course, and still wearing his officer's robe—despite his insistence that there was no command here beyond the flight crew. Soft chimes and the low sound of conversation drifted in with the distinct scent of iodine and something that might have been curry.

"Make it quick." She remained in the doorway, blocking entry to her rooms. These four monochrome walls were hers, even if she hated them, and she wasn't about to let Dar's snippy self sully what was shaping up to be a perfectly miserable wallowing session.

"Yeah, you're so damn busy."

"PROXIMITY ALERT."

The bell rang for its allotted three times. Nel didn't know how they managed to make something as dire as a proximity alert sound boring, but they'd succeeded with flying colors.

"Where even are we? And what day is it?"

He snorted. "You don't know?"

"What am I supposed to do," she sneered, "check the position of the sun? Oh wait—we don't have one!"

"You have a comm and computer. Don't act like you're imprisoned here by anything other than your own shitty attitude."

She glared. Truthfully, she barely looked at her computer to do anything other than swipe away notifications that she'd missed yet another appointment or meeting, or dismiss the incessant proximity alerts. She slept or she didn't, neither mattered or helped her mood.

"We've been traveling for five weeks, twenty-three days of which you've been conscious. More or less." He rolled his eyes and gestured to her room. "You want answers, you're going to have to let me in. This isn't for general consumption."

Something that resembled curiosity, if curiosity was born of apathetic boredom, unfolded in her mind, and was just as quickly squashed. *It's not like I can help them with any of this. Not anymore.* With a final pointed, if childish, glare she backed up and gestured dramatically to the room.

He swept in, scanning the untidiness with disdain. "You don't have a chair?"

She smacked the side of her wheelchair. "Only this one and you can't have it."

He shook his head and went to the window. He was probably checking his own reflection instead of watching the seriously close asteroid tumbling above them.

"You still haven't seen your mother. Or anyone, actually."

"What, you're talking to her now?"

Dar snorted. "Hardly, never met the woman. I just hacked your door's data logs."

"Gross," Nel snapped. "How is who I visit any of your business?"

"It's time you got out of here. You've been wallowing in your own misery for weeks. You saved Earth. You lived through it. You're approved for the highest-tech prosthetic we can make—which you would know if you went to a single one of your appointments. Get over yourself long enough to be grateful."

Nel snarled and turned away. She hated Dar. She hated the lack of empathy. She hated the pretentious, spoiled thoughts in the man's perfectly groomed head. Mostly, though, she hated how much he reminded her of Lin.

"I mean, it's obvious you have some feelings," Dar observed. His voice had dipped into something other than his usual bark. She couldn't place it, but it sounded as if he were about to impart some sacred knowledge.

Nel wished he would just leave her alone. "No shit, Sherlock." She had a lot of feelings, if you counted each specific flavor of her anger and apathy separately. Fuck, by that measure she probably had more feelings than space had shitty dark corners. And, judging by however long they'd been traveling, space had about a zillion of those.

He sighed. "I have an investment in you, and I'm less than pleased that it appears to be almost impossible to make that pay off."

That made her scowl deeper. "I'm a person, not an investment, you creep."

"Right now you're pathetic," Dar muttered.

The numb chill that permeated from the hole inside her chest spread in a brittle layer just under her skin. Dar's words shattered its surface. A flame of her anger licked up through the cracks. "Stop being a fucking alien!"

"Stop being a bitch maybe I would!" Dar snapped back. "The minute you get over yourself, I'll start treating you like an adult."

"Your ship blew off my leg, goddammit, I can't just get over that," she shouted, shoving her tray table away. It crashed against the far wall with a clatter. The flash of anger fizzled back into numbness.

"I respect that. But I need you to respect that what I've got is a lot of problems. And not enough people to solve them."

"That why we're drifting around some fucking rocky minefield?"

The question had the desired effect—Dar's face settled from his judgmental sneer into something that was either stony anger or reserved frustration. She never could really tell with Dar. "We're out here because it's the only place we can hide right now. We're out here because we don't know where we're going next. We're out here because your infuriating and ridiculously determined ex-girlfriend has been point-three sectors behind us the entire way. You really don't read a single notice, do you? This is all old news to pretty much everyone in the fleet."

"Well, I've been busy." She braced for the inevitable quip about what she could have possibly been busy with, but to her surprise, it never came.

"We're safe out here, but it won't last forever. And we burn too hot when we're running to waste any power on our analysis systems. We could really use your help. No one else saw as many stages of this investigation as you."

She shook her head. "Look, I'm not one of you. I have no idea what half the stuff I saw down there even was, let alone what it did or how. It was fun, I guess, to play for a while, but I'm not cut out for this sci-fi shit. Just get out of my room."

"Nel, next week it won't be your room."

"What?"

"You're no longer in need of acute medical care. You're scheduled for a psych eval and assuming you pass it—and despite your nasty attitude, you will—you're moving to the residential units and starting service shifts."

"What?" For the first time since she woke, very real concern spread in a chill through her body. *Psych eval?* Would they flag her because of her temper? What about how she had handled Mikey's death? Or Gretta's? Or Paul's? Or facing down her own in the bitter cold of New England's wilderness, or consumed by raging fires in exchange for Earth's safety? Nel wasn't a therapist, but there was a lot to flag on her chart, surely, and most of those flags looked pretty fucking red. And that wasn't even including the dreams, the number of times she woke drenched in sweat with a thousand voices screaming accusations in her skull. "Why a psych eval?"

"It's protocol. To make sure you're not a danger to yourself or others. You've been through a lot—all of us have."

She glared up at him, wondering if that was actual sympathy in his voice. "I'm just not a fan of therapists. And I don't see why I need to move at all."

"Look, I pulled every string I could to keep you here so far. But it's selfish now. You're wasting the medics' time and frankly, we really need the bed."

She paused. "Why do you need the bed?"

"We're a refugee fleet, Bently. Most of us escaped during firefights. You're not the only one who lost a limb. You're just lucky you only lost one." He paused in her doorway. "You need to be done wallowing."

Nel glared at him, wishing IDH had outfitted her with something useful, like laser eyes to zap jerks. She squeezed her eyes closed. Pressure built in her ears, between her eyes, the background mutters of several dozen accusing voices crescendoing every time her lids slid shut. When she opened them again, she was alone. She wasn't done wallowing. No longer wallowing meant she'd have to actually do something and she hadn't the faintest idea where to start.

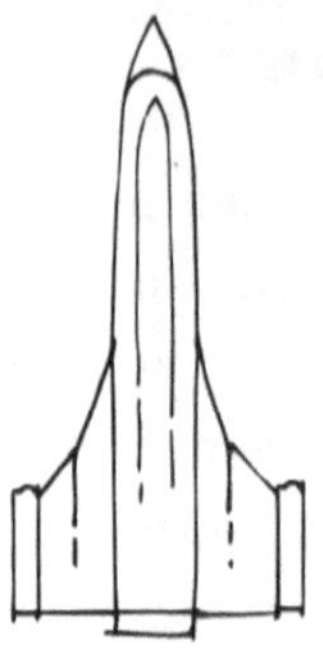

TWO

The thousands of unanswered emails cluttering Nel's university inbox as an associate professor had nothing on the utterly overwhelming slew of notifications and missives currently crowding her screen. She'd always preferred dirt and pages and handwriting in the field to the carefully cataloged tablets back at the university labs. *I just wish there was something besides tech out here.*

Wincing at the pull on her healing scars, she leaned over the edge of the bed and fished her field book out of her pack. Her hand was stiff, and writing wasn't as easy as it once was. Her handwriting was so bad to begin with, she assumed it was impossible to make her already poor scrawl worse, but apparently she was wrong.

Psych Eval
Orientation
See Mom

She squinted at the list, then crossed off the last item, replacing it with:

Apologize to Mom.

A glance at her computer told her that a confirmation for the first task had already been sent to her sometime after Dar's visit. Hopefully, whatever old quack they had doing her eval knew as much about her as anyone else did up here: nothing beyond a bad attitude. She could fake being snarky and shitty—as opposed to depressed and shitty or furious and shitty—for however long it took to prove she wasn't about to send herself or anyone else out the airlock.

Her heart twisted when she saw the name on the confirmation message:

Sender: LZachariah
Subject: Psychological Evaluation 2-9-43-0900

Dr. Bently,
I'm delighted to hear you're ready to be discharged. I heard you were among our fleet and hoped you'd reach out when you were ready to speak. While I won't be able to see you in person, as I'm a passenger on The Yarmouth, I look forward to seeing you via our secure vid-chat tomorrow morning (September 2nd).

After confirming that the current day was the first of September, she sat and glowered at the name for a moment. She was looking forward to seeing a familiar face. Really. She was. But she'd preferred a face that wasn't trained to see right through her bullshit. She didn't have the energy for a proper lie.

With her appointment confirmed, she eyed her dwindling to-do list. She really couldn't avoid the final one, especially if they were expected to move in together. *But I'd rather seem like I have my shit together first.* Scrolling down, she found her service assignment—stockist in the cantina.

Heaving a breath, she dragged a change of ship-issued clothes out of her bag and began the awkward process of changing. The iron-gray sweats and soft tank were identical to the set she'd had on previously, but at least these were clean. She wished suddenly for a good button-up or a jacket, just for the illusion of armor. There was no mirror.

She glanced at the shelf in the room's corner. It held a black hoodie she had found folded over the end of her bed one morning. At the time, too angry to accept what she considered charity, she'd shoved it into the cubby without looking. Now, she shook it out, brows rising. It was from her undergrad college, soft with wear. *Mom.*

"Computer, where is the cantina located?"

"*Recursive*'s cantina is on deck D, sector 32."

"Thanks. Download map to my personal comm, please."

"Downloads unavailable."

She scowled, unsure of what pissed her off more—that the luxuries of *Odyssey* weren't available here or that she'd gotten used to them in the first place. With a last glance at the stranger in her mirror, she wheeled to her door and tapped it open. The conversations outside were still faint, and the smell of antiseptic was stronger. With a steadying breath, she wheeled into the hall and turned left.

The patient rooms clustered around a central node where a medic station stood, currently manned by a girl who looked no more than sixteen. She glanced up as Nel approached. Her colorless eyes were framed between uneven bangs and sallow circles.

"Yeah?"

Nel stopped at the edge of the desk, mercifully low enough that she could speak over it. "Do you think I could talk to someone about moving?"

"Who're you?"

"Ah, Dr. Nel Bently. That's one 'l' on the first name, one 'e' on the last."

The medic pursed her lips, scanning the patient log. "I got an Annelise by that surname—"

A shrill alarm pinged from a room just beside the medic station. The girl's exhausted eyes flicked over and she jabbed a finger at the cluster of buttons beside her screen. "EM to 27B: Code Blue." She waited until a team of medics rushed to answer the alarm before turning back to Nel. "I'm sorry, you said your name was what?"

"Annelise Bently," Nel explained with a grimace. If it wouldn't be blasphemy against her paternal grandmother—whom she never met—she'd have changed it long ago.

"Right." She raised her voice over the still shrieking alarm. "The discharge papers have been waiting for you to confirm since you were signed off physically. All you need is a psych eval and you'll be set. I see that's scheduled for tomorrow."

"Yeah. After that?"

"Once we receive Dr. Lieberman's notice the following day, assuming you pass, you will be cleared to leave."

"Oh, I'll pass," Nel muttered. Frankly, the only reason she was willing to be stuck between the four gray walls of her medical room was her own refusal to move. Not a random doctor's orders, and certainly not due to a psych hold.

"Your discharge will arrive on your personal computer and once you've signed, you'll be good to go." She stared at Nel for a moment, blinked, then asked, "Anything else?"

"Which way to the main cantina? I don't have a map."

Again, the medic delivered a long blink before her answer. "Follow this corridor down to the main one. You'll see indicators from there. It's the yellow light. If you get lost just ask the system."

"Gotcha. Thanks again." She headed back down the hall where her room was located. Shoving aside the wave of discomfort that came with asking for help, she turned back. "Oh, do you know—"

Both of them fell silent as the alarm in 27B turned to a low, long beep. One medic emerged, wiping bright yellow bile from their smock. "Emalie, update Mr. Sanez's records. TOD: 1328."

Nel forgot her inane question. Dar's comment about her selfish monopolizing of a medical room echoed through her head. He might be a jerk, but he wasn't wrong. Ducking her head, she escaped as quickly as she could.

The Recursive was big—at least, it felt big, compared to the few transport ships Nel had seen. The corridors were broad and sparse, utilitarian almost. Perhaps its previous use hadn't called for the comforts of *Odyssey.* The bands of lights along the floor were the same soft glow, but chips in the paint showed their colors weren't from different species of phosphorescent bacteria, like the space station's. Finding the thin tube colored gold, Nel set off.

The proximity alert sounded again and Nel winced. It was much louder out here. *How can they risk audio?* she wondered. That was something that, along with the events of the last few days, she probably would have learned had she bothered to read any of her messages.

She longed for a map, some overview to understand this new space and her place within it. Except, like most ships, IDH or otherwise, she was fairly certain she didn't have one. The lights on the floor split, the gold and orange extending straight, while the softer green and blue cut right, toward what she felt might be the center of the ship. She stopped, rolling stiffness from her wrists and forearms. It might have looked easy—or even lazy, if you were an asshole—but piloting a wheelchair used an interesting set of muscles, ones more used to shaking a heavy screen of dirt.

She flipped open her field book on her lap and made a few tick marks on her rough sketch of the corridors she'd navigated thus far. It seemed to cut an arc from one end—where the medical and technological areas were concentrated, based on the signs she'd noted along the way—to the residential areas. She eyed the door through which the blue and green lights disappeared. A tiny Spanish sign under a faded and scratched plastic cover was tacked to its center.

Sector 32 Deck C
Hydroponics
Recyclers
Databank

Nel jotted down the information beside the line that indicated the corridor on her map, but where those places ultimately were in relation to her was unclear. After another half-remembered PT stretch for her wrists, she continued on. Despite not making a single wrong turn—much to her delight—it took the better part of twenty minutes to find the cantina at the very end of the corridor.

The cantina, like most of the larger communal areas, was a broad, curved chunk of the outer ship.

A strip of windows lined the edge, overlooking space. The lights were the gold of afternoon and the sound of the kitchen cleanup dominated the space. Nel edged up to the open doorway, watching stragglers pick out food and find seats. Conversation and laughter were faint and she saw more serious faces. Many dined alone.

A faint rumble rose from her gut, but she bypassed the circuit of food and made straight for the expressionless person chopping protein blocks behind a counter. "Excuse me?"

He didn't answer. After she cleared her throat and repeated herself, adding a wave, he glanced up. Using his chin, he tapped a button on the collar of his vest. "Sorry, upped the cancelation. Can't think with all this noise. What's up?"

Nel flashed a strained smile. "I'm supposed to have service orientation. Where would I go for that?"

"We're dealing with lunch stuff, but why don't you grab a bite and a table if you want. I'll let the boss know you're waiting. Shouldn't be too long."

"Cool, thanks."

She watched him chin-tap back into auditory solitude, then turned and moved slowly down the line of food. Most of it was arrayed in covered single servings, digital readouts scrolling through various languages. Nel was dubious. Despite the labels, Nel did not believe for one second that the gray squares were actual pork chops. After some brief reconnaissance, she grabbed a small plate and packet of instant coffee and headed to the inventory check.

She hung back, watching as the person in front of her gave their name before disappearing into the seating area. When it was her turn, she flashed what she hoped was a not-too-strained smile and offered her name.

"You're already registered for lunch," the woman said apologetically.

Nel frowned. "What does that mean? Sorry, first time here."

"It means you've already had your second ration for the day. I can use one of tomorrow's slots if you'd like."

Nel recalled the meal she had turned away just before noon. *Rations.* "Uh, yeah that's fine. Thanks." With the awkward interaction through, she retreated to one of the single tables tucked along the wall closest to the kitchen entrance.

Forget the haint blue of her mother's front porch ceiling, forget the quirk of Lin's mouth, forget Dar falling flat on his ass—the thing Nel wanted to see most in the world was a goddamn pizza. She stared down at her plate. The thin slice was doused in runny tomato and a sprinkling of the dusty non-dairy cheese. There was even a red slice of protein to simulate a pepperoni. It contained 30 percent of Nel's daily caloric intake, had added daily vitamins, and a blessed sprinkle of MSG to combat the slightly earthy flavor of plain protein. What it sure fucking wasn't, was actual pizza. She heaved a self-pitying sigh and shoved most of it into her mouth. It really wasn't awful. After far too few bites, she took a long, slow sip of the thin, greasy coffee. *Yikes.* Now that was fucking terrible.

"That bad?"

Nel shook her head, swallowed helplessly, then glanced up. A man who was surely the size of an entire shuttle loomed, arms crossed, over her table. "It's fine, just used to the real stuff."

"That's as real as we get here. You Bently?"

"Yeah, here to report for work, I guess." She glanced down at her wrist, though whether it was in search of a wrist-comm or an analog watch, she couldn't say.

"Been on our service list awhile—medical just clear you?"

"Yeah," she lied. "So what am I supposed to do? And when? No one really told me what this whole thing is about."

"I take it you still need to watch the general orientation vids?"

"Guess so."

"Well, after you finish your Michelin 5-star meal we'll get you started. Just about everyone is expected to contribute a shift every other cycle—or two on, two off. Evens out. You got wheels, so I'll probably throw you on stock for now, unless," he glanced back, holding the swinging door open for her as he did, "you have cooking experience?"

"Not with the stuff we have up here. I'd make it worse."

"Fair enough," he chuckled. The kitchen was designed for economy of movement, tiny but meticulously organized. Four others bustled about the cramped space, only one sparing a glance at Nel as she followed the kitchen manager. "You'll have time to meet them all when we ain't cleaning up the lunch rush. I'm Mikey, by the way."

Nel's heart attempted to flop from her throat straight onto the scratched floor between them.

He turned back with a frown at her gasp. "You cool?"

"Sorry," she managed to breathe out. "Had a friend, same name."

"Ah," his eyes softened. "Well, I mostly go by M, or Big-rig round here. If it's easier."

"Awesome. I like Nel, but Bently's catching on—use it too when I'm mentally berating myself."

That earned a snort. "Through that door is the larder and what we've managed to cobble together to work as an interim recycler for our food waste. Shuttle to the ship that does most of our recycling work only leaves about once a month. Was pretty ripe in here for the first two weeks until we figured something out," he confided with a humorless chuckle.

Nel poked her head through the doors. Half a dozen shelves held crates of uncut protein blocks. Another few pallets contained carefully stacked vegetables and fruit. Racks at the other end held preserved food, waiting for reconstitution. A mess of buckets, basins, hoses, and pipes squatted against the other wall, occasionally letting out a contented, if malodorous belch.

"Wait, Big-rig," she asked, turning, "where'd you say the stock room was?"

"You're in it."

She stared. "Larder" brought to mind overflowing shelves of jars and preserves, tinned fish and clotted cream—whatever the fuck that was. Rationing made much more sense now: no matter how you stretched it, this wasn't enough food for the several thousand passengers.

"We get deliveries from the other ships. Less often than our recycler transfer, but at least they're regular."

Nel didn't answer. Clearly there wasn't an answer bleak enough. She cleared her throat and tried a firm nod. "Well I'm glad to help."

He gave her another soft glance. "Why don't you get up to speed before we go into the details. You can watch the vids on our inventory computer in my office. Hopefully they'll help answer some of your bigger questions. And I'll do my best, too." He wrested open a rusty door in the nearest wall and gestured her in. It wasn't so much an office as a housekeeping closet putting on airs with the aid of a folding chair and computer propped on the middle shelf of the rickety rack in the back. He tapped the computer into wakefulness before edging his bulk from the room. "Just request the general orientation vid. I've gotta go make sure Jeff isn't burning something—man's like a broken clock—only right once a day and he already used today's up. Come find me when you're done."

"Will do." Nel nodded. When the door was half closed, she turned to stare at the flickering screen. She appreciated the flawless tech IDH had the privilege of stuffing into every single corner much better now that she was faced with something that looked like a holoscreen prop from '90s TV.

"Computer: run the general orientation video please."

"Playing video 1 of 23."

Nel groaned and slouched back in her chair.

A smiling Black woman appeared on the screen, wearing a bright yellow sleeveless robe over her Founder's issue electrosuit. "Welcome to *The Recursive*. I'm Sal and I'll be guiding you today on your virtual orientation. First, we want to remind you that until further notice, all recorded audio communications between ourselves and any other vessel is strictly prohibited. Live-audio format is permitted only in emergency or medical instances. Audio within our ship is welcomed."

The image flickered and Sal's cheerfully beaming face pixelated into a schematic of the ship.

"Holy shit, an actual map." Nel leaned forward, taking note of the ship's shape. It was massive enough that even at the farthest end of the cantina, she could barely glimpse a third of it.

"This may seem restrictive, or concerning, or even lonely," Sal speculated. "But we are far from alone out here!" The image zoomed out, now flying backward as the cartoon ship was joined by four others. "Our ship is one in a fleet of five. We are joined by *The Yarmouth*, of terrestrial-tech. It is versatile and currently houses much of our nonperishable resources. *La Fe De Amor* and *Āl Sinai* are both Los Pobledores origin, and are the largest and best-suited for our journey. Both contain impressive hydroponics that currently allow us to augment your nutrition bases with vegetables and fruits. While we all have recycling systems, the civilian cruiser *Chéngnuò* is our main recycling unit and where most of our waste is processed, and therefore where the majority of our protein is produced. And that brings me to our own ship. We're a research vessel, and as such house the majority of the medical resources, laboratory facilities, and databases. Transfer to another ship is not currently possible, with the rare exception of those who have particular skills." Sal still beamed, but Nel caught the glint in the woman's eye.

The videos wound on, concise and optimistic, an unhoused parent telling their child it was "camping" when they slept in their Corolla. Half a dozen clips were entirely about IDH and the history of their relationship to Earth and the Founders. Nel tuned most of it out, though she was distantly impressed how many actual facts made it in. Then the screen transitioned back to Sal for a final time. "Our people are our greatest strength. We're confident that, together, we will establish a new community built on egalitarianism, transparency, and cooperation."

Nel's gaze bore into Sal's. Behind the bright smile and wide eyes flickered fear. Sal knew. And Nel knew it too. Call it what you like: revolutionaries, intrepid explorers, pilgrims of the stars. They had rationed food, dwindling fuel, and fading resolve. They were refugees.

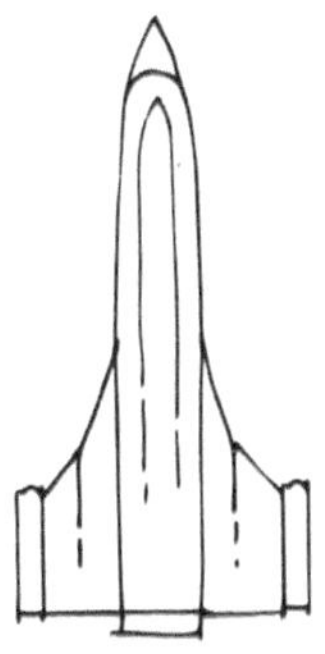

THREE

Nel's next hurdle came at 1613 bearing a tray of chop suey and key lime pie. The dinner rush had barely begun, and Nel heaved the last rack of protein onto the prep station. "Should be the lot of it," she offered with a sigh. "Gonna dip into tomorrow's if we're not careful."

Lee made a sound that belonged nowhere near anyone's food. "Telling ya, this place is gonna go bells-up 'fore we ever reached that fucking prick's utopia. Or whatever he's selling now."

"Prick is right. Gotta grab that pallet of—" Nel turned back to the storage room. Her words died. A middle-aged woman in standard-issue pants and a loose, collared blouse moved along the line of food. She picked out a few items, fussing with a sauce packet, before stopping by the inventory check. Nel watched her mother turn and scan the mostly empty tables. Without her usual neutral makeup, Mindi looked much older than when they last spoke, and gray overtook her hair. *How many of those grays are my fault?* If Nel were being honest, she'd bet they all were. She hadn't been an easy kid. *Or an easy adult.* Mindi chose a smaller table by the window and, to Nel's relief, sat down alone.

For all her searching, her research, her mental begging to see her mother again, she didn't have the slightest idea what to say. *"Hey, how do you like space?"* seemed like a poor place to start. Nel was a runner. And when there were no more places to which she could retreat, Mindi had made a point to always be there. Without questions—well, without too many—and certainly without judgment. There had been times when that security was the only thing, besides Mikey, that held Nel together.

"Teska, tell Big-rig I'm sorry. I gotta go."

"It's mealtime, Nel, c'mon—"

"That's my mom, man." Ducking her head, Nel scooted across the room to the line, grabbing a tray and piling it up without really looking at the fare. She was barely hungry, but food would give her something to focus on other than panic and guilt. Previously, when Nel slunk back into her mother's good graces, she was hiding hickeys and beer, not an entire missing limb. *She knows,* Nel reminded herself, wheeling the long way through the rows of tables. She longed to run across the room and fling herself into her mom's arms. Or just run in general. Her grip on the wheels was clunky, but she managed a good clip. Nel drew a breath and cleared her throat.

She paused a few yards away from her mother's table, tray balanced on her knees. The glimmer of the tubes of light cast her mother's face in gold. "Care for some company?"

Mindi whirled, eyes widening at her daughter's familiar drawl. Her tray clanged against the table as she shoved her seat out and rushed to Nel. Before she could think, Nel was enveloped in warm, soft arms and the scent of rosewater. How she managed to bring perfume on board a refugee spaceship, Nel would never know, but if anyone could, it was Mindi. Nel's stubbornness hadn't appeared from nowhere, after all. "Baby. Oh, Anna, my darling."

Nel could barely hear through the rushing blood in her ears, the roar of emotion rampaging through her chest. The 117.3 trillion kilometers, twenty-seven months, and two bouts of cryosleep had never seemed so large until she felt the press of her mother's hug, the soft hum of her voice—the first voice Nel had ever heard.

She locked her arms around Mindi. Had she always been this small? Had Nel always been able to squeeze her this tight?

Mindi drew back abruptly, pushing Nel's mop out of her eyes and peering into her daughter's face. "I'm sorry. You're probably still sore."

"It's okay," Nel smiled, hoping it looked less awkward than it felt. "Got some hugs to catch up on, after all."

"You sure do." She straightened with a tired sigh. "You really joining me for dinner?"

"If you don't mind."

"I mind that this is the first time," Mindi pointed out.

Nel winced. "I'm sorry. I should have seen you sooner—"

"If you're about to tell me the line the nurses—medics, I suppose?—tried on me every time I insisted on seeing you, just can it. I didn't raise you for thirty-nine years not to know when you're lying. Let's just put it behind us. I'm glad you're up. I missed you every second."

Hot tears burned down Nel's cheeks and she pressed the heel of her palm against her eyes. "You too, Mom. I'm so sorry."

"We're both here and safe. That's all I ever wanted." She pulled away, fixing Nel with a stern glare. "You do owe me about a hundred answers, however, and you'd best start quick, missy."

Nel chuckled and nodded to the table. "Food too, at least?"

Her mom reached for the handles of the chair and Nel batted her away. "I got it."

"You could use some practice. You parked on my toe."

Nel winced and apologized again before pulling up at the table. "Hopefully this is just temporary. PT said I'll be limping around with crutches and prosthetics soon enough."

Mindi grabbed her hand. The care in Mindi's gaze was usually a warm blanket, but right then it was stifling. "You're allowed to be upset, hon."

She looked away, forking salad into her plate. "Yeah, well, I'm a bit tired of upset and sad and mad. Sounds like everyone else is too."

"Then let's ignore it," her mom stated briskly.

Nel stared at her mother, marveling. Here sat a research librarian from western Massachusetts, hair cut into the style that inspired fear in the heart of any server, dumping a flavor packet over an insect-protein patty on a spaceship like it wasn't anything. Like it was just another damned Tuesday. She glanced up and caught her daughter staring. "What?"

"You're incredible."

She snorted. "Is it Mother's Day?"

"No clue. You're just taking all of this," Nel gestured to the cantina, to the foreign rocks looming outside, "in such stride. Like, we're in fucking space, Mom, and you're acting like it's the Springdale Co-op food court."

Mindi pursed her lips. "If this were, I'd be getting one of those soft pretzels that little corner place always has."

Nel chuckled. "I just never thought you'd be okay with all of this. I wasn't."

Mindi met Nel's eyes. "Honey, neither was I. By the time you arrived I'd been here three weeks. It's been eight now. There's a lot you didn't see. A lot of confusion. Fear. But what good does it do?"

Nel's heart clenched. She'd been so wrapped up worrying about how it would feel to have her mother see her minus a single leg that she hadn't considered what Mindi was going through, minus an entire planet. "I'm so sorry. I should have been there for you. I should have explained it. Fuck, I've been an asshole—"

"Language, Anna," she reprimanded, but her eyes softened and her hand slipped over Nel's.

"What happened?" Nel asked, setting aside her fork. Her painkillers were starting to wane, judging by the ache building in her leg and hands, and her heart was too battered for her to stomach even something as sweet as pie. *Space pie*, she reminded herself.

"It was complicated, after you left, of course. There was a disaster in your wake. Not in so much as legal stuff—everyone knew you went on a business trip. But with the government and the surveillance and everything, it was just so bizarre. I tried saying it was a site on government land, then I tried saying it was because of what happened to Michael, they were concerned you were in danger. There's only so much lying you can do. Then, people started getting sick. A lot of people. It's not something I'd wish anyone to live through. The isolation, the fear, the uncertainty. Political factions warred over whose fault it was, so much that no one was bothering to find a cure, a fix. It got bad, and then it got worse. People were dying everywhere from illness, but also their own hand. And there were attacks—whole communities and families suddenly just gone without a trace." Her face grew shadowed, and Nel was struck again by how much her mother had aged.

You're technically two years farther apart than you were last time you saw each other. It was a terrible thought, a hideous reality that she had feared but was unable to fully comprehend until now. "I'm sorry I wasn't there."

"I'm not. It wasn't anybody's idea of fun." Mindi tried another smile. "It was months later, I was in my book club—though it was virtual then, to try and flatten the curve of the virus. Our phones all went off with a breaking news alert. Someone had found a vaccine. And it worked."

"Co-Chair McNally?"

"We had never heard of him, of course, and few even knew about IDH at the time, even their cover story. But we didn't really care. It was that bad. The treatment worked, so we didn't really care that it was the devil who handed it to us."

Nel winced. "I guess not."

"It was only afterward when the headlines started running—IDH was actually this huge superpower. They had spaceships. They were from space. And I knew these were the same people who took you. It seemed so wild, but after a year and a half, we weren't in the position to argue. Of course, there were many who didn't want to get vaxxed. Some survived. Many didn't. It was about a month after I got my shot that everything went dark. It was rolling—we heard about blackouts, entire countries cut off. And then it was us. For our safety, they said." Stress lined her face and Nel reached out a hand.

"Mom, you don't have to—"

"It's important. And it happened. Even if it hurts to acknowledge. Even if it changed us forever."

Nel squeezed Mindi's hand, throat tight with tears for her mother, tears for herself. Tears for their entire planet and the way of life that they could never return to, even if they were ever able to find their way back to Earth. That world would not be the one either of them had left.

"A woman came to my door three months ago. Said she represented some group that you worked with. I thought she was some religious nut—there were a lot of them that sprouted up during that time. Then she said she knew you."

Nel frowned. Lin had been with the mission for most of their time on Earth, and the precious few days Nel had gone to ground with Los Pobledores, she had been busy trying to blow up Earth. Right? "Who was it?"

"Tall dark woman, beautiful hair, about my age. Ms. Gamal of the elk-something?"

"Alkhalaaq?"

"That's the one."

Nel grinned, her heart warming. "Max. She was on the project back on Earth. Mikey's aunt, actually."

Mindi's brows rose. "Really? She seemed like such a nice woman."

"Hey," Nel snapped. "I'm not nice?"

"You, I expect to take off at the drop of a hat. She seemed a bit more centered than you will ever be, my dear."

Nel glared but had to admit her mother was right. She always was. "Well, maybe my shrink will help with that."

Her mother paused, genuine surprise crossing her face. "You're in therapy?"

Nel lifted a shoulder. "Kind of?"

"Because of Michael?"

Nel floundered, wishing suddenly she hadn't mentioned it at all. In IDH therapy may have been the norm, but in rural New England it wasn't. At best it was somewhere rich housewives went to process their narcissism. At worst it was court-mandated as an alternative to prison. *But we're not in Greenfield. Or Jasper Hill. Or anywhere even close anymore.* For an odd, dizzying moment, Nel realized that, for the first time in perhaps her entire life, she and her mother were on equal ground. Both alien. Both human. Both lost in a world running from something neither could understand or even see.

Mindi cleared her throat softly. "What about where you were? I know pieces of what happened—the medical parts. But no details."

"Well, guess I'm healed up enough," Nel offered, unsure of where to start.

"I was told you'd be discharged weeks ago. Were there complications?"

"No." Nel winced. "I didn't want to see anyone. I mean, more like—"

"You didn't want me to see you. Like this."

"I-I'm getting better about it, though. I have to pass a psych eval tomorrow morning. But then I'll be set. I can come home."

They both winced at the word, Nel watching as Mindi's gaze dropped to the empty plate between them. "They said you could room with me. I can show you around the ship," she offered with a slight smile.

Nel chuckled. "That's the last thing I ever thought to hear, you know."

Her mom raised an eyebrow. "Your old mom is pretty capable, you know. Even if this is all a bit strange and unexpected."

"I should have been there."

"Let's not worry about 'should have,' alright? You might have a lot of explaining to do but I'm just happy you're here to do it."

Nel nodded tightly, swallowing past the lump in her throat. "Guess I almost wasn't."

"I'm told I have the captain—or whatever that snippy Filipino boy's rank is—to thank."

Nel laughed, a proper laugh. Dar would die a thousand deaths if he heard anyone call him a snippy boy. *Accurate, though.* "He's not Filipino. I mean, not exactly. He grew up out here. His parents did too. And I'll answer your questions. All of them," she promised, chest tight at the mere thought. "I just want you to know the answers might not be pretty. Or actually any better than questions."

"Well, let's start somewhere familiar," Mindi offered, serving Nel then herself thin slices of chocolate-flavored protein as if it was from Burdick's. "If I recall, there was a woman."

Nel dumped a packet of dehydrated raspberries onto her food with a rueful smile. "Isn't there always?"

Prickling sweat accompanied the sound of screaming weaseling through Nel's skull. She squeezed her eyes shut. The view of massive asteroids was almost hypnotic, despite the discomfort. Or perhaps because of it, like a glimpse of a very far drop. Because of the danger. The screams she kept hearing weren't real. Just like Mikey's answers to her every plea and frustration and moment of self-doubt as she trekked alone over the White Mountains: it was just in her head. *Except I'm also in my head.*

It would be easier if she could recognize the voice. Instead, it was a twisted sound of a thousand voices, unintelligible save for the certain feeling of condemnation. Beeping scattered the other sounds—real or imagined—and she rolled back to her computer from the window. She scrubbed the lack of sleep from her eyes before peering at her comm. She had never been so grateful to hear an alert.

NOTICE: Psychological Evaluation Reminder.

Raking a hand through her mop of hair in a futile attempt to look tidy, she rolled her shoulders and adjusted the tiny lens held upright beside her computer's holographic screen. Even given the poor quality of the connection, she looked like shit.

A black square preluded Zachariah's appearance. She had known he was technically among them—she had seen him leaving just moments before she retreated to IDH and Lin and the fiery confusion that awaited them. Even if she wasn't quite sure how to feel about him, he made the yawning void surrounding them seem a bit less empty.

"Hello Nel!" Zachariah's voice rumbled through the speaker and Nel winced. All signs pointed to this being a soundproofed room, but embarrassment still flushed her throat.

"Hey. How's it going?"

He chuckled, leaning back in his seat. Behind him was a thin tapestry in autumnal colors, and a narrow, dark bookshelf with a mix of clinical texts, well-worn fantasy titles, and some leather tomes. She blinked. When was the last time she saw actual books? Her hands itched to touch their covers. She was an occasional reader, loving thrillers and historical fiction—mostly for the anachronisms—but rarely found the time to start a new book. Longing for the scent of paper, the low hum of the surprisingly massive library at UNNE struck her. How long had it been since she thumbed through her typology books or Whittaker's *Flintknapping*?

"Nel?"

She blinked again and Zach's pixelated face loomed larger as he peered at the screen. "Sorry. I, ah, it's been a while since I saw anyone. Bit awkward."

"This is just me. Just a friend checking in."

"A highly educated friend who happens to be a shrink."

"Well I'm sure if I found some projectile points in my mom's yard you'd help me figure out what to do." He smiled, twirling one lock of his hair absently. It was much longer than it had been when they last saw one another, and his beard was thicker.

His comment brought a faint smile to her lips. She'd forgotten their hometowns were within 400 miles of one another. "How is your mom?" She knew very little of his family, but it seemed like safe territory.

"Safe. Adjusting. Like all of us, I'd imagine. How have you been since last I saw you?"

Last I saw you. The words were so gentle for the fire and chaos that followed. She drew a breath. A twist of frustration rooted in her chest, souring her relief at seeing him. As much as she wanted to shove it away, she swallowed and followed it down. "Why didn't you tell me? I mean, Dar never had the chance, really, so I guess I don't blame him for that. Shitload of other things, just not that. But you and I spoke. Like you said—friends."

Honesty draped his face, when he offered, simply, "We couldn't be sure of you."

She sat back, stinging at the insult. "It's not like my distrust for IDH was much of a secret. Kind of infamous if I recall. Just because I loved—I was fucking Lin?"

He stared at her for a moment, surely registering what she had almost blurted out. "Nel, you went into space because a pretty, clever woman asked you to. At the end of the day, we assumed you'd choose her. And there was no way we could sway her yet. If you and Komodor Muda Nalawangsa couldn't, what luck would we have?"

She frowned. For all her reputation and frustration, he was right. Given a choice she had chosen IDH over Los Pobledores. Lin over her life in Jasper Hill. *Odyssey* over Earth. She wasn't the one who had rejected Lin in the end. She would have brought her along in a heartbeat if she'd agreed. "I guess I just wish you'd asked."

"Nel, Emilio did ask you. In a hundred different ways. And finally, though we told him it wouldn't work, he tried to trick you into it. Figured once you knew everything, you'd understand."

"I did. Understand, I mean," she rasped. "But you're right. It was always Lin. I tried everything to prove I was smart enough to be there. Strong enough. Skilled enough. To prove it wasn't just a fucking handjob to keep me from causing trouble. The perfect daughter's pathetic pet, given a shiny title and patsy site so she doesn't piss on the floor." She shuddered, anger washing over her impatient, insistent muscles. Her arms bunched as she gripped her bed rail. "The smoke," she whispered.

He hummed, eyes soft even through the grainy pixels. "That's how your message ended—follow the smoke."

"You said anger was the smoke. To the fire. Which was fear."

"I'm glad that resonated with you. It sounds like you might know what your fire is now."

Nel jerked a nod. "Don't think I'm ready to talk about it. But um," she picked at the knotted end of her right pant leg, "I don't really know what to do with the anger right now. 'Cause there's a lot of it. And more often I just end up bawling and furious. Not a good look."

He chuckled softly. "I cry all the time. There's nothing wrong with that. You're processing. Acknowledging that is important, even if it's just for yourself. Is it impacting your ability to function?"

Nel barked a laugh. "My life is a fucking joke right now. Did you see my chart?"

"We're unable to access the database. Just what everyone brought with them. A great pool of files if you're looking for the latest terrible slasher flicks, but not really rich in the way of privileged-access medical files. I know you were in an explosion and survived with some lasting injuries."

"Oh," she answered. "Well, ah. Yeah. 'Lasting injuries' is apparently code for some moderate burns—nothing deep, but some pretty interesting scars on my right arm. Stiffness. And ah…" She frowned down at her lap, searching for the sanitary, conversational way to say she was missing her shovel-stomper. "They amputated my right leg. Mid thigh."

"Oh Nel." His voice dropped into what even she registered as true empathy. "I'm so sorry. That's quite the adjustment. When did that happen?"

"I guess when we were here. I was unconscious. It took a few days to get me here in stasis. I woke up a few weeks after the ship blew up—it was Dar's ship. Did they tell you that part?"

"We were all briefed when the final ship joined the fleet. We'd been here for a few weeks by the time all the conversations were wrapped up. I imagine that was a lot to deal with when you first woke up."

"I don't think I did deal." The joke fell flat and she realized it hadn't really been one in the first place. "I don't know. I don't really want to talk about it. Like everyone's focused on it and I'd rather pretend it never happened. Which is probably unhealthy. Or whatever."

"Then what do you want to talk about?"

"How I can pass this evaluation and get on with my day," she muttered. "No offense. Seeing you is nice. And it'd be fun to have, like, a real conversation. I miss those. I miss shooting the shit. I miss having a beer with coworkers after a long hot day. Don't you miss drinking? It's all just space-vials up here."

"I don't drink on account of my faith, but there are other things I miss. The crunch of autumn leaves. Rain. Seeing my mother and her friends walking back from our mosque in the evening and meeting them in the driveway."

Nel's chest ached for him. For both of them. "How do you do it?"

His smile was thoughtful. "This is where I need to be right now, I think. This is what God has given me to work with. I can only hope to do my best."

The idea overwhelmed her, and thoughts tailspun at the lack of control. "I guess I don't know where I need to be. Or how to make the best of it."

"You have a clinical, scientific mind, Nel. Let's focus on questions that fit into those boxes. This is an evaluation to determine if there are concerns, medically and psychologically. So, do you have concerns? For example, have you been able to sleep?"

"Not much." *Because every time I shut my eyes shit starts looping.* "I need to be busy. But out here it's all this really big important stuff. And I'm worried I'm gonna fuck it up. Honestly, I don't know what to feel," she whispered. It wasn't a lie. A dozen feelings rampaged through her chest, which were a good ten or eleven more feelings than usual. "Sad. Angry. A lot of angry. But it's a bit different now. Sharper. Brighter." She shrugged. "Lately it kind of has a point."

"And where is it pointed?"

Nel picked at the bandage again. "Mostly at myself. Lin too, obviously. But that's complicated and I so don't have the energy to go there right now."

"That's good, that you're picking which mental battles to focus on. Your body needs you focusing on healing, and yourself, and adjusting to whatever you want this next part of your life to look like."

"I don't know what I want it to look like," she confessed. "Honestly, I'm not sure I ever have."

"What about before the events in Chile a few years ago? Before you knew about IDH."

She shrugged and looked away. "I was content. Maybe not happy. But I saw a way to get there. I know you've been a fan of this life up here and have family back on Earth too, but this is pretty far outside my comfort zone. I can't even figure out how to be happy up here."

"Maybe you should think about that for a while. Every choice—I mean down to when you bathe and what you wear—think about which one would make you happier. And when appropriate, choose that. I'm sure seeing your mother helps."

She winced. "I hadn't until yesterday."

His eyes widened slightly. "That must have been complicated."

"It was shitty of me. You can be honest. She said as much—well, without the cursing."

He chuckled. "I'm sure you had your reasons, just as I'm sure that, if she's anything like my mother, she didn't care what they were. Will you be moving into her apartment?"

"Yeah, when I'm free here. I guess space is tight, but they've been holding her spare room for me. Otherwise she'd have a roommate. So I guess I will, assuming I pass this."

"I'm confident you will."

She frowned. "Really? 'Cause I feel like a Grade A headcase."

"Well, tell me about that. Everything you're feeling is normal. Intense and hard, but normal. Any serious injury comes with grief, as does losing someone you cared about. And you've had more than a few losses recently. Would staying in your medical room make any of it better?"

She shook her head.

"Do you wish harm to others or yourself?"

She shook again, but it took a second longer this time.

"Is your hesitation about yourself?"

"I don't feel like I'm worth keeping around. Like I've any use. But I'm not going to act on that thought."

"Nel, I think the best place for you would be with your mother. She could probably use a familiar face as much as you, and surely having someone who is a bit more used to this life would be helpful to her. And Dar has been vocal about his need for additional aid."

"Bitching is more like," she muttered.

He chuckled. "He's been testier than usual, yes. But Nel? I think you need to take some time to yourself as well. There's work for you here, but not enough to drown yourself in. Your worth wasn't tied to your limb. Or to who you were dating. You're a person and a very capable and driven person at that. You'll get through this."

Nel resisted the urge to slam the camera shut at the sentiment. "Thanks. I'll believe it when I see it."

"You can talk to me whenever you need to. The connection isn't always fantastic, but just send me a message and we'll figure out a good time. God willing, this journey will be a temporary adventure."

"Aren't they all?" Nel snarked. When she smiled, it was almost real. Maybe he was right—getting back to normal things, even if they were small, was exactly what she needed.

"I suppose so." He fiddled with a few things on his screen for a moment, probably ticking off whatever boxes needed to be checked to release her into general society. "How're you doing now, after we talked?"

"Fine I guess? Relieved. Antsy. The usual."

"Fair. Well, I've got everything I need here. Was there anything else?"

An entire case study's worth, dude. "Not really. I'll let you know if something comes up though."

"You know where to find me. Talk soon?"

"Sure thing." She held her smile until the camera faded to black. As relieved as she was—and she was very relieved—she was also let down. The tools he gave her helped, there was no denying that, but she had to wonder how good of a therapist he really was if he couldn't tell she was batshit and hearing things. Even when she wasn't sleeping. *Bently, he's a tired man very far from home talking to a lying bitch through a shitty tele-vid connection.*

She grimaced and ran through her checklist again, signed off on the forms that appeared, then slipped the tablet into her bag. *What now?* Everything was packed, not that she had a lot to begin with. She would watch her additional orientation that evening, when she could ask Mindi about anything that didn't make sense. Her mom was fixing an issue with the cataloging system used for resources and passengers among the different ships. Though she had their apartment number, it didn't feel right showing up when her mom was out.

Her gaze lingered on the field book. It was busy work, her map. But busy was better than nut-case. Looping her pack over the back of her chair, she wheeled to the door. A glance back told her she'd left nothing behind. Maybe, if she was lucky, the nightmares would stay here too, between these four walls, and not dog her down the corridor and to Mindi's spare room. If she was very lucky, maybe they wouldn't follow her into whatever life awaited after this was over.

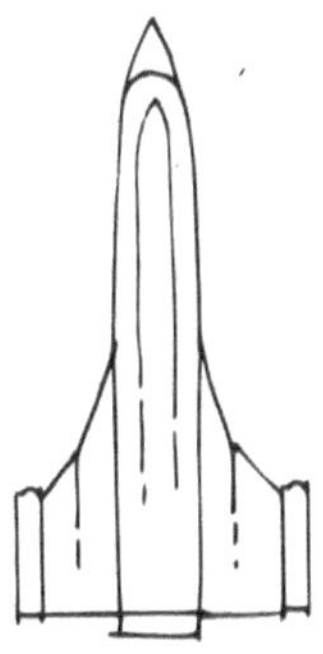

FOUR

"Alright, great, now do it again, this time extending your thumb as well."

Nel bit down on the inside of her cheek to keep herself from snapping at the medic. It wasn't his fault. Sure, he was the current face of a Bizarro IDH, but he was trying to help. At least, that's what he kept parroting to her every time she lost her temper. And if she wasn't careful, she was gonna lose it again. For the third time today.

If Nel were lucky enough to live another decade and never smell antiseptic and silicone again, it would be too soon. She leaned forward and extended her hands. Unbandaged, her knuckles were as gnarled and scarred as ever. Now, they just sported a marbled pink and white sheen. Scarring reached up to her elbow on the right, while on her left the injuries were localized to her palm and wrist.

She was lucky.

Anywhere on Earth she'd still be changing the bandages daily and have no feeling other than pain. She extended her fingers slowly, feeling the tug of stiff flesh against her muscles. Then came the squeeze, around the foam bulbs. She'd worked up to them, and if Medic Jesse was to be believed, she would be through with her out-patient PT by the end of the week. At least, for the hands. She finished her tenth squeeze and let go.

"You're doing awesome," Jesse remarked, making a few notes on his tablet. Like most of the tech on *The Recursive*—and probably all the other refugee ships—it was battered, the holographic screen flickering from time to time. "How often are you doing the exercises on your own?"

"Three times a day," she lied. When he glanced at her over the single lens covering his left eye, eyebrow arched, she blushed and looked down. "Okay, twice. Morning and night. I have a little routine."

"Think we can make that three times for real? How do you spend your days?"

"Pretending like I don't have to go to PT because my body's burned and broken and missing a few pieces."

"And your pain?"

"It's there. But I taught people to dig holes for a living—pain is always there."

"Well, twice daily is sufficient, but when you're ready, more would certainly help you heal. The ointment, though, is key."

She grimaced. The ointment smelled like ass. And not in a good way. "Gotcha. I'll work on it."

"Ready for the leg?"

"Never," she muttered. Still, she checked her brakes, then scooched forward on the wheelchair's seat until her right thigh hung over the edge. She hiked up her sweatpant leg and wedged it under her before rolling down the compression sock. Seeing her residual limb wasn't the worst part, though she had expected it to be. The worst part was, after hours of distraction, she remembered what she was missing.

"Looking great. You've been active? And I don't just mean with your chair."

"Yeah. I mean, both. The ship's big, so I use my chair for that. But around the apartment and our Block I'm mostly on crutches."

"How are those working out for you?

"Eh." She shrugged. "Fine. My balance could be better, but I imagine that's practice. My hands weren't up for it until about a week ago."

"Indeed." He leaned forward, reaching out. "May I?"

She nodded, and his hands settled on her leg. He massaged the tissue, which made Nel's skin crawl. "You're healing well. I know the process must seem slow, but honestly, you're doing great."

"Thanks," she replied, words tasting bland in her mouth. She didn't want to be healing well. She wanted to run.

"Our Med-eng team said you hadn't reached out about being fitted for a biomech leg yet. Or even a removable prosth. I think for someone as active as you—and keen to get back to that lifestyle—the former would be a good option." His tone was the kind of neutral that reminded her of stale classrooms and glass ceilings. *Judgment.* "Both are fine choices, of course," he continued, expanding on the virtues of various prosthetic options.

It wasn't a question, so she let him yatter on until he got to his point. Assuming he had one. She didn't want a smart leg. She didn't want an iRun. She didn't want some heavy metal and electric thing hanging off her body.

"What do you think?"

"Hmm?" She realized he'd been speaking for a while as he worked the stiffness from her abbreviated muscles. "Sorry, have a lot on my mind."

"I asked if you had put thought into what you'd like to use." He sat back, handing her the compression sock before disinfecting his hands.

"Oh, not really." She drew a breath, rolling the sleeve back over her healing flesh. "I'm good with just wheels for now."

"Fair enough." He made a note, then flashed a bright, if fake, smile. "Same time in three days?"

"Be there or be square," she replied with a false smile of her own. Ignoring his confusion at the quip, she tugged the leg of her sweats down and headed out the door.

Muttering to herself, she wheeled away from the medical and laboratory units, heading toward one of the elevators. The corridor wrapped in a single fat helix around the ship's core. Every few hundred meters a long—and dangerously thin, if you asked Nel—strut of an elevator shaft led down to the body of the ship. It allowed the broad, curved band of the corridor to rotate, producing the illusion of necessary gravity. Of course, as one descended down to the mechanical systems in the core itself, the illusion dissipated.

Nel turned right, following the gentle arc of the ship. *Infirmary, then labs, then up—down?—to the gym,* she recited to herself. Unlike the space station's tidy division of departments, whose workers lived efficiently beside the systems they managed, there was something utilitarian about this one.

The windows faced away from the very distant sun now, and the daytime corridor lights threatened with a headache behind her eyes. She shook it away and headed toward the gym. PT was an awkward combination of therapy and medical procedures that left her overwhelmed and with too much nervous energy.

Luckily, the gym was mostly empty. She rolled to one of the free-weight alcoves and parked so her left side faced the mirror. If she didn't look too hard, she almost recognized herself this way. She might not have been keeping pace with her PT, but an extra layer of bandages later, and she was halfway through a set of bicep curls. Bright aching spread through her shoulders and arms, finally giving her a reason for why her body always seemed to burn.

The Recursive wasn't alive, not in the sense that *Odyssey of Earth* teemed with life. Hundreds of interconnected systems with the pulsing heart of a forest warmed by Phil's sentience, all of it fed with generations of dead. But the refugee ship was a hive. Writhing with people, crammed into the arc of its main corridor and down to the still, central cylinder housing the throbbing engines.

Nel pressed her hand harder against the smooth matte plastic of her bedroom wall. Even from here, thousands of meters away, she felt the distant hum of the engines. They used fuel cells, that much she knew, but beyond that, the power that thrust them silently through space was as much a mystery to her as whatever unseen force bonded a colony of ants.

It was past midnight. At least, that's what her body told her, with its restless aches and the steady burn in her hands and arm. Her meds were wearing off. Already mentally arguing with an imaginary doctor about how this wouldn't happen if she opted for a port, she swung her leg over the side of her bunk. Gripping the bar along the side, she dropped down, did two of her usual five pull ups before touching the floor, one aching hand keeping her precarious balance. The endorphins woke her up and gave her brain the kick in the ass it needed. *Plus I gotta rely on my arms these days.*

"Computer: Personal lights, please."

Silence. She frowned. Her eyes were already accustomed to the dim light of the ship's insulated corridors and rooms as they glided through darkness in a sector without sun. Somehow this seemed darker.

She cleared her throat. "Computer: Lights."

No response.

What the fuck? Nel glanced at her bed with diminished longing. It's not like she had been sleeping anyway. She hooked her chair over and lowered herself into it. That, at least, powered on. *Okay, so batteries still work.* And as far as she could tell, the air she breathed was no more stale than usual, so life support wasn't compromised. *At least not much.*

But it was cold. She grabbed her sweatshirt and wheeled over to tap the door's panel. Nothing happened.

Her hand shook as she pumped the manual override, but a second later the door slid easily open. The living space beyond was dark. Their apartment consisted of a combined kitchen and sitting area, flanked by two bedrooms. The bathroom was off the back. However much this trip had come as a surprise to Mindi, she clearly had time to pack. The heirloom wool rug that previously covered her parlor floor now lay between the narrow kitchen bar and the single overstuffed couch.

Mindi's door stood open, as it always had—an old habit from when she would lie awake, waiting for Nel to sneak in well after curfew. Soft snores drifted from her room. Tension in Nel's chest loosened just a fraction. Everything felt different—easier—when she knew her only family in all the world rested meters, not lightyears away.

Nel rummaged through the case she left by the couch, finding the bottle of pills and the tube of analgesic healing gel for her burns. Knocking back her dose, she set about working the gel into the faint pink marbling of her right forearm.

Around her there was no whir of fans, the ghostly hiss and pop of the comms so faint it was barely perceived—until it was silenced. With the edge filed from her pain, she dropped everything back into her case and made for the apartment door. There was just enough space for her chair, so they hadn't kept the shelves, but Nel had helped put up a row of hooks the day before. A tidy collection of slippers and shoes hung from their laces. Nel's steel-toed boots slumped there, though she couldn't bring herself to properly look at them. She double-checked her mother's easy, restful breathing before slipping into the hall. Another manual override and their apartment door thunked shut softly behind her.

Like all long-range ships, *The Recursive* had day and night cycles, the chipper blue-green phosphorescence replaced with a gentle gold in the afternoon, and finally a dim peach, lighting only a single overhead strip and the runners on either side of the corridor. Outside their apartment, however, the ship was completely dark. Unlit.

The hall still smelled of a dozen dishes cooking. That evening the lights had dimmed like they always did. She peered either way, breath held, listening.

Unlike the other ships she had been on, the halls were quiet. Distant sounds of business and bustle drifted from around a corner or two, but nothing close to *Odyssey*'s hum or *La Fe De Amor*'s cacophony. Each deck held four common areas, around which the apartments were centered. She had yet to do more than peer into theirs, but she often heard the unmistakable sound of a ping pong game.

Now, everything was still.

At the edge of the Block, an elevator waited to bring her up to the main corridor. But without power, she was stuck. *And so's everyone else.* She patted the pocket on her chair's arm, pulling out her field book without looking. They lived on one edge of Residence Block 410, Deck H, sandwiched between the large-family dwellings above and the singles below. Quarters were tight, but Nel didn't mind. They were nestled between a quiet duo of engineers and a raucous Ukrainian family. She peered down at the ever-growing map in her field book.

Most of the main corridor was sketched, plus the medical and laboratory bays in the aft, which she had completed on her way to a PT appointment. Then gymnasiums and data banks and a dozen other things Nel didn't understand. The central portion was the largest, with each of the four decks containing the passenger quarters themselves. The cantina, gardens, and gravity-run recycling systems were all housed in the fore.

Someone else was bound to have noticed something, but she wasn't up for the condescension or drama of talking to Dar. Instead, she turned left and wheeled farther into the residential units. She was almost to the far side when she heard voices, low but urgent, emanating from the residential observatory. Like the rest of this area of the ship, it curved gently. For once, the view through the window seemed bright by comparison. Nel paused in the doorway, head tilted and ears straining to catch any hint at who was speaking—or what about. Both voices were deep, one clipped, the other rolling.

She eased forward, peering into the room.

Two figures stood by the observation window. She recognized Emilio's easy stance, his splayed feet and mop of wiry dark hair. And she'd bet her last dollar that the rigid uniformed figure beside him was Dar.

"Hey."

Both men whirled, Dar's hand tilting open. It was then that she noticed both men were fully dressed in atmosuits and armed.

A snake of apprehension coiled in her belly. "What's going on?" she asked in Spanish.

Dar pinched the bridge of his nose, a sign she was coming to realize meant stress or annoyance. "It's almost over, I think. Just go back to bed."

"You think that's comforting?" Emilio shot him a look, then turned back to Nel. "There's an IDH ship in our skies. Our little fleet went dark to avoid detection."

Nel clenched her jaw and wheeled up to the window. "They know we're here?"

Emilio gave an easy shrug. "Hard to say."

"There must be a shit ton of backwaters like this though. What brought them out here? Unless they've been tracking us. Is that possible? To leave a trail in space?"

"It's not just possible, it's far easier to track out there, where there's nothing to muddle the trace."

It was Nel's turn to heave a sigh. How could they have ever thought to disappear? To run? Of course they were followed. A battered fleet of Founder's cargo haulers, engines cranked, racing for the stars against thousands of state-of-the-art spaceships? "Where are they now?"

Dar tilted his head closer to her level and pointed. Metal gleamed well outside the asteroid field. It was a speck, half the size of her bitten pinkie nail if she were to hold her hand up to compare.

"That? Can they even see us from there?"

"With our engines off, and running solely on emergency power, and with the amount of shielding these older models have?" Dar's gaze was fixed to the speck, eyes narrowed. Was he afraid? Did Dar even feel fear? Or just annoyance at anything dangerous? "I don't know."

She squinted. "How'd you know it was IDH? You have binoculars or something?"

Emilio snorted, tapping the console of the observation room. It was meant for analysis of potential asteroids and moons, not high-definition surveys of a craft through the changing landscape of an asteroid field. Still, she caught the delicate lines and bright hull. Unlike most of the larger ships she had seen, which were circular, save for a hexagonal central unit, this was all sleek lines, a long needle of a thing with a single exterior ring. Even through the blurry image on the console, Nel could see the tip of the needle itself was the only piece not rotating. "What is that? Never seen one like it."

Dar hadn't blinked, maintaining a staring contest with the distant craft that Nel, at least, hoped very much was one-sided. "It's a battleship. That tip is almost entirely solid steel, dotted with explosives. It's essentially a warhead at the end of the most powerful ship in the galaxy."

"Cute," Nel muttered. "So probably not out here looking for some nice acreage to settle down and start mining or whatever it is you people do when seized with manifest destiny."

Emilio reached for the console again and Dar looked over sharply. "Don't."

"She deserves to hear it."

"No one's going to hear it. Most of them won't even know this happened, if we can help it. Thank goodness it happened during the night cycle—"

"And if the next time it doesn't? You want a full-blown panic on your hands? No. First thing tomorrow you announce this. You were just complaining that there was no protocol for this sort of thing. Make one. If we're really all in this together, you could start acting like it."

Nel stared at Emilio, brows raised. Until their brief time as enemies in Chile, he had always struck her as easygoing, thoughtful. Under the chill exterior, however, seemed to be a will of steel and the brainpower to match. "What do I deserve to hear?"

This time, when Emilio reached down, Dar didn't stop him. "It's been looping for hours."

Lin's voice boomed through the quiet.

"GENERAL TRANSMISSION: THIS IS THE *IDH-LAHIFA*. DOES ANYBODY COPY? WE ARE CONDUCTING A RESCUE MISSION OF A KETAFI CLASS SHIP LISTED AS *THE RECURSIVE*. AND *LA FE*

DE AMOR, IF YOU ARE RECEIVING THIS, REPORT BACK IMMEDIATELY."

"THIS IS *IDH-LAHIFA*..." The message looped, so similar that, for a few minutes, Nel even thought it may have been recorded.

"WE ARE CONDUCTING A RESCUE MISSION..."

"LAST REPORTED IN SECTOR-92-1-K-5..."

"REPORT BACK IMMEDIATELY..."

Silence bloomed then withered as her voice crackled, alive, so alive even through the hiss and pop of the radiowaves in the darkness. "Nel? Dar? If you're out there, please respond. Everything will be forgiven. Just—"

"Turn it off," she rasped. "Please."

Emilio switched it back to silence.

She glanced up at Dar. "Do you trust her?"

He stared at her for a moment but did not answer. Instead, he simply stalked from the room without another word.

"I can't fucking stand that man," she muttered.

Emilio didn't look down at her, but she caught the hint of humor on his mouth. "Komodor Muda Nalawangsa is a complex man."

"I think you mean asshole."

"The same has been said about you. Frequently." He snorted. "Perhaps you and Dar are too similar to get along. Learn to like yourself and you might just realize he's not all teeth."

Nel didn't know which was less likely. "Yeah, but I'm not..." she faltered. Not what? *Too dedicated to my career to have a proper relationship? Too focused on my own insecurities to ever actually see another human being? Too pissed off at what I think people want to realize what they need?*

Emilio sank into one of the seats across from the observation window. "Was I wrong? About letting you hear the transmission."

She shook her head. "No. But that doesn't make it easy."

"You never said how things…ended between you. Did they end?"

"Well, she's in a warship hunting me down and I'm cowering in a ragtag refugee fleet. You tell me."

"In my experience things aren't so simple when it comes to affairs of the heart."

Nel took in the large capable hands, the concealed strength of his shoulders. He fit just as easily here as he had in his restaurant. As he had at the gala on *Odyssey*. Wherever he went, he fit. She wondered briefly what experience he did have with affairs of the heart, as he'd phrased it. In all her summers in Chile, she had never seen a wife or girlfriend—or boyfriend, for that matter. Perhaps, like so many out here, it was easier to be married to his work than a complicated, impossible person.

"Ah." She dragged herself hastily out of her introspection. There were too many parallels between herself and these sad, lonely men for her comfort. "If they're close enough to send a message, doesn't that mean that they're close enough to pick us up?"

"Yes. But we have our best security techs on it. Not having a senti-comp has its perks—our ship puts off a far smaller energy signature, so it's easier to mask it as something else. And most of these are repurposed colony ships and research vessels. Wouldn't be odd for us to be out here, maybe refueling at a processor station."

"I'll pretend like that made enough sense for me to be comforted."

He chuckled. "Me too."

Nel found her gaze drawn by the same gravity that kept her heart's orbit around the woman piloting the distant warship.

Lin's adoration—no, deifying—of IDH had been a curiosity. Then a boon, then a frustration. Nel had hoped it would never be a breaking point. Of all the things she expected to break the tentative relationship, she honestly had expected the first thing to be her. Her avoidance. Her fear of commitment, of betrayal, of disappointment. Her terror of being left behind. Smoke stung her eyes.

Her hands curled into fists around her scars. *Fuck, we're such a damn mess.* But still her bones balked. Still her fury forced her onto an untrod narrow trail reaching up, up into the jungle that Nel let grow wild around the tiny glimmer of hope that never quite guttered. She knew somewhere inside of Lin was good, was empathy, was faith, if not in humanity, in Nel. She knew.

Her smile was a ghost still haunting Nel's heart.

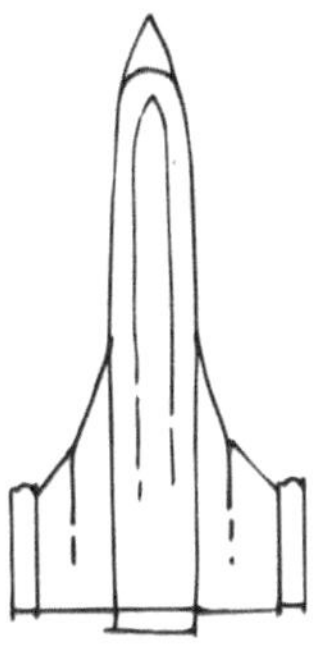

FIVE

Every lift of the barbells sent heat flickering over Nel's skin. Music would have been nice, but instead of the beat of some song, she timed her reps with the thudding of the generation gym cycles in the next room. At least that gave her something to focus on. By the end of her set her arms burned. Her shoulders flamed. And her heart. Her heart was an inferno that pinched with rage. Every pump of the iron made the image of Lin brighter. *How dare she.*

Zach's words about focusing on healing rang in her mind and she growled. Skills and duties and healing aside, she was sick of listening to everyone else about what was best. So sick of it was she that it took Emilio crouching down and waving at her to wrest her attention away from her mental bitch session.

"Morning."

She flashed a tired smile and set the weights down. "Hey, how's it going?"

He shrugged. Gone was the thick Founders electrosuit, and in its place was a tattered, baggy tee with the sleeves cut off and loose shorts. "Slow and steady. You?"

She made a face. "Didn't know you were a gym guy."

"You would if you glared at anything other than yourself in that mirror when you come here," he teased. "PT have you strength training?"

She snorted. "More like I want exercises to do that have nothing to do with PT. Or my injuries. Or leg."

"Sorry for the reminder."

She waved the apology away. "It's fine. It's not like I can actually forget. So, ah," she cast a glance around the room, "I take it we're all good?"

Emilio offered only a discrete nod.

"Dar going to explain it to people? Because I can't be the only insomniac on this colossus."

"He's planning an explanation tomorrow."

"Explanation. How come I feel like it won't be the truth."

"Because you're a paranoid, distrusting misanthrope."

"Am I wrong?" she challenged with a raised brow.

He shook his head, not bothering to hide the rueful grin. "No. You're not wrong. But he has his reasons—good ones, ones I agree with, before you even start."

She scowled, too angry about the whole thing to really pursue the topic. Her brain burned with too much frustration at the feminine Nalawangsa sibling to spare much for Dar. "How're things with your project?"

His dark eyebrow arched. "Project?"

"Or whatever it is. Dar keeps trying to rope me into it."

"Ah." His expression shuttered closed. "Project is a fancy word. We're just trying to survive, really."

Her eyes narrowed. Maybe she had been wrong about him being more honest than Dar. *Maybe you were wrong about being entitled to information.* "He seems to think whatever it is will crack the whole thing wide open."

Emilio chuckled to himself. "Well, that's Dar now, isn't it? I hope he's right, but he bounces between the fleet logistics and combing through signals and frequencies, unable to focus on either fully due to the lure and duty of the other."

A half-formed bitter retort turned stale on Nel's tongue. It was the second time he was cutting Dar slack. *Showing actual empathy,* she realized a moment later. Shame pinched in her chest and she flexed her hands as if the physical exertion could erase the sensation. Dar might not be worthy of much compassion, but by that metric, was Dr. Nel Bently? An entirely different and more painful feeling chased her guilt away and she grimaced. "I guess I see why he's so pissy all the time."

Emilio grinned, gracious enough not to point out how forced her not-insult sounded. "It's a nightmare. But I agree with him that you'd be a help."

"Kiss ass." She glared. "Look, it's not that I don't want to help. I do. I just don't feel like I'd be much good at anything right now."

"Because of your injuries?"

"Yeah but," she shrugged, realizing the truth only as it tumbled from her tongue, "mostly because I'm me. This entire fever dream of the past two years has basically been me failing upwards."

"Imposter." He rested a hand on the bench beside hers. "We all are, Bently. Often to ourselves most of all."

There was that echo again, the hint at a varied life far beyond his involvement with Los Pobledores. "Are you?" she blurted. "An imposter to yourself?"

He blinked, but it was the flutter of thoughtfulness, not offense. "Less than I used to be, perhaps. Something I'm working on. I'll let you return to your exercise. But it wouldn't hurt to consider Dar's plea."

Nel offered a vague wave of farewell before her gaze dropped down to the weights on the floor beside the bench. The words struck far too close, so close that they weaseled between her myocardium and curled at the base of her cerebrum. So close she couldn't ignore them. Remembering how to live wasn't just about recovering from her injuries. Her rough hands curled around the silicone grip of the barbells. She had never been a gym rat—too many people—and digging kept her body fit enough for her level of vanity. What was the point in going to such effort when no matter what, she wouldn't measure up to anyone's standards? Or her own. For now all she could manage were fifteens, and that was a struggle, but she enjoyed the new definition in her arms.

It suddenly didn't matter that her myriad past iterations weren't into lifting much beyond a shovel and women's skirts. She raised the barbells with a soft grunt, wondering what new callouses she'd make. Maybe Mindi wasn't the only one using the isolation and upheaval as an excuse for reinvention. Maybe New Nel needed the competition against the person she had disappointed the most.

Nel shifted the pack of protein from the shelf onto the hovering platform to her left. After a second glance at the shelf, she levered up another and let it thump beside its twin.

"Bent, there's someone here for you."

"Thanks Big-rig," she huffed, tugging a box of flavoring packets onto her lap. "Tell them my shift is done in ten."

"I think now would be best."

The annoyance in his voice made her turn. Sure enough, the galaxy's most obnoxious pilot leaned against the storeroom door frame, examining his wrist comm.

"I think never would be best of all," she muttered, drawing a chuckle from Big-rig and an eye roll from Dar.

"Oh I'd agree. Yet here we are." He gestured dramatically to the cantina beyond.

Nel tapped the platform's keypad and ushered it into the galley kitchen where one of her coworkers waited. "Here, this should do for the next day or so. Got you some of the flavor packs too—anything else?"

"Nah, we're set." The chef barely looked at her, and his tone hadn't wavered from disinterest, but at least he didn't glare every time she spoke. *Like Aline.* The woman hunched over the prep station shot Nel a scowl as the archaeologist parked the protein packs next to her.

Heaving a sigh, Nel wheeled backward out of the narrow room. Though the corridor was brightly lit at midmorning, her heart easily recalled the silence and the dark as they hid from Lin's searching gaze just a few nights before. Perhaps the dread would never fully abate.

Dar waited at one of the small two-person tables by the kitchen door, face an unreadable mask of assholery. It was only when she slowed beside him and crossed her arms that he looked up. "Do you like working here?"

"It's fine. They don't seem to like me much, outside of Big-rig. But then again, who ever does?" She shrugged. "It's nice to help out, I guess."

"You guess," he drawled. "For someone ready to blow herself up for the good of mankind you're awfully disinterested in actually helping out."

"Blowing myself up would have removed the necessity of having to actually interact with said mankind. Something I think we can all agree I'm not stellar at."

He snorted. "That's an understatement."

"Is there, like, a reason you're here or..."

"I was hoping you had your fill of playing sous chef or whatever it is they have you doing here and were ready to help us. There're some pressing matters to attend to that you'd be better suited to." He glanced at the kitchen door. "Or that would at least require less interaction."

"You're obviously getting at something. Probably whatever project you were dangling over my head when you booted me from the med ward."

"I didn't boot you, necessity did. And yes. I am. You in?"

Nel glanced back at the kitchen. She didn't like her coworkers. Rather, she was a bit tired of them not liking her. But the work? She enjoyed the rhythm of it, the problem solving of what food and when and how much, as depressing as the answers often were. Most of all, she liked the distraction. "Don't think so."

He blinked, head tilting as his expression tried to catch up with the utter surprise at not getting his way. "What? You can't possibly like this job and your skills are wasted here."

Nel's working class upbringing roared to life at that comment and her face relaxed into its familiar sneer. "Look, asshole, just because you're above the earthly need to consume food, the rest of us aren't. This is important work. Even if I did want to switch my current career path from stock boy to something more befitting my 'skills,' being your lackey, or scapegoat, or assistant is the last thing on my list." She sat back, thoroughly enjoying the way displeasure twisted his face. "I'd rather clean the recyclers."

Silence stretched between them, taut and humming with the unavoidable impossibility of their entire situation. Finally, Dar grimaced. "The recyclers clean themselves."

"Answer's still no."

"Why?" The dark eyes he turned on her did not belong to Dar Nalawangsa, former Komodor Muda of IDH and pilot of *Promise for Tomorrow*. They belonged to a desperate man. A man who would gnaw off his own pretty hand to get what he wanted. A man who would do just about anything to survive.

"Because I don't trust you. I barely trust Emilio, and that's mostly because he doesn't seem to lie, unless by omission." She leaned forward, voice dropping to a hiss. "Look, I get that you were raised to think you were some elite messiah or whatever, but I doubt there's anyone on these boats that doesn't know what this really is."

The condescension was back. He nipped each word off like a bitter bite of dry protein. "And what do you think this is?"

"We're rationed, we're silenced, and we're running. It doesn't take a shiny degree from Space U to add those up." She hated his needling that she should be doing something better with her time. She hated the condescension. She hated the secrecy. She really, really hated that he wasn't entirely wrong. She heaved a sigh. "For fuck's sake, even Sal knew it, despite what you told her to say."

Dar frowned. "Sal?"

"The orientation lady. I assume you approved the video we all have to watch."

"Oh. Social Artificial Liaison. S. A. L. She's a computer program."

Nel recalled the flicker of expression that crossed the woman's eyes as she spoke. "Good coding. But I guarantee half the people on board know she's lying."

"Lying." It was no longer a question, no longer a casual inquiry.

"What about 'Egalitarianism, transparency, and cooperation?' Transparency, Dar." She jabbed a finger at his rigid chest with every word. "Your idea of explaining what happened last night was a brief bulletin that we would occasionally 'run dark' to conserve power and maintain a low profile. Nothing about how close we came to disaster. I'm no shining example of how to handle a shitstorm, but I know enough not to tell my crew it's chocolate."

"You ever seen an entire ship panic? People die. Trampled to death. Blown out airlocks because that's better than whatever they think is coming. Or suffocated in suits they didn't seal properly because their hands were shaking and their minds were frayed and there was no one who cared enough to double-check because they were all too fucking focused on their own damn selves—"

A bright voice over the ship's system cut him off. "ATTENTION ALL *RECURSIVE* PASSENGERS. THIS IS YOUR VOYAGE STEWARD, JUNE. IN FOUR HOURS WE WILL BE WITHIN HAILING RANGE OF TERSA ETH."

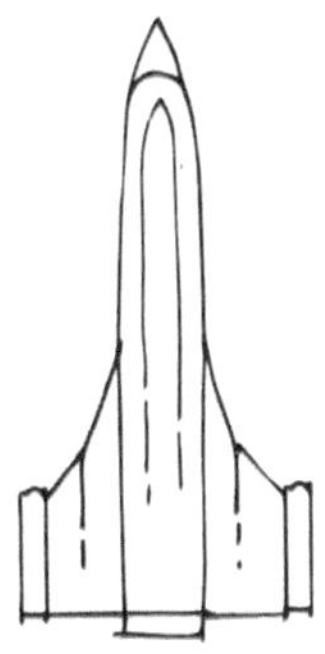

SIX

"THIS IS A ROUTINE STOP. WE WILL DEPART FROM THE REST OF THE FLEET TO DOCK THERE. THE PURPOSE OF THIS DOCKING IS TO RESTOCK AND ASSESS OUR CONDITIONS. AS SUCH, WE REGRET TO SAY THAT ONLY THOSE WITH PROFESSIONAL PASS KEYS WILL BE PERMITTED TO LEAVE *RECURSIVE*. THOSE OF YOU WHO MAY BE ORIGINALLY FROM ONE OF THE BOROUGHS, PLEASE SEE OUR SECURITY TEAM SO THEY MAY AID YOU IN A SAFE DECOUPLING FROM THE REST OF THE VOYAGE."

Decoupling? Nel shuddered at the mechanical word, momentarily distracted from the rest of the ridiculous message. Dar's smug face at her surprise, however, rocketed her right back to distrust. "We're stopping."

"Yes."

"The fleet being tracked through a fucking minefield of ship-destroying rocks by a mad woman in a war machine needs to stop. For what? We run out of gas?"

The expression crumpled into a full-blown smirk. "Maybe I'd tell you if you were actually part of the team and not an overgrown busboy."

"Oh fuck right off, I'm serious. Is this safe?" Another thought trailed in on the tail of the first. "Can I go?"

"Oh, absolutely not." His sneer dropped. "We have limited passcards, and it's not worth the risk. There will be time to visit stations when this is over."

"Dude, I'm antsy. Cooped up, you know? What's the worst case—we get seen?"

"The ship has miles of accessible halls, Bently. I fail to see how that's 'cooped up.' And with you? The worst-case scenario is your ass gets left and I'm stuck explaining to your mother why I don't feel like wasting the fuel to turn around." He stood, flashing a smile with as much disdain as teeth. "I'll get you something nice."

"I couldn't possibly," she snarled back, jerking her wheels back in a childish display. Her heart hammered, though, anxiety leaping with every pound of her heart. She hated this. Hated that they were going without her, hated that they were going at all, that they would risk stopping for whatever it was, risking their lives—thousands of lives.

She turned back to the prep area to see Big-rig leaning against the door, thick arms crossed. Under the heavy hair, she caught sight of an array of scars. Some were the usual burns from kitchen accidents, but many more looked gnarled and older. One, a long thin line that stretched the length of his ulna and half way up his tricep, was clearly surgical.

"You wanna poke around." It wasn't a question.

Nel nodded, trying to edge past him. "He's right though. The thought of someone recognizing us just freaks me out. Fugitives from the government and all that."

Big-rig's eyes narrowed on her. "Recognize you? IDH isn't our government, Bently. We don't really have one, I guess."

She stared at him, trying to process that bombshell. *Christ, Bently, you really just dove into this shit without a single second of research.* She may blame Lin for not telling her anything, but Nel willingly walked blindfolded into the deception. Now, realizing how utterly vast their society was, Nel couldn't blame Lin for not knowing where to start. "What?"

"Stations like this are huge. Dozens of factions, from IDH to the Liberatora. Even some Ta Molag on the ones further out. Ain't no one gon' think nothing of a bitch on wheels."

"Ouch, my ego." She hadn't told any of the kitchen staff much about who she was. She'd spent enough time in infamy while working under IDH and it was nice to just be on equal footing with her coworkers. Even if, for some people, that meant equally disliked. Her brain scrambled to record the new strange names as Big-rig pulled something from his pocket. It was a plain white square of plastic and clear silicone. He tossed it, and she caught it one-handed. "What's this?"

"Kitchen passcard. Every department has at least one. We've got a short list and shorter favors, if you wanna take the run for us."

Nel's heart leapt. "Me? Seriously?"

"Why not? Teska and Lee's roommates are docking crew and will be gone so those two'll prolly spend the whole evening sticking it in every place they can think of, and the last time I sent Katarina May she refused to go within a block of the butcher due to the smell. So. Do me a favor?"

It was a good cover for his kindness, and Nel wasn't about to admit what a charity case she was. She turned over the cube, visually tracing the delicate lace of three-dimensional circuitry filling the clear half. She didn't even know how to use the damn thing. "How do I—"

"Just pop it on their reader. There are guides in every language on most corners. Here, I'll get you the list." He ducked into the kitchen and returned before the door had even swung back around. He then handed her a thin cylinder that, when she tapped its single button, unrolled a strip of light covered in what must have been Big-rig's handwriting. It was beautiful, one step down from calligraphy when compared with her own.

"Awesome. Thanks." Glancing down at herself, she grimaced anew. *Fuck. Four hours.* Sweats might have been cool in college, but her cheeks flamed at the thought of going out in public—proper public—without so much as jeans. Tucking the pass key into the safety of her chair's pocket, she wheeled from the cantina in double-time.

Three hours later, Nel was wheeling desperately down the corridor to the docking bay. The space swarmed with people, and she was struck again by how utterly huge the ship was. Hundreds of people crowded between the tethered and docked shuttles, faces she had never seen, uniforms and insignias that were utterly foreign. At least getting lost in the crowd wouldn't be hard.

She kept to the edge of the bay, finding a spot to wait that seemed neither underfoot nor conspicuously out of the way. There was no formation or order, it seemed, just people falling into rough lines. A splash of violet cut through the sea of gray and black atmosuits. Dar, unable to resist being the flashiest person that ever crawled from under some sullen space rock, wore a long coat. His atmosuit helm, donned but open, gleamed under the dim docking bay lights. Nel shrank back against her seat, hastily tugging on her own atmo helm.

Blaring klaxons. Flashing lights. Roiling air.

Sound spiraled from the airlock, and she allowed it to wash over her. Their ship was nothing compared to this. This was chatter, life, surviving and thriving and everything in between. She followed the crowd out onto the open grate of the docks. After filing through the narrow opening in the station's shields, atmo helm visors snapped up, groups breaking off to whatever errands gave them the privilege of momentary freedom. The mass of people disgorging from *The Recursive*'s belly broke up, clumps wandering to lifts and transports, disappearing into the pulsing innards of the station.

Tersa Eth was a lattice-work sphere, with ships dotting docks and cylinders made entirely of thick acrylic, so light and life writhed within, moving like honey in a vial. Landing signals flickered over its surface, a mimicry of a whole new galaxy. A band of shop stalls rotated slowly around the towering block to their left. Nel craned her neck trying to catch a glimpse of the top.

Her eyes followed Dar's haughty stride, matched by Emilio's easy lope. For a second, she contemplated following them. The passkey hummed in her hand, updated with a map and AI navigation as it synched with the station's network. When she glanced back up, she was alone. *Sort of.* Eye-wateringly bright letters blazed above their heads: Dock KW-7610-3B.

Nel noted the dock numbers and repeated them to herself half a dozen times before turning to take in the station itself. Her heart thudded against her ribs. Thousands—millions, probably— of people surrounded her. Termites swarming their automated, metal mound. She never could have imagined this. Maybe in the far distant future. Comparing Earth's progress with that of IDH—or whatever these people all called themselves—was like viewing an alternate reality where Earth didn't fuck up. Nel narrowed her eyes. Or fucked up differently.

Flexing her hands in her PT gloves—stiff with disuse—she palmed her wheels and set off along the main road. Tangy sweat and hot spices replaced the cloy of electricity and burning ozone. Shield there may be, but recycled the air was most definitely not. Humming cargo transports zipped over the steady stream of pedestrians and rickshaws—both electric and human-powered. There were no signs indicating any designated traffic flow, at least none she recognized as such, and so she kept to the disorganization that inevitably flanked the street. Better to be bumped into than swept away.

She turned a corner when one of her wheels shuddered. Hands grabbed her by the shoulders, yanking both Nel and her chair back. Nel let out a shout. The kiosk shot upwards as the block rotated, the edge less than a meter from Nel's boot. "Jesus," she groaned, torn between being furious and wanting to puke.

"Nah, it's just me." Jem stepped from behind Nel as the block settled into its next configuration. A tiny Catholic shrine now stood in the kiosk's place. "You good?"

Nel flashed Jem a weak thumbs up. "Thanks."

"No worries. Sorry for manhandling you—I always hated it when people grabbed my crutches when I was recovering. I just thought—"

"No, seriously. Thanks." Nel's face burned with the uncomfortably familiar mixture of adrenaline and embarrassment. *This was stupid.* She reached to shake their hand.

Jem batted the hand away and bent to give Nel a tight hug. They laughed sheepishly when they pulled away. "Sorry, should have asked if you were a hugger. Familiar faces are harder to come by these days."

"I hear that."

"The edges flash yellow then red before they move. For future reference." They jerked their chin at the pass key in Nel's shaking hand. "Where you headed?"

Nel grimaced, glancing down at the list. "Peter's Premium Proteins—what a name—and a chem dealer. Also looks like a courier station."

"Mind if I tag along? I'm headed in that direction too."

Nel sighed, grateful Jem was kind enough to disguise their pity. She cleared her throat, grinding out an awkward, "That'd be great. I could use the help. I'm pretty good with a map no matter where I go, but I think this is a bit out of my league."

"Unfamiliar stations are a nightmare. Luckily you can find most things within a hundred blocks of any dock."

Nel fell in beside the medic, glancing twice at their hair. A shock of teal accented the tech's brown skin.

"That new?"

"Yeah!" Jem scraped it back, grinning. "I always stop by a barber when we're docked somewhere big. You want to get yours done? Sha's the best, and I've been to every barber between here and *Odyssey*."

"Maybe another time," Nel offered with a wan smile. Nel hadn't had a proper haircut since her half-assed attempt in a New Hampshire Irving's washroom. She didn't know how to pay and felt awkward enough as it was.

"Not the barber shop type?"

"What gave it away? The detainment center dye job?"

"More like the shifty eyes."

"Probably why I started glaring so much, so people wouldn't notice I was always about to book it," Nel mused with a sigh. She followed the tech through a winding mess of stalls and onto a narrow, hovering pad. Her bitching trailed off as the platform buzzed into motion. The movement hummed through her chair, setting off the over-sensitive nerves in her leg. As they slid away from the main street, more of the station loomed into view.

Thousands of blocks marched down each spoke of the sphere, some lit with neon, others glowing with gentle phosphoresce. Nel even caught the glimpse of a forest, backlit with brilliant radiation. She turned, following the line of districts, communities, recyclers, services, generators and probably more than a few nefarious syndicates. Maybe even Lin was somewhere on this same station, gleaming ship separated from their hulking transport by two docks or two thousand.

"Shit..." Nel trailed off. It was the same mixture of horror and pride that filled her at the sight of looping powerlines spanning otherwise untouched wilderness.

Jem chuckled. "Just don't—"

Too late. Nel turned. The walkway was strung between two of the station's massive spires, gossamer against galaxies. Nel's lungs shuddered, terrified to exhale, lest her breath be sucked out into the surrounding stillness of space. So many stars. Even with the bright pulse of life radiating from the station, she lost count. Faint sprays of light marked billions of suns, and others stood alone, bright and bold. Her soul pitched forward, longing for the weightlessness, reseated each time she blinked.

"*We were unmade.*"

Nel's trance shattered. "What?"

"I didn't say anything." Jem glanced out, frown disappearing. "Trippy, eh?"

"Too trippy for me, I think," Nel transitioned clumsily. "So what's on your list?"

"Gotta get refills for the prosth-printers and some other basic medic stock."

Nel let out a sad chuckle "Think they'll have a second-hand leg I could barter for?" She added a lecherous wiggle of her brows. "Or maybe they'll take it out in trade?"

Jem grinned. "Your outdated Earthling ways are showing—most districts don't police sex work. Some do, of course. There's all kinds out here. But I know more than a few people who would take you up on that offer, if you were serious."

Nel's bravado faltered at their nonchalance. She was used to being the one in control, the one who took the lead. Being a fish out of water really threw a wrench into her game. *Have you ever actually felt like you were in the water, though?* Discomfort sometimes seemed like her only constant.

Jem nudged Nel's shoulder with their elbow. "So how've you been?"

"Ugh," Nel started, then stopped. Maybe along with pumping iron, New Nel could try some positivity. "It's alright. Adjusting, I guess. It's really awesome to see my mom again."

"I'm glad you found her!"

"We're roommates now." Nel made a face. "Talk about adjusting! What about you?"

Jem's eyes lidded. "I haven't heard from my family much—even before the comm-ban. We send each other updates, vids, all that, but the distance stretches more and more, the farther we go. Sometimes I forget what it was like before. Got my mates though," they concluded with a bright grin. "Found family is everything out here."

Nel was about to note she understood the camaraderie from her days among tight-knit digging crews during her CRM days, but Jem stopped.

They gestured to the large, crowded store to their left. "Here's my first stop. Might take a minute, if you don't mind waiting."

Nel shook her head, silently following the tech through the open doorway. The shelves were crowded with battered parts, some clearly prosthetic, others looking like they belonged under the hood of a pile driver.

"Hola," Jem greeted, gaze fixated on the tiny blocks arrayed across the counter. They were all various grays and beiges, fairly uniform, though others were marked with swirls of faintly varied opacity. "Got any Centron 4?"

The clerk made a face and shook her head, mass of cherry-red curls bobbing with the motion. "'Fraid not." She tapped a button and the belt around her waist and thighs whirred softly as it lifted her from the chair and carried her down to the far end of the counter to point at the cube to Jem's left. "Centron's hard to come by lately with the strike on Jasmine Ring, but this stuff is a good alternative—provided you don't exceed a 20K load. For that I'd recommend Tasmanian Alt-Steel."

Jem hummed thoughtfully. "Pop always preferred TAS."

Nel listened to the jargon, letting herself move deeper into the shop. Buckets of bolts and rings with a hundred different shades and textures of synthetic skin cluttered one wall; another held rolls of different gauges of electromesh and wires. *Neurowire,* according to one of the signs. Nel turned a corner and halted before a gleaming case of an entire human figure made of prosthetics. Its chest and abdomen were open, like the front of an intricate desk. Within, systems whirled, pumped, tapped, and clicked. She leaned forward, breath fogging the glass as her eyes darted from faux femoral down to titanium tibia. Would she ever have something so terrifyingly alien affixed to her own body? A strange sensation tugged somewhere near her solar plexus. Her abysmal emotional intelligence, however, couldn't discern whether it was longing or nausea.

"Can I help you?"

Nel glanced back at the clerk with an apologetic smile and switched to Spanish. "Sorry, I'm with them. Just looking."

The clerk's attention dropped to Nel's hands, appearing to check that she hadn't pocketed anything of value before turning back to Jem. "Will that be it?"

"That'll do it, yep." They slid their own pass key into a port on the counter, then withdrew it and flashed a smile.

"Jemina Berwah? What the hell you doing in this sector?" A big voice boomed from the next aisle over. She flinched and tried to squeeze against the wall, but her wheels bumped into the prosthetics case. A middle-aged white man just over four feet tall emerged, arms spread wide.

Jem chuckled and returned the offered embrace. "Stars above, Teke, it's been too long! And it's just Jem now."

Teke stepped back and gave the tech a cursory look, concluding with an approving nod. "You look good, Jem. What's brought you out here? Still cruising with those academics on the *Promise*?"

The tiny shred of chill Nel had left to her name frayed and threatened to disappear altogether. As she was opening her mouth, however, she caught Jem's headshake as they looked over at her.

"Nah, with a long-range hauler now, with my friend here, Andy. We're freelance, thank goodness."

Teke's face lit up. "Naima's got grits for tonight, and we can spring for a cut of veal, if you wanted to stay for dinner." He nodded to Nel. "Bring your friend here, too."

"I wish, Teke, but our boat's gotta jet within the hour. You know how it is—hauler's life." Jem gave him another tight hug. "Catch you next time?"

"You better! She's gonna scream when she hears you were docked up and didn't visit."

With a laugh, the tech ducked from the store and nodded down the dock in the direction opposite their bay. "Shall we?"

Nel wordlessly fell in beside them, waiting until they were well out of earshot before asking, "He a spy or something?"

Jem's laugh was loud, and Nel glanced around as heads turned. Just as quickly, they turned back, disinterested. "Teke's nothing but a damn good biomechanic married to a hell of a cook. I did that to protect him, not us. Plus, he gets to talking. We'd miss take-off."

Nel frowned at the tech's empty hands. "Where's your stuff? And how'd you pay?"

"It'll be delivered at the dock. And our passkeys are linked to the ship's resources." They didn't bother to hide their teasing smile. "Think of it like a company credit card."

"I'd be dead so fast out here on my own."

"Hardly—you were just offered a hot meal by a stranger. It'd be rough and you'd have to drop your shitty attitude, but you'd make it." Jem made a face. "From what I've seen of Earth it'd be harder to hack it on your own down there than it ever would be here."

Nel glowered. "I'm not thrilled that I get a chance to compare."

Jem chuckled and led them into a tight acrylic cylinder that shot them down several levels to another block. Or maybe the same block with a new set of storefronts, Nel couldn't really tell. Music thumped from one dark bar, brilliant neon pulsing from behind the massive woman blocking the doorway.

"A bar. Now that's a bit more my speed," Nel remarked.

Jem snorted. "Good luck. Most bars don't care who comes in, but that's not a bar."

Nel craned her neck as they passed. Glittering icons decorated the lintel, showing whips, cuffs, and paddles. *Oh.*

"Unless…"

"Not in that setting, nope," Nel answered quickly, feeling her cheeks flush again. She might have been experimental in college, but the trust and intimacy required for safe kink weren't easily fostered with one-night stands.

A few stores down, Jem gestured to the elusive Peter's Premium Proteins. "Want me to walk you through it?"

"Please," Nel answered, giving up what felt like the last bit of her pride. To her surprise, the main counter held actual butchered meats, with sections designating vat-grown, farm-raised, halal, and kosher options. Nel's thoughts lingered on what a farm in space would look like. Was it like *Odyssey*'s forest or something more utilitarian?

"With ya in a min," the butcher called. They wedged a hose into a whole duck with practiced ease, inflating the skin to roast for Peking.

Nel scanned her list, then the racks to the left with different shelf-stable blocks that were stored alphabetically by base protein. It took a minute and Jem's easy lie about this being Nel's first time off-mine, but by the time they left the butcher, their order of protein was on its way to *The Recursive.* Another half hour saw the rest of Nel's errands completed. They were heading back to the ship when her stomach let out a rumble of protest.

"What do you say?" Jem jerked their thumb at a long, covered counter wreathed in cook smoke. "Want a hot meal with someone who isn't a perfect stranger?"

Nel parked at the counter with a grin and hopped to the barstool at the very end.

"Dar said this was a shit part of town."

"Sure, I guess, if you're a privileged hotshot who didn't have to wipe his own ass until he was twelve. It's like any place: only as dangerous as the worst person you walk past. Plus," their grin widened with delight, "this place has, hands down, the best souvlaki."

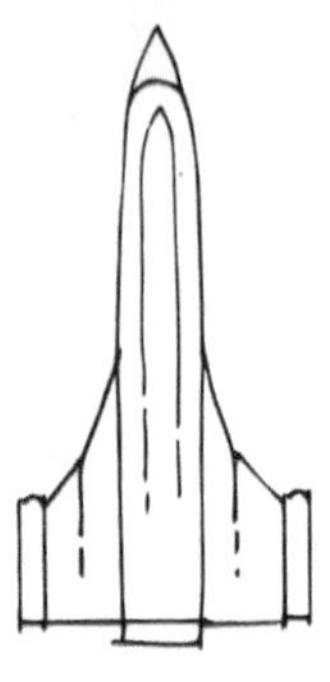

SEVEN

It took two weeks before Nel truly believed they hadn't been followed from the station. The days wound on, marked only by the ebb and flow of her shifts in the kitchen, the weeks marked by the cycle of meals they prepped. *The Recursive* may have been massive, but with every passing day Nel's world seemed to shrink in on itself, imploding under the pressure of uncertainty. Sometimes she'd see Jem or Emilio pass through the cantina, or on even rarer occasions, Dar. Each time he looked more wan, strained, or exhausted.

Each time her chest tightened further with avoidant guilt.

It had been a month since they had docked at Tersa Eth, and despite her increasing hours in the gym, Nel felt ready to crawl up the very walls from boredom. She popped a wheelie, rocking on her rear two wheels while she waited for Jesse to arrive for her physical therapy. Despite whatever lie Dar had spun, *The Recursive* was quiet. Perhaps it was the percolation of the truth, or some semblance of it, that lowered people's voices and led to hushed conversations where there was once raucous teasing. Or perhaps it was the inevitable emotional doldrums that came with a long, destinationless journey. Outside the windows a new sector of the asteroid field drifted around them. Nel thought even the other ships in the fleet looked more subdued.

"Good to see you, Dr. Bently!"

Nel turned from the window, sending the table of PT bands skittering across the room.

Jem beamed from the doorway. Their shoulders filled out more of the plain civilian clothes over their electrosuit, and their puff of hair was still brilliantly turquoise.

"Hey!" Nel found an actual smile on her face as she settled back into her chair. "Are you running my PT now?"

"Kinda." Jem shrugged. "PT as in prosth-tech as opposed to physical therapy. Most of us are techs-of-all-trades up here. Also, Jesse thought you might make more progress with someone you knew."

"Someone who didn't take my nasty personally, you mean?"

Jem snorted and reached back into the hall for a cart before shutting the door behind themself. "Jesse could stand to take himself less seriously."

Nel grinned, peering past the tech into the cart. It was filled with what looked like half a cosplayer's wardrobe or the set of some campy sci-fi movie. "So proths-tech, you said?"

"I did." They settled backward in the other chair and drew the cart closer. "Your chart indicated you were ready to try some manual ones."

"I guess. Integration freaks me out."

"I get that." Jem held out a battered metal and silicone arc to Nel. "Let's start with this. I'll show you how to hook it up, but you should get some practice doing so yourself too."

"I will," she muttered. She'd have to. After all, this was her new reality. "The fancy one—the electron prosth whatever—will I be able to remove that?"

Jem fiddled with the bundle of delicate wires attached to the cup of the limb. "Sure. There's a disengage switch and a power down. It'd be like hauling around a very heavy hunk of metal then. But in case of an accident you can completely unclip it even. If you were pinned, for example."

"Fuck. You guys think of every horrible thing."

"Actually, most of those things were thought of too late for at least one person. You don't want to see what happens when someone is in a puddle of blood and their exposed wiring starts firing. Blood's still technically conductive."

"And I'm done with that topic," Nel interrupted. The last few years had given her imagination plenty of creative boosts in regard to what the human body could endure. Or couldn't. "Alright, let's jack me in."

"You currently have temporary feeds, but part of the eventual integration process will include conductive lines. Makes everything a lot safer, too." Jem produced tiny filaments encased in silicone tape. "May I?"

When Nel nodded, Jem unrolled the cap over Nel's leg and did some cursory examinations. "You're doing great so far. The eventual conduit will go right here in the center, made mostly of surgical steel and silicone. Other pieces will actually be grown from your own genes, of course. Whole limbs are something we're still working on."

Nel perked up at that. "Wait, would having this kind of um, prosth—"

"Leg," Jem offered. "It's easier to just call them what they are."

But they aren't. That's not me. "Right, I just..." She swallowed. "I guess I'm not there yet."

"It takes a while. You were asking something."

"Right. Does having this kind of leg mean I couldn't have a flesh one? A grown one? If that became a thing?"

"Not at all," Jem promised. They leaned forward and held up a new cup in which her thigh could rest. "This is a smart-cap. Has places for your conduits to attach. Not the fanciest, but it simulates the major sensations pretty well. A proper fit would of course feel more seamless." Jem fixed the cap into place, rolling the soft, tacky material over Nel's skin before plugging each conduit into its port. "They're color coded, and each has a different pattern at the jack so you could even do it in the dark if you needed to, say," they grinned, "sneak out of someplace again."

Nel grimaced. "Last time I snuck out of someone's room it ended in a hostage situation and a missing limb. Not about to try it again."

Jem snorted, face still inches from their task. "Never been much for sneaking out of rooms myself. But you make it sound exciting."

Nel awkwardly seized the attempt at small talk. "You don't date much?"

"Flings. This job doesn't leave much in the way of putting down roots. Pretty amazing you and Lin made it work for so long."

"She was stubborn. Probably still is, I guess." Speaking about Lin in the past tense felt just as strange as it did in the present. Speaking about her at all turned Nel's chest to fire. "So wires—will I have to do this every morning?"

"Until you have an integrated one. Once you do though, you won't have to decouple it except for when it's being serviced, if you want."

"Wait, even for swimming?"

"Sure," Jem replied with a grin. "If you splurge for the fin attachment though, make sure you also get stabilizers in your other limb—the added strength and efficiency can do a number on your body trying to compensate."

"Shit." She watched Jem feed the wires through eyelets and into ports. It looked very *Terminator,* the aesthetic clearly utilitarian. The lower portion ended in a smooth broad arch, with no attempt to conceal its true nature. Nel fell down a mental hole of all the different feet she could have now— shovels, flippers, boots, even high heels, she supposed, if she were ever inclined to put one on her real foot. *Flesh foot. They're both still real. I guess.*

After a moment of protracted silence, Jem finished fiddling with a final wire and rocked back on their heels. "Alright, let's get you up. Ready?"

"I guess so." Nel cleared her throat. "You said it takes a while for them to feel like ours. Like you knew. Firsthand, I mean."

"I do." Jem turned and hiked up the back of their shirt and binder. Two patches of metal flanked the top of their sacrum, like an arrow, then narrowed and rose along the entire length of the tech's spine. "Ever see me moving stiffly, that's why. One of the older models. Also why I haven't gone forward with some of the other mods I'd like," they continued, pulling their shirt down and gesturing to their chest. "Some of the connections are a bit finicky and undergoing full anesthesia would be potentially traumatizing. Saving up for a newer model though."

"Saving?" Nel asked with a frown. She hadn't once considered how much this would cost. Everything had been tidily taken care of with IDH.

But there was no more IDH, not as far as their wallets and wellbeing were concerned. *Or love lives.*

"I was applying credits from my contract toward it. Made for a longer stint as a cryotech, but it would have been worth it."

"Credits? I'm sorry, I think there was some fine print I missed."

Their mouth quirked. "Isn't that very IDH. Everyone who ever lived up here has a contract—their health, food, lodging, recreational needs and so forth. When you want to switch jobs, you put in for the transfer, and all your needs are transferred to that faction as their responsibility. Of course, some have more resources than others to spend on their teams. Or fewer to spend it on. I promised to stay at that department longer if they covered the materials for my mods. Does that make sense?"

"Yeah. In a kind of nefarious way." Nel stared down at her limb. "How are we all paying for these things?"

Jem shook her head. "I think we're using all the resources we can for those who need them and are hoping something gets fixed soon."

A shudder that had nothing to do with integration or amputation juddered up her own spine. She was lucky. She knew that now. There were others, surely, on other ships, or even this one, who would have to wait longer. Whose injuries were, perhaps, too great to fully fix yet. *I should be grateful.* Her clumsy attempt at introspection was aided by the sudden burn of sensation.

"Ouch!" Fear followed the zing of pain. Any moment she expected the limb to combust, to rend her flesh anew, to trigger the screaming and accusations. When a few seconds passed and nothing happened, Nel put out one shaking hand and touched her thigh where it transitioned into metal and silicone. What would it feel like when she was integrated? Would phantom sensations wake her like they did now? Would they even be considered phantom at all? The concept tugged discomfort through her belly. *Acknowledge it, then fold it away.* Easier said than done.

Jem winced. "It's weird at first. These models have very little nuance." They tinkered with a few controls, then produced a tiny screwdriver. "I can turn the feedback off, if you'd like. So you control it but you can't feel it."

"Yeah. For now, I think that's better."

A twist of the screwdriver and the burning stopped. At least, the artificial burn through her sciatic. The other burn, the heat consuming her core, was always there.

"What do you think, Bently?" Jem asked with a bright grin. "Ready to walk again?"

"Fuck yeah."

Nel locked her chair in front of the parallel bars and levered herself upright. "Any tips?"

"Go slow. It's gonna feel different for everyone, and you're going to have to have patience."

"Patience? Never met her," Nel grumbled.

Jem rolled their eyes and crossed their arms over their chest. "When you're ready."

Weight supported by her arms, she took a step. There was a delay, almost imperceptible, but there. She had never had to think *walk* before and barely knew how. Now, she was a stranger, negotiating with something both her and not-her. *Step.* She rocked forward, weight easing onto the new limb. It was springy in a way her flesh leg wasn't. Bouncy almost. *Step.* She almost fell, her balance unsure how to distribute her weight without the aid of heel-to-toe. She clenched her jaw and quickly scooched her left leg forward. *Step.* "I think it's a bit too short."

"Maybe," Jem mused, eyes narrowed on Nel's gait. "Get to the end of the bars and we'll reevaluate."

Never had four meters felt so far. Nel lowered her head with a growl and lurched back into motion. Movement. It was Nel's balm. Years ago, she would run into the woods or take a long drive. Movement gave her the illusion of progress, of working through whatever had sent her running in the first place. And sometimes, by the time she made it back, she actually would have an answer. Now it was a reminder of how far she couldn't go.

It was an hour later, exhausted and annoyed, that Nel returned to the apartment. Her temples pounded and her muscles ached.

Bright, playful music drifted through the Kolisnyks' open doorway. It brought a smile to Nel's face, albeit a faint one. *Life.* It's what she had missed in the acerbic halls of *Odyssey.* Perhaps there were decks like these on the station too, places that teemed with culture and sound and scents of food and humans. Seeing it thriving here made her wonder if they had just been housed in the temporary rooms.

"Hey honey, how'd it go?" Mindi greeted. She was propped by the counter, looking at something on her tablet. Her face fell when she caught Nel's expression. "I'm sorry, sweetie. Hungry?"

"Starved. Headache." Nel lifted the right leg of her sweats. "Got some bling."

Mindi peered at the new limb with curiosity. "For all this high technology, that looks fairly Earthly to me."

"You should know better than anyone how thin resources are spread," Nel pointed out.

"Guess that doesn't help the protective mother in me."

Nel chuckled darkly and nodded to the cleanser. "I'm going to wash up. Want some tea when I'm out?"

Mindi nodded and rose. "I'll put the kettle on—or the—screw it, you know what I mean." She bustled off into the kitchen muttering about the rehydrator.

Nel smiled and grabbed a change of clothes before wheeling into the bathroom. Avoiding what she looked like standing in the mirror, she stripped and wobbled over to grip the overhead handle. Her new prosthetic was safe in the cleanser at least, though Jem forbade her from wearing it in the shower. Nel rubbed her neck. The headache didn't seem to be going anywhere. If anything, the smell of the cleanser and residual discomfort from her new leg made it worse. Light and disinfecting mist played across her scarred skin. Weeks without any actual sun faded her usual tan and freckles. Under the stark lights, her coloring was almost sallow.

The lights flickered again and Nel doubled over as nausea slammed into her.

"Murderer! Heretic!"

This time each of the voices screaming were Lin's. Nel's vision bleached white, the screaming turning from sound to pure white-hot pain. The ship's gravity failed and she tipped backward, spinning end over end. And then there was nothing.

Screaming woke her. This time it was her own. The sound died in her raw throat and she clawed herself back into consciousness. The first face she saw was Zachariah's, pixelated and far too large on a massive holoscreen.

"Hey, Nel."

Nel couldn't find which words to say, not even among the few dozen cusses she favored. *A stroke?* Her first fear dissolved in the face of at least four plausible science fiction explanations for what she just endured.

Movement flurried beside her and the screen was blocked by her mother's gripping arms and worried face. "Anna? Anna, sweetie, what happened?"

"I," Nel rasped, then tried again, "I don't know. Sorry." Deep aches filled every inch of her, even places she never knew could feel. She sat up, noting with some relief she was on the couch in their apartment. Her naked body was covered in a blanket. At least that ruled out anything terribly medical.

"Mrs. Bently—"

"She's my daughter, Dr. Lieberman," Mindi reminded, but after another smooth of Nel's hair, she stepped aside.

"Hey, Zach," Nel greeted, wincing at the sheer intensity of the screen's light. "What the hell happened? Did we hit an asteroid?"

Zach's face grew very still. So still, for a moment Nel thought they lost connection. Something terrible, something uncertain, underscored his assurance. "Your mother activated your emergency med contact. Why don't you tell me what you recall. So we're on the same page."

Tell me what you felt, so I can tell if you're a fucking loon, more like. She liked Zach. Even trusted him, as much as she trusted any medical person, which was to say, only as much as was necessary to get her the hell out of there. She glanced at her mother then dragged the pitiful force of her confused gaze back to the psychologist. "I was in the shower—cleanser, whatever. After PT. My head hurt, but I had a headache all morning. I was just washing and then, wham. There was this awful noise. And just—" She shook her head. "I thought we crashed."

"Can you tell me what you saw?"

"I..." She shook her head. "I didn't. Or couldn't. Just white. And the sounds. Screaming, metal ripping, wind. It sounded like—" She stopped herself. Her eyes fixed on some point far behind the corner of the holoscreen. There hadn't been a crash. Or any asteroid. Or anything at all, outside of her own mind.

"Nel? What did it sound like?"

"Nothing, I think I'm just overtired. I haven't been sleeping much. A lot going on. I think I just did too much and had low blood sugar."

"You're still having trouble sleeping?" Zachariah asked.

"Yeah. Weird dreams."

"That's difficult, I imagine. Disruptive dreams can be a result of unprocessed trauma. I know some people have found sitting with the thought, acknowledging it, then setting it aside easier than trying to shove it away repeatedly. Maybe pairing that with the breathing you already use could help."

She nodded, though it sounded way easier said than done.

Zach stared at her a moment longer but seemed unwilling to press it further when they had an audience. "I'd like to see you again in a few days. If that's alright. We have a good chance now to make headway on some of the underlying things that might be bothering you. Instead of just throwing on a Band-Aid. I can speak with the doctor and have him give you something to help you sleep."

"Okay." It might be worded as a suggestion, but Nel knew better than to argue. Maybe he was right. Maybe the hundred cracks in her psyche finally reached all the way through. Maybe she was breaking.

"Good." He watched her for another moment, then made a note before glancing back up. "How are you feeling right now?"

"Sore. Tired. But fine, I guess."

"I think you should rest today, even if it's not sleep, just closing your eyes might do you some good. Mrs. Bently, will you be available for her?"

"I don't need that," Nel insisted. "I can nap unsupervised. I'm just going to grab some food and crawl into bed. Promise."

"Anna—"

"Mom," she pleaded. The last thing she needed was a fuss. The last thing she needed was for everyone else to realize what she already knew: she was nuts. Planning. That was a good place to start. "I'm okay. Just working too hard. I'll look at my schedule tomorrow, Zach, to figure out a time, alright?"

"I think that would be best. I look forward to speaking with you and please, if you need anything, if something happens again between now and our next appointment, please call me."

"I will," she lied with a smile. "Thanks for talking to me."

"Alright, archaeology princess, you be well." The screen blinked out.

Mindi stared at Nel for a long moment before pushing the folded pile of clean clothes toward her. "I'm going to get you something to eat. You get dressed."

Nel wordlessly slipped on her boxers and A-shirt before pulling the blanket back over herself. She felt wan and shaky. *Empty.* By the time she was settled at one end of the couch, tea steamed on the table between them. She couldn't meet her mother's eyes.

"Will you call him again?" Mindi asked.

"Yeah." Nel cleared her throat. "I'll stick to it. Probably not as much as Zach would like me to, but that's part of what we're working on. That and my anger. Out here everyone does therapy. And I wish I'd done it sooner."

"Good." Her mother seemed unable to look away from her face. "You know, I think the past few months—years, I guess—would have been a lot easier if we could have done this more...or at all."

Words couldn't fit past the tightness in Nel's throat, so she just nodded.

"It was agony, you know. Having you gone. Not knowing where you were or why you went. If Lin shows up here, the first thing she's doing is meeting me. I have to see what's so special about her that you took off to space."

"If you figure it out, let me know, okay?" Nel muttered.

Mindi laughed, but the sound was soft and sad and faded too fast. "Are you okay? Really?"

Nel floundered. *No. I haven't been.* Not for a long while, probably. She was breathing, she was fed, she was sheltered. She had so much more than so many. "I wish I knew what I'm doing, Ma. Usually it's some half-cocked idea, but this is way worse. I'm so glad you're here, but so scared too. The whole way back, since I learned Earth went dark, finding you was my only thought. I mean, saving the world is fine, but you." She tried a smile. "You're my world."

"I'm so sorry, honey."

"For what?" Nel frowned.

Her mother reached out one hand, then the other, both grasping her daughter's, the delicate thin skin taut over the sharp lines of her knuckles, bird bones compared to Nel's blocky, calloused fingers. "You are enough. You were always, always enough. My beautiful, complicated baby, full of fire and fury and laughter and so, so much pain. I love you. And maybe I should have told you more. Maybe I should have told you all the ways you awed me. All the ways you made me proud." Her fingers squeezed with deceptive might. "You might be feeling like less out here where space is so big, where these monsters are so mighty, where we seem so small. But you're enough. Even here. Even now. And to me, especially so. You will always be enough, just as you are. Just as you will become."

Nel's throat was too tight to speak, her vision too watery to meet her mother's gaze, but she squeezed back. She squeezed until she worried both their bones would break. Until she felt real and flesh enough to swallow, look up, and smile. "I love you, Mom."

"I love you too, Nel."

Nel's smile broadened a bit at the change in nickname. "It's okay. I don't mind you calling me Anna. No one else though. That's just you."

"Good, because that one felt a bit weird," Mindi confessed, nose wrinkling. "You want a snack?"

Nel nodded, and Mindi retreated to the kitchen. The blanket was warm over her leg, and the tea settled her churning stomach. Nel had that, even if she didn't have patience, or a girlfriend, or a high-quality prosthetic. She watched her mother breathe in the aromatic steam from their tea. *And Mom. I've got her, too.*

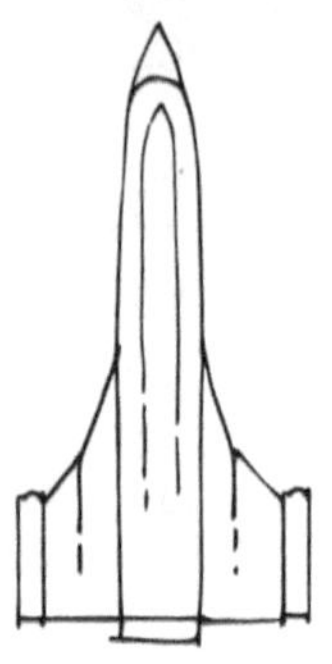

EIGHT

"Bently?"

"Fucking Christ, Dar, I'm naked!" she snapped, one arm covering herself as she peered, accusing, at the comm speaker in the ceiling. She was half dressed, doing exercises in her room to avoid thinking about the world outside the recycled plastic of her door.

"What? It's not like I can see you."

"It's not like I know that," she muttered back. "What do you want?"

"I got your message. About helping."

Nel grimaced. She had sent it off late the night before, lying awake wondering what the fuck was wrong with her brain. She'd forgotten, honestly, until now.

"Any chance you're free tonight? Assuming you meant it."

"I meant it." *Not really.* But maybe he was right, maybe her brain was atrophying without a puzzle to work on. "Busy tonight, though. Sorry."

Wherever he was, she pictured the smile he reserved for particularly entertaining barbs. "What could you possibly have to do?"

"It's Friday, or would be back home. Mom's cooking her famous cabbage pie and roast chicken—made with insect protein this time." It felt weird dressing while talking to him, but she shoved the thought aside and donned a clean set of sweats. Far weirder things had happened.

"Can't she just do it tomorrow?"

"You say that to your mom about her cooking?" She really had no idea if Mom-Nalawangsa cooked or was anything like most of the mothers she'd met. Judging by the silence that followed, however, she was right.

"I need another twenty sets of hands if I'm to comb through all this data. As it is, Sepulveda's been up almost every night trying to help me make sense of it." He drew a long, seemingly painful breath. "Alright, here's your deal: I show up tonight wherever it is you live. You get dinner with your mom and I get your help."

Her eyes narrowed with distaste. "I'm not in the habit of inviting folks over."

"Well, good thing I invited myself."

Nel bated, weighing her options. Maybe he wouldn't be as insufferable with a chaperone. *Or he'll be worse.* "You insult my mom, or her cooking, or act anything like your usual shitty self and you're out on your ass."

"Deal." Dar cut the call before either realized it was probably the last way they wanted to spend the night. Nel hopped over to her tiny bedside shelf and peered into the mirror. As a kid, she avoided them because she didn't look girly enough. For a while, as a teen and into her twenties, she didn't mind because she finally liked what she saw. Now, though? Now all she saw was a stranger.

Scraping her tousled hair back, she eyed the dark blonde steadily reclaiming her head from the dyed light brown. Maybe it was time to cut it. She'd always liked having it long enough to tie back, but maybe her number of limbs wasn't the only thing that needed to change. Regardless, she wasn't about to take clippers to it in the bathroom like she had at thirteen, so she grabbed her crutch and hobbled back out into the living room.

Mindi was in the kitchen, unpacking the crate of their weekly provisions of protein packs and dry goods. "Hey, Mom."

Her mom glanced up. "Hey, honey. You manage to get some sleep?"

Nel nodded, wondering how much of the conversation had filtered through the door. "You off today?"

"I am. Double shift tomorrow though. Finally distributing whatever we picked up from that stop."

Nel looked down. "Dar just called. He's coming over this evening. I told him I'd help with the latest mystery but that it had to be here. Couldn't postpone Family Friday."

"That's very generous of you with my time, Annelise Bently." Mindi's brow arched and she glanced at Nel.

Nel stopped. Her mom had been here for longer than she had, and for all she knew had started a book club. "We still do Family Friday, right?"

Her mom's face softened. "Oh, of course. I just meant inviting others over for dinner. I think we'll manage fine, especially with whatever extra we'll get next week." She glanced at the pantry, eyes darting about as she did whatever mental calculus kept them fed.

Nel winced. "Yeah, I'm not thrilled either. He kind of invited himself. I can make dinner—"

"Like I'd stake my reputation on your cooking," Mindi teased, pulling out her tab and making a few notes in what was probably a digitized version of her grandmother's recipe book.

"It's just Dar." Nel watched her mother's motions for a second, then drew a breath. "Look, he's not the nicest person. I know I said everything was safe up here when you asked—"

"Annelise, I can make my way up here just fine. It's you I worry about. First you were on the run and then next thing I know you're going to the moon—"

"Samsara."

"Moon, Jupiter, Samsara, it made no difference." She frowned. "I know it's dangerous."

"These are different people," Nel started to explain, but stopped. Explaining warring space factions was something she'd only ever done when trying to catch up on their daytime TV specials. "Out here everyone's dangerous, I think."

Mindi eyed her for another quiet minute, then straightened. "Well, if I know anything, it's that you can't dwell if you're busy. C'mon, Anna, this protein block won't chop itself."

The afternoon flew by and, despite her whirling thoughts, Nel lost herself in the routine of helping her mother cook. The distinctly different smell of the protein combined with the achingly familiar scent of rosemary and garlic. By the time Dar knocked just before dinner, the entire apartment smelled like home, and some of the tension between her shoulders had eased.

"Hey," Nel greeted.

"Bently." He flashed a smile and held up a basket covered with intricately embroidered red cloth. "I've got some things for your mother."

Nel's brows rose. Regardless of how he treated her, his manners seemed to match the upbringing she imagined he and Lin had enjoyed. "Thanks, come on in." She hopped backward to allow Dar room to enter the tiny hall. He toed off his boots and slipped on plain flats before following her in.

"Evening, Mrs. Bently," he said with a deep nod. "It's an honor to meet you properly and to be over for dinner."

Mindi's face lit up and she offered a hand. "I'm glad to finally see the face of the institute who press-ganged my daughter into scientific servitude."

Dar's polite mask froze until Nel smacked his arm. "She's teasing. Learn to take it if you're gonna dish it out. Besides, Mom," she continued, looking over, "we're all just people out here—at least that's what Dar told me when I woke up here."

"You were high on painkillers."

"Probably also why I remember you not being a total—" she caught her mom's narrowed gaze, "jerk."

"Obviously." Dar's polite smile returned and he held out the basket. "From my household to yours. I know rations are a bit tight, and I so rarely cook for myself."

Mindi accepted it graciously, pulling back the cloth to reveal several more packets of protein, a tin of spices, and several pears. "This is lovely, thank you. Are you hungry now? Food should be ready shortly—I'm almost as good with these appliances as I was with my old Amana."

"Famished, and it smells incredible," Dar answered. He gestured to the couch. "Would you mind if I set up some of my work? Nel offered to go over some things with me this evening."

"I'm no stranger to working dinners. Why don't you two get started? This kitchen's too tiny for all of us to squeeze in anyway. Dar, I hear you were raised out here?"

"I was," he confirmed, setting down his tab and several data drives. He opened up a few screens, all of which were filled with an overwhelming amount of very tiny words and several complex schematics. "My sister, Lin, and I were born on *Odyssey of Earth,* one of our largest space stations. She was raised there, while I spent more time on my mother's home planet, Samsara."

"That's the one you were excavating, right, honey?" Before Nel could do more than nod, Mindi was off again, grilling Dar on his childhood.

Nel half listened, wishing she was hearing these stories from Lin instead. She settled on the couch and peered at the screens. Coordinates and timestamps she recognized, as well as the hundreds of audio files his computer seemed to be scanning. One screen was dedicated to what looked like the blocky, battered databank Mo was examining before his death. Nel shuddered, secretly grateful most of that data appeared corrupted.

"Nel's been, I believe. It was luxurious, but honestly I think the reasoning was as much due to the limit of human imagination as it was wanting something familiar."

"Been where?" she asked, glancing up.

"The center of *Odyssey.*"

"Oh, yeah." She met her mom's eyes. There was an odd expression in them, as if of all the fantastical things she had witnessed, the forest in the heart of a space station was too much for Mindi to process. "It's beautiful."

"I can't imagine. What was it like?"

Nel searched for the right words. How to describe something indescribable? The sheer power of the place, the false sun high above, feeding the whole with the power of Phil's thoughts. "It smelled like home."

Mindi shook her head at that, then turned to check their food. "Now your parents—where did they grow up then?"

Nel chuckled and turned her attention back to the data. The last screen contained a searchable collection of audio transcripts which, judging by the sheer nonsense of what she could decipher, was automatically generated. "This is a nightmare. What even is half of this?"

He glanced over. "Aberrant audio data from various outposts and stations. Got my hands on some from Samsara too, but it cost more than I would have liked. Good and the bad of big stations like Tersa Eth: everything you could possibly want, but competition for it's steep. It'll be far harder to get any of the data from the IDH mission."

"I knew you had other reasons for stopping," she muttered, peering at a particularly steamy conversation between a pilot and his senti-comp during what sounded like a routine systems test. "Are any of these from our fleet?"

"No. Those are being scanned, but they're in each ship's databank. Why? See something?" His gaze sharpened to its usual predatory gleam.

Hearing something, more like. But what if she wasn't? What if all the crazy she thought was finally crashing down wasn't so much a long overdue mental breakdown as it was a symptom. Evidence. She wished she could wave away the chatter, wave away the dread that was sinking into her belly.

"Anna?"

She blinked and looked up. "Sorry, just thinking."

Dar turned to Nel with a vicious, delighted grin. "'Anna?'"

"Fuck. Off."

"Language!" Mindi insisted. "I don't care if you hang around with space ruffians all day, you don't have to talk like one under my..." she waved a hand, "hull."

Dar glanced down at himself, smoothing a hand over the front of his sleek robe. "Ruffian?"

"Your manners may be impeccable, Komodor Muda Nalawangsa, but you are the only person I've ever met with an attitude worse than hers."

"Ouch," Nel joked, though she was silently cheering she at least came out on top. She jabbed a finger at Dar. "And if you so much as think of calling me anything but Dr. Bently or Nel, I'll tell everyone on this boat my mom thinks you're a ruffian."

"Fine." He grimaced and stalked over to look at the data with her. "Once we get it organized we can actually start making headway."

"How far back does it go?"

"Well, excluding the Samsari data, it's from the initial reports of aberrant signals on Earth up through just after you all came out of cryo."

"Which time?"

Mindi glanced up in alarm. "You were in cryo more than once? For how long?"

"Ah, twice now, if you don't count the coma they induced for transport, which I don't. Was unconscious anyway. Two years the first time, two weeks the second. It's cheaper than feeding us for the trip, I think, that's why they're obsessed with the idea up here."

"It's far more complex," Dar muttered. "And I believe the second."

"What about where?" Nel asked, before the conversation devolved further.

"Who knows." Dar heaved a sigh. "Half of what we've been combating is the sheer volume of data. It's a good problem to have, but it's daunting. And the cataloging system is utter—" he glanced at Mindi, "—ly useless."

They both jumped when Mindi snapped, "Oh let me see it!" She strode across the room, tossing her dishtowel aside to peer at the screen. She tugged a folder out with a scowl. "You've two, no, three different filing systems. There's no sense in going through all this if you can't keep it organized. Get a universal cataloging system like..." She eyed the documents, typing an example with one hand. "Date, location, relevancy—that last based on content, I presume. A fourth column would be helpful to indicate any associated events that were unusual. You'll still have to manually edit anything that doesn't fit the correct format, of course..."

Dar looked up with surprise. "Mrs. Bently, I didn't know you were a scientist."

She snorted, waving her hand. "I'm better—I'm a research librarian. Organization will solve all problems, my dear."

"Now you know what my childhood was like if my room ever got messy," Nel muttered. "Hell."

"I've been meaning to comment on your room here," Mindi warned. She made a last adjustment and sat back. "It would take me a few hours to finalize this, but I could have it done by the end of the evening."

Dar's eyes widened. "This whole time it was the wrong Bently I was asking for help. Is there anything I can do?"

Mindi glowed, but swatted his arm with her cooking mitt. "Eat first. Then I'll save your skin, Komodor."

He unmade us.

Thrumming darkness enveloped Nel's senses. Even with every light turned off, their tiny apartment constricted, recycled bioplastic walls pressed inward despite the soft stream of cycled air and the faint vibration of very distant, powerful engines. Her mouth tasted of sand and ash.

Were the words real? In her head? Instead of growing clearer, with every episode she grew more and more uncertain. She drew a shuddering breath, shoving away the images that surfaced against the darkness of her room and sat up. "Computer: room lights."

The bedside light flickered on, brightening gradually over the next two minutes as she dropped to the floor for her pushups. Another five minutes were claimed by her half-assed hand PT exercises. Thick scarring marbled the flesh but grew more supple every day. Donning thin gloves was more a fashion statement than a necessity now. Nel set about attaching her leg before slipping her computer into her bag and heading for the door. One crutch helped balance the worst of her lurching steps. *At least no one's awake to watch if I eat shit.* Soft blue numbers glowed on their living area wall:

0321

In another two hours the colors would ease into white and then pink and gold, mimicking the light of dawn. She hadn't asked yet if all apartments did that, or Mindi had chosen the settings. Not wanting to wake her mother, Nel snuck through the door and down the hall. Even the lively Kolisnyk apartment was still. The scent of molasses and cleanser clung to the air. She made her way down the hall to the rec room. It was larger than she had first thought, with battered game tables on one side and peeling vinyl chairs and couches on the other. One corner boasted a bank of cabinets.

Curiosity peaked, she dropped her bag on one of the chairs and went to investigate. Glasses and boxes of powdered drink mixes were the only contents. A second perusal assured she wasn't missing so much as a bottle of Kamchatka. "All the tech in the world and you can't provide a single decent drink, Dar?" she grumbled. Resigned to sobriety, Nel hauled her computer over to one of the half-dozen study alcoves set into the rec room's walls.

She set the holobar down and booted up the screen. Dar, with some reluctance, had agreed to give her personal computer access to the project's data viewing and searches only, not editing, of course—only after she threatened to come personally find him whenever she had a question. It still made little sense to her, but after her mother's saving grace, at least it was organized. Shrinking the audio signature column, she instead focused on the transcripts. Many were still garbled. Many more, however, were clear enough to make out the majority of the phrases.

She cracked her stiff knuckles and drew a breath. *Here goes nothing.* She brought up the advanced search portal. Her fingers hovered over the keys for a moment before she let them loose:

SEARCH: he unmade us; heretic; now we are this
SIMILAR PHRASES: YES

She toggled on the choice to run the search in the background and sat back. There was no way to do the whole thing manually, but reading through brought a few chuckles—humans were nothing if not messy and complicated and horny. Space, apparently, didn't change that. Years compiling data sets for academic publications and official reports for CRM clients granted her the skillset to sort data, but it certainly hadn't improved her patience for how tedious such tasks were. Thoughts glazed her eyes as they lidded, unfocused on the shifting frequencies and transcripts.

Her mind slipped into the liminal space between daydreams and memories until it blended a new reality into the dark, small hours within *The Recursive*'s bowels. A reality where Nel looked up to see Lin in the doorway. Lin on the rooftop in Chile, with her black-hole eyes. Lin, sandblasted on Samsara, turning back to save Nel. Lin, hair tousled by earthly wind as they raced along the Euphrates. Lin. Lin. Lin. Even in her daydreams Nel couldn't decide whether to scream at the other woman or tell her it didn't matter. To fall on her with fury or adoration.

"You need a break?"

Nel glanced up, blinking away tracers from the digital readouts. Emilio leaned, one arm braced, against the doorframe. Two ping-pong paddles dangled from one strong hand.

She let out a long, exhausted sigh.

"The data can run itself, you know."

She chuckled and pushed herself away from the desk. "I still don't trust this tech completely," she confessed. "I can't shake the feeling that the human component is what makes the difference."

He laughed and stepped back into the hall to let her pass. "Me too."

She limped up to the pong table, appraising its battered surface. "So I'm not very good at this. Most of the pong I played was of the beer variety."

"I'm not great at it either," he agreed. "Just helps keep my mind busy. I imagine that's why you're out here during the witching hours too?"

She hummed, taking the proffered paddle and practicing a few swings. "I can't sleep. Like, I lie there with my eyes shut kind of pretending. 'Cause at least that's resting. But even when I'm drifting my brain just keeps looping images, words, mostly stuff from the last few years. The bad bits."

"I think we've all seen things that make it hard to sleep. You're not alone in that." His tone wasn't diminishing but welcoming. "I have nightmares too."

"What're we doing out here? Honestly? Because from where I sit, this whole thing sucks. There's gotta be something better. I mean, just look at the number of people on Tersa Eth. Like we could disappear out there. Big-rig even said IDH wasn't the biggest bird in the sky."

Thwack. Bonk.

"So you did sneak out. Dar owes me a drink."

"I could have just seen it through the windows." Nel's face flamed at his pointed stare, however, and she gave a rueful smile. "Technically, I didn't sneak. I had a passkey. Dar bet I wouldn't?"

Emilio chuckled. "He bet you wouldn't succeed. Not so much that you wouldn't try."

"Guess you know me better."

"It was more his own hubris at how intimidating he is."

Thwack. Bonk.

The ball skittered across the surface and she sighed. If she was ever going to improve it might be worth seeking out the nearest DIY distillery. "Does Dar even drink? He strikes me more as the kid buying his friend's Adderall to overachieve."

Emilio was quiet, dark eyes following the battered ball as he returned the volley. After another smack, he answered, "He's always got something in his port."

The tone wasn't judgmental, and Nel suddenly felt ashamed for even speculating. Who was she to talk, the woman who spent the days after Mikey's death drunk and bent over a tinny jukebox instead of solving the myriad problems at hand? "I guess with ports, drinking isn't really a thing up here, huh?"

"We're all still human and will do anything to forget that fact. Tashante—my neighbor here—makes some pretty good bucket-wine. Have to listen to his stories to get any. They're borrowed and mostly consist of one-upping whatever one you just shared, but they're good stories at least. Better than the wine."

Nel laughed. She knew the type. Archaeology was filled with them. Or maybe that was just humanity.

"So," Emilio began, nodding to the computer chugging away on the table next to them, "what are you looking for?"

She lifted a shoulder. *Thwack.* She didn't want to risk telling Zach, and she didn't want to worry her mother. But Emilio was honest, even when it hurt. "We're scanning for signals. Frequencies. Patterns. Have you tried actual phrases?"

Bonk.

"Something you think we're missing?" Emilio's thick brows drew together and his lips pursed in thought. "You think someone's triggering these events with words? What happened with Mo—"

Nel's nose burned with the smell of rent pipes, ruptured flesh, scorched metal and clay and helplessness. Her throat longed for the erasing burn of booze. "Half of that shit I'm ready to blame on IDH. That whole thing was just a fucking cover-up."

"Paranoid much?"

"Am I wrong?"

He shook his head. "Mo's death was due to the safeguards within his biomech augmentation. Who triggered that safeguard is certainly up for debate. But the mechanics of his death itself have been proven by both IDH's forensic techs and our own. Dr. de Lelis's as well."

She smacked the ball back far harder than necessary. It flew wide, bouncing from the wall behind Emilio to disappear under the cracked vinyl sofa. She grumbled and hopped over to the couch, lowering herself in stages until she could peer underneath. *Gross. Space-dust bunnies.* She stretched, fishing the ball out and ignoring the sock, broken necklace, and the brown, moldy mystery lump beside it. When she straightened, she didn't turn, staring at the ball as if awaiting the words "Try Again" or "Good Chance" to appear on its surface. "Emilio, can I talk to you?"

"I hope at some point we will be good enough friends that we can forgo your awkward overtures."

"I'll never not be awkward, at least not with this dry-county of a ship. So good luck with that." She cleared her throat, searching for the right words that weren't "auditory hallucinations." The words she wanted to speak were too large to fit past her denial and common sense. "On the train to

Alexandria you said the Teachers were like spirits. In some of the Founders lore I've been reading they come across as gods, or what maybe we'd think of as ghosts or superheroes. Greek demi-gods. Angels."

He did not answer, but his bright brown eyes seemed to glow from within, the weight of his honesty forcing her own from her chest.

"What did that sound like? Or feel like?"

"I wasn't there, you know."

"I just thought maybe you'd have some stories."

"It's as you say—something other than human, but still a person. A being. I think it differed from person to person, culture to culture, even through the years it's been romanticized. Simplified. You've come to me in the past asking academic questions. But this doesn't sound like the same line of research. Why do you ask?"

"I, ah…" She shifted, shrugging deeper into her sweatshirt in hopes that somehow she might still remember that she was Nel, skeptic and scientist, after she spoke the words. Her scarred fingers tightened around the battered ball. "Just curious. A lot of speculation out here about tech and faith. I kind of empathize with your ancestors."

"Yours too, you know," he teased. "The Teachers didn't just visit us brown folk. We're just better at remembering our history."

"Probably because you're not trying to hide half of yours." Nel snorted. The secret in her chest longed for freedom, longed to search through Emilio's stories and Dar's hypotheses, and even Zachariah's faith, in the off chance it discovered a story, an anecdote, anything at all that told her the voices she was hearing were real. Pride, and not a small amount of fear, however, hobbled her mouth. She settled for searching the database and hoping someone among the transcripts shared her secret. Nel lurched to her feet to return to the game, brandishing the ping-pong ball. "What do you say—best three of five?"

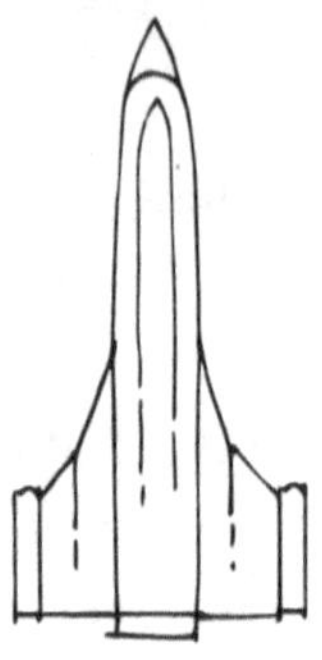

NINE

A faint, tinny alert interrupted Nel's third round of prosthetic training—or bootcamp, as she was coming to think of it. She snarled and reached for her comm. It was probably just another bulletin about restricting water bathing to once a week. She didn't care what they said about how advanced the science was, the cleanser left her feeling vaguely sticky.

"Finish your rep first," Jem suggested.

"It might be Dar."

"Dar thinks everything he does is important. For all you know he farted and decided it's the greatest ode to the human experience."

Nel laughed and forced herself the next few steps to the end of the bars. Apparently, Jem had quickly discovered the only thing that got Nel moving was spite and frustration and had leaned hard into dissing Dar.

"You all making headway?" Jem asked.

"On…?" Nel hazarded. She had no clue what anyone knew anymore. Rumors had quieted in the weeks since their stop, with the blackouts just regular enough to dispel all but the wildest conspiracies.

Jem's mouth quirked. "Our stop was strictly monitored but not terribly necessary. Dar strides around broodier than usual. Now your computer tells you something interesting enough to distract you into actually standing on your own. It doesn't take a rocket scientist to realize you all are working on something."

"Well, headway is nonexistent," Nel mused, turning and making her uneven way back along the bars. "Mind if I just look at this for a second?"

The medic slid Nel's chair over, but Nel shook her head. Carefully balanced, she removed one hand from the bar and tapped her comm. Instead of Dar's dulcet disdain, a notification projected above her wrist:

SEARCH COMPLETE
RESULTS: 3,201 (similar phrasing), 2 (exact matches)

She expanded the window. A quick glance at the similar phrasing indicated her next search attempt needed to be far more specific—conversations varied from "gross—he made this soup last week" to "now let's try this." Nel's cheeks pinked at the realization that a fair amount of her and Lin's pillow talk—actually, all of their talk—

was probably contained somewhere in the database. When she glanced up, she was met with Jem's smirk. "What?"

Jem just jerked a nod at Nel's legs.

"Oh." Nel was standing. No hand holding the parallel bars. No wobbling. Just a wide stance, hip cocked to put more weight on her uninjured leg. The realization broke her unconscious ease, however, and she teetered for a moment before grabbing the bar to steady herself.

"Told you it was as much psychological as physical."

Nel made a face. "Hard to fix that when my brain has a one-track mind."

"And would that one track be paranoia or sex?" Jem held her gaze for an extra moment before pointing at the faint glow of the hologram. "Good news?

"Maybe?" She opened the exact matches. *Holy fuck.* Heart hammering in her ears, she fumbled with her comm. "I need to make a call. Are we—?"

"You're all set. Don't forget to do your exercises. You really are making good progress."

Nel barely listened as she pulled on her sweatshirt and settled back into her chair. "Thanks, see you next week."

"And Nel?"

She stopped in the door, popping a quick wheelie out of sheer excitement.

"Good luck."

She flashed a grin and set off down the hall. A left and then a long ride down the fairly deserted corridor. It was there that she thumbed the call button beside Dar's name on the wobbling holoscreen.

"What."

"Rude," she snapped back.

"I wasn't aware our friendship progressed to greetings."

"Or into friendship at all," she muttered. "Fine, if you're too busy I won't tell you about what I found in the database."

"Meet me at Emilio's in five."

"No. Just finished PT. I'll be there in half an hour," Nel relayed. The sweat she worked up during PT was something she wouldn't subject even Dar to—mostly because she didn't want to listen to him bitch about it.

"We'll see you then." He cut the call and Nel stared at the data. She wasn't crazy. She was an asshole and probably an alcoholic, but she wasn't crazy. *Mom would be so proud.*

Despite her insistence that Dar could wait, she raced through the cleanser and was three minutes early when she rolled to a stop outside Emilio's room. The door was open, screened with a sheer red drape. The faded Los Pobledores symbol was embroidered across it. Two sets of low, deep voices drifted from inside.

She paused, drawing a breath in an attempt to control the feelings and frustrations roiling under the surface of her thoughts. She lifted the curtain and peered inside.

Dar sprawled on a chair. His head was lifted, face open and curious in a way she rarely saw. Emilio muttered something and Dar's head tilted back as he laughed, long and loud. Nel's heart faltered at the sight. He was so much like Lin, and her heart pinched at the thought that Nel might never see her laugh again.

All thoughts fled from her head, however, when she saw Emilio cross the room and set a gentle hand on the pilot's shoulder. She could have written it off as a friendly gesture, but the same could not be said for the look on Dar's face when Emilio turned back to his computer screen.

Well that's more interesting than any database search. Nel pointedly knocked on the doorframe. "Hey."

Dar glanced over, cheeks darkening a shade. "Bently. Half expected you not to show up." His Spanish was better than Nel's, though his accent leaned more toward Spain's than Chile's.

Nel let him have the barb, just waving some jazz hands in response. "Surprise. Don't make me regret my effort at socializing."

"I don't know if I'd call this socializing," Emilio remarked.

"Even better." She pulled up beside the coffee table.

Dar's eyes were bright with fixation. "This about that search you ran?"

She glared and gathered what thunder he hadn't stolen. "How'd you know about my search?"

"Emilio mentioned you were trying some alternate methods."

Nel snorted. *That's a kind way to refer to my fucking goose chase.* "Look, before we start, I need you to hear me out. Or just, I don't know, pause the whole moon-sized-ego thing." Dar said nothing, but his lips pursed. "I heard something. A few somethings."

"I assume you're not talking about a rumor."

"No. A week ago I collapsed. Had some sort of episode. You know when your brain misfires and you hear your name, clear as day? But no one's there?"

He regarded her for a long moment, looked at Emilio across the room as if to accuse him of keeping this secret. "I do."

"Like that. I told Zach I was just tired, but fuck," she glanced at Emilio, pleading he, at least, believe her, "Emilio, this was real. I heard it. Keep hearing it. Loud, clear, a fucking voice from the sky. And it's as if there are many voices. But not like, out of sync. Made me think of demons, you know? 'I am Legion.' And it wasn't just a voice, it was a whole fucking feeling. Ran up my spine, like it was inside me. In my head, but not in the made-up sense. In the everywhere sense. And it hurt." Every attempt at ordering her thoughts failed. None of them made any sense, at least none she was willing to face. "It's been happening for a while. I just thought it was me. Something wrong with me. But I don't think so anymore."

Dar's eyes narrowed. "And you're sure it's real?"

Nel shrugged. "No. But it feels as real as anything."

Dar sighed, but Emilio said nothing for a moment, his face unreadable. "And there is no other explanation?"

"You don't think I would have exhausted that line of thought before embarrassing myself enough to tell you? Before trying a hairbrained search? It's been happening for weeks. Since I woke up." She gestured to her wrist comm. "Look, it'd be easier to show you. Is there some way I can share this—"

Dar leaned across her and tapped a few commands. A second later a hologram flickered into being above Emilio's table.

"I set up a parameter based on the phrases, rather than the actual characteristics of the sounds," she explained, scrolling down. She hadn't dared to look at them before, but now she wished she had, wished she'd thought to screen the results for absurdity. For insanity. A tap brought up the exact matches.

There.

Glowing almost cheerfully against the translucence of the holographic screen, were the words that wormed into her dreams and haunted her waking mind, stitching the two together until she wasn't sure if there were boundaries. If there ever had been.

"There. That's when I had my, ah," her finger trembled as she brushed it against the screen, sending ripples through the pixels, "my reaction."

Dar leaned forward to scan the details of her search parameters. "'Now we are this…he unmade us…' these phrases." His words petered out, eyes narrowing. His mouth opened, but for once, it seemed as if he didn't have a snide retort. Or he was exercising a surprising amount of suspension of disbelief.

Nel forced herself to barrel onward. "There are a lot of duds and a few that belong in a voyeur's wank-bank, but I did get some real results. I don't know what it is, but you're hunting aberrant sounds and I'm hearing one."

Neither man spoke, Dar transfixed by the first actual evidence of their quarry that wasn't bodies and blood. Emilio, on the other hand, seemed just as intrigued with the man himself. Nel allowed the exclusion of their silence for all of about two breaths before the burn of anxiety flooded her mouth with desperate words. "Do you think I'm nuts?"

Emilio's warm eyes slid from Dar to her. It wasn't until his features softened that she realized his jaw had been clenched, staring at the pilot. He nodded toward the counter, beckoning her away from the nonsense of databases and search algorithms, to the homey comfort of his kitchen bar. She locked her wheels and hopped up onto one of his stools. "We've lost him for at least an hour," he confided softly.

Nel glanced back at Dar. "How? There's hardly anything to make sense of."

Emilio chuckled and set out three mugs. His motions were easy, practiced, comfortable even here among the stars his ancestors rebuked. "To us."

A pile of damp herbs sat in the mug he slid toward her, the dented aluminum and thick plastic a far cry from the silver-decorated chimarrão gourd Emilio had used in Chile. *There and here. Past and future.* At odds with one another, yet linked, tethered like magnets. Like Nel, at once drawn and destroyed by Lin. She bowed her head and took a long meditative sip. "Emilio, I mean it— my search might have delivered a zillion results, but most are shit. And that doesn't change the fact that I'm hearing voices."

Swirls of plastics layered the mug in browns and beiges. Her eyes picked out the arch of a blade-mean brow, the curve of peach lips. She blinked, as if that would do anything to erase the tea-leaf hint of fate. The heat she'd chalked up to anxious fear licked at the top of her stomach, sending curls of fire up her throat. Except now she thought it might be a deeper burn, a far more ancient fire stoked not by fear, but something else entirely. *Or it's acid reflux.*

"No, Dr. Bently," he answered, "I don't think you're crazy. I don't know what you heard, or why, or how. I don't know if it was this signal or a brain glitch, as you said. Or maybe even God." Emilio's face settled into a new expression. It wasn't scorn or disbelief. It was understanding. "But I believe it was real."

"It's simple," Dar insisted, drawing up the highly complex search he had run following Nel's clumsy attempt.

"Really, though, it's not," Emilio translated with a smile. He retrieved the almost empty mug from its precarious position at Dar's jabby elbow and replaced it with another steaming one. Judging by the lack of herbs and the faint sharp scent of citrus, this wasn't mate, but lemon water.

Nel doubted it would counteract whatever made Dar's pupils black pits and set his hands trembling. "Can you make it sound simple, at least?"

"Sure," Dar answered in a way that said even he knew it was a lie. "I combed through both sets of results with an advanced search and using your mother's system—praise be to God for her, Bently. I ordered everything by relevance and frequency and sure enough, there was a consistent signature, albeit more consistent in what wasn't there.

Mapping the negative space within the frequency—" he glared at Nel's glazed expression. "Oh come on, even an idiot could understand that."

Emilio snorted. "Perhaps when your brain is fueled by medical-grade stim and bottomless ambition, everyone's an idiot by comparison."

Dar's mouth snapped into a thin, displeased line. Sullen silence filled the room as he dragged several displays into place on the screen. "Here are your voices."

Nel frowned at the results. It wasn't one occurrence. Or even two. Dozens of timestamps filled the screen, going back as far as their database allowed. "It's not an anomaly?"

"No." Dar's voice slipped into that strange softness, the one reserved for secrets. "They're everywhere. Why you're the only one hearing them, I don't know, but we're...surrounded. They fill the void between conversations, even. It's like we have voices in place of—"

"Static," Emilio finished, staring not at the screen, but through it. Did he, like Nel, feel the echo of prophecy, of sanctity? The same whisper their ancestors felt when creatures of light and sound and terrible promise flickered into their lives?

"Can you trace it?" Nel asked.

Dar's sneer broke the fragile awe. "Already did. And I don't know what it means, but it's something. An answer. Or at least another, more pointed question." Another flick brought up a map which, after a moment, Dar expanded to fill the entire holographic projection area.

Nel had pored over maps of Samsara and traced schematics of *Odyssey of Earth.* She memorized site overviews of Los Cerros Esperanza VII and, decades before, carved the drive to her parents' home into the atrophied fibers of her heart. Nel's entire life could be marked in maps.

She had never seen a map like this one.

It was their sector of the galaxy, stars arrayed in brilliant golds and blues, and space stations marked with tidy white squares. Ephemeral lines denoted shipping and travel routes in digital spider silk. And blinking faintly was a silver dot labeled *Lahifa.* It didn't matter where they were in the yawning dimensions of whatever godforsaken sector this was. It didn't matter that, if she looked hard enough, she could find *The Recursive* light-weeks or whatever away from the colossal warship. It didn't matter where Nel planted her boots when she could point to a single glowing dot and say, "There. There flies the woman who tore open my chest."

"We're here," Emilio indicated. Even given the scale of the thing, Nel was uncomfortable with how close Lin seemed to be. "The rest of the fleet here, here, and," he searched for a moment before tapping a third location, "here. *La Fe De Amor* and *Āl Sinai* are flying tandem, of course."

"Of course," Nel echoed, though she had no earthly idea why.

"And these are the locations of each of your aberrant datasets." Dar overlaid a new layer, a swath of glittering pinpricks. They stretched and curved in a seemingly random line.

"Looks like a river," Nel remarked. "Or like the Milky Way."

Dar's features pinched in dismay. "What you call the Milky Way Galaxy is a series of spiral arms, not a—"

"The way it looks from Earth, Dar," Emilio interrupted before turning back to Nel. "Do you see the pattern?"

She looked closer. Several dots clustered around Earth, and another few where the gate was labeled with an asterisk: *fka Samsara*. And a dusting trailed after *The Recursive* itself. "Us. The voices are following us."

"You, mostly. And sometimes they follow and sometimes they precede, in the case of Earth, at least. Every single dataset falls within a few weeks of your presence."

Dread knotted in Nel's belly. She was a glorified troglodyte when it came to advanced technology, so why did she feel guilty? There was no way she was responsible. *Right?* Her memory lingered on the feel of the Samsari console under her suited hand, the grind of sand-gunked gears and corroded circuits. If her life had taught her anything, it was that she didn't need to know what she was doing to cause a fucking mess. "Look, I—"

"There is one exception," Dar admitted. The map zoomed in dizzyingly fast, to show the surrounds of Samsara. Its skies were empty save for a few transport ships and the distant loom of *Odyssey*. Hundreds of radio transmissions flickered at the bottom of the hologram. "This is the day Ada died."

Died. Nel's brain flickered with the images of Polyana, awoken to putrefaction. "That was years before I even knew about you guys, right? I thought your data only went back to—"

"When I saw the pattern, I called in a favor. This data is hacked from Dr. Patel's research."

"That's a breach of our radio silence," Nel protested.

Dar's eyes narrowed on the map. "Well, it got us answers, didn't it?"

Answers at the risk of all of our safety. She shoved the concern aside, too exhausted by danger to care anymore. If Lin found them, so be it. At least it would be Dar's fault. "Well," she prodded, "you two gonna tell me what the fuck this means?"

Dar leaned back, clearly above actually explaining his work and revelations. Emilio chuckled and switched to a third screen. "Bently, this is a high-clearance short-range personal transport. It departed from Samsara the day the planet went dark, trajectory undisclosed. And this is mining outpost Morphose-131, where the ship last docked."

Nel stared at the crags, the gnarled surface, the bleak gray landscape. It looked like every other asteroid she had seen in the last few weeks. The mining base was a chunky metal mite latched to its smaller end. A battered iris of a universal docking station protruded from the bulbous back end that must have served as a transport hangar. Something shuddered through her, something akin to the sensation when Jem altered the sensitivity of her prosthetic. *Otherness.* "This is some special base, right? Something unique? Otherwise why go?"

"Asteroids are always special—they have all sorts of trace minerals, clues about where they came from, what's passed by them. Little Roombas of the universe. The base itself is an old one, but one of thousands manufactured a few decades ago."

Nel peered closer at the image of the base. Her gut was screaming at her, screams that sounded like voices that weren't hers, weren't even human, maybe. "Samsara went dark because it received a signal, right?" she whispered. "What were the last transmissions to this place?"

"Bingo." Emilio offered her a golf clap. "A sound. Your sound, to be precise."

"We're going, right?" Nel's heart already hammered in response to her certainty, the promise of something finally happening. "When? We'll need to set eyes on the place, I assume—"

"I'll give you all the details, but only if you go with me. Not wasting my time updating someone who plans to just sit around with her thumb in unmentionable places."

Nel grimaced. "Help? Dar, look at me." She gestured to her body and chair.

"What's that, number fourteen in your books of pathetic excuses? Last I checked, the person who took over your excavation of Samsara was a man in a wheelchair. Besides, we're mostly scanning, maybe some slight recon if we find something. But," his delicate brows twitched suggestively, "I'd bet your life we will."

"Generous."

Dar let her wheedle with herself for all of two seconds. "Look, Bently, it's not going to grow back. I need someone who is trained to examine human remains and artifacts and interpret their meaning and significance. Someone who understands maps and systematic searches. You gonna help or not?"

She wished there was some excuse that made sense, that explained why she hadn't gone to half of her appointments, why she hadn't bothered to look through the vids on physical therapy, on how to use the latest accessibility devices, or flipped through the sample images of the various prosthetics she could order. Why she hadn't moved out of the hospital room until forced. She wished there was an excuse that wasn't fear. "Dar, if shit hits the fan, how am I gonna run? I can totter about on a crutch, but this chair runs on batteries and my own muscles."

"Space, Nel." He grinned, and it was honest, bright with the prospect of answers. "No gravity. Just pull yourself along."

"There's no gravity down there?"

"Most mining stations don't bother. Why make ore heavy when it can weigh nothing and save you some effort. Some of the newer ones have grav-habs, but this looks like one of the older models. At least twenty years old. Maybe older."

She scowled, then shoved one hand through the greasy tangle of her half-dyed hair. Her suit—rather the one that replaced the suit that melded to her arms in Chile—still had two legs, but maybe she could make it work. *And maybe if you had gone to more of your appointments you'd have a better one.* Dar was right. Her excuses were shit. Sure, she had a lot to process and face, but her biggest lie was saying that's what was really holding her back. "Fine. What do I need?"

"Gotta go in expecting anything." His fingers flew over his personal keyboard while the tech expanded the holo image. "I'll have to put in a request to the munitions people on the *Yarmouth*. They're what, two days away?"

"Seven," Emilio countered.

"Borrow a handful of heavy blast suits, maybe some enhanced gloves. Wish you had one integrated, have to say."

"Gross," she grimaced. "You don't want that, I'd be a hazard."

"Excuse number fifteen in the book, I'd say," he answered, voice pulled taut as he examined what appeared to be a refueling port. "Besides, you insist on showing up in the middle of shit, you might as well be armed."

"Well, I doubt an abandoned mine qualifies as the middle of any sort of shit," she muttered. "How long till we're there?"

"Ten days, once this scan ends. We can't use travel power until my dear sister has her attention focused elsewhere. And we'll take the long way, to be safer. This'll bring us within scanning of some of the bigger IDH ships, but mines aren't their faction, so I'm hoping we'll be ignored." His fingers flew over his own much smaller comm projection. There was an odd expression in his eyes as he looked up at the Los Pobledores leader. "You coming with, Emilio? We got enough full atmosuits."

"With you down there it's the perfect opportunity to take over this boat. Mutiny might break up the monotony." Emilio softened the threat with a wink.

"You're welcome to take over," Dar retorted. "I'm tired of dealing with everyone's problems."

Emilio snorted and retreated to the kitchen counter to concentrate on his comm, putting in requests for the litany of equipment required for making landfall—or asteroid-fall, Nel supposed. "What can I do?" she asked, glancing between the two of them.

Dar's sneer blossomed. "If I'd known giving you a project would pry you out of that hideous mire of self-pity, I'd have told you there was some mystery signal emanating from the recycler just to shake sense into you."

"I'd have seen through that, sorry," she quipped. "Besides, I'm still fully into the wallowing, this is just distracting for a bit. I'll be back to my morose norm as soon as my boot's back on *The Recursive*."

"I'd expect nothing less," he drawled, expression bordering on unhinged with excitement. "Better dust off your trowel, Bently. It's time to dig."

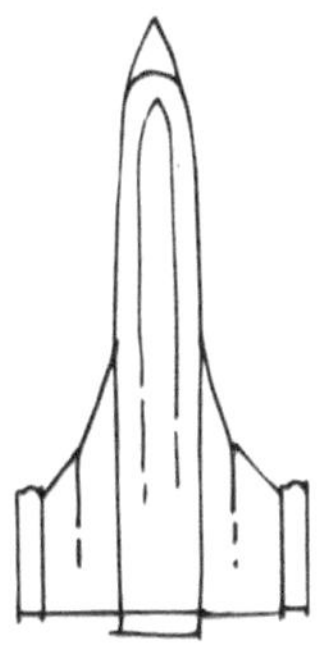

TEN

Dar's shuttle dropped from the docking bay. Darkness rose up to envelope them and Nel craned her neck to peer up at the ship. Watching it rise away, the bay doors easing shut in their wake, drove home how massive *The Recursive* truly was. Nel drew a breath through her nose, counting to herself as she tried to focus on the pocked surface far ahead, rather than the safety they left behind. The asteroid rolled slowly, twisting until its belly, pierced with the metal mite of the mining station, drifted into view.

"It's so tiny," Nel marveled. "I thought it'd be this giant complex."

"Most only host small crews, maybe a few scientists or researchers from various factions. And their respective families. Stations of this size produce several million tons before they're decommissioned. The size helps us move them once we've extracted all we can. Draw up all the drilling equipment, jettison what we truly can't take—stuff always builds up—and wait for the next hauler to pick you up. But this one was decommissioned several years ago."

Nel chuckled. "Reminds me of CRM. Call someplace home for a week, a month, a year, then pack it all up and move on."

Dar didn't answer, his hands caressing the shuttle's yoke, eyes scanning the instruments and surface ahead. They'd spent a week discussing how to proceed once they landed and three days alone on the shuttle approach. Hours were dedicated to how they would navigate each potential obstacle and outcome. Hours more on the challenges they couldn't begin to predict. It didn't matter now. They were free of the hulking protection of their ship and gliding toward the unknown—hurtling, really, Nel realized as the asteroid grew and grew and grew in the cockpit's windows.

And then the pocks were craters and the crags mountains and the shuttle landed with a lurch. Nel shot him a nervous glance to see his jaw was clenched and his knuckles white on the yoke. "We all cool, Iceman?"

"I hate landing in rural areas," he responded, drawing a long breath in through his nose before exhaling through his mouth with a woosh.

Nel regarded him curiously while the shuttle's hydraulics settled them into a stable crouch. "You know, based on the evidence, you're a shit pilot."

He glared back. "You think they'd promote a shit pilot to Komodor Muda, Dr. Bently?"

"They hired me. Plus, your family's all important and stuff. Just noting that half the planes you've flown crash-landed."

"One, Bently. One crash-landed. And it was still whole enough to have working power systems, might I add, hence why it helped you save the world."

"And why it blew off my leg."

"Picky picky," he drawled, unclipping his safety belt before rising. "Double-check your suit seals and I'll depressurize."

She did as he asked, watching the practiced flurry of movements as Dar powered their shuttle down and prepped for their exit. A glance to the back told her the crate they brought was still safely stowed. She jabbed at her wrist and confirmed her suit was sealed and the noise cancelation powered on, then jerked a nod at Dar. "Ready."

The air rushed from the shuttle, whipping tie-downs and straps. Then everything was still and they were engulfed in weightless silence.

"Alright, map should be on your helm…now." The glittering overlay spread across the craggy face of the asteroid and Nel blinked. After the dark cabin and black sky, the guidelines were eye-wateringly bright. "We're cutting straight across with our equipment—tethered, and with mag-boots in case of emergency. Let's keep the comms clear in case something comes up, alright?"

"Roger," she answered, bouncing down the gangway. She had switched the electroglove out for a mag one, her dominant hand coated with a slick black layer. *Suit: engage mag-nav.* Her left ankle twinged as her boot clapped to the asteroid surface. A faint tug on her wrist told her the glove was active.

Dar had already maneuvered the crate outside on the hovering cargo-lift. There was just enough space for them both to stand. "You gonna be okay with your prosthetic?"

"I have the added propulsion," she confessed. "It's a glorified crutch right now. But Jem thought it would be good practice."

"Well, let me know if we need to reevaluate. There are hooks along the way, of course, but it's hard to say what might have been damaged since anyone was here last." He clipped his tether to one of the crate's handles, watching as she clumsily did the same. "Secure?"

"Yep. Ready?"

"Affirmative."

She rolled her eyes at the lingo and wedged her left hand into the webbing that prevented their equipment from drifting into space. The lift whirred—rather, she felt the tremor through her suit. *No sound out here.* It was a peaceful thought. They rose slightly, then set off across the asteroid's surface. Without atmosphere, everything was terribly contrasted, with pitch darks and brilliant glints of light.

"Bently, 310."

"What?"

"310°. There's an anomaly on the surface adjacent to the mine."

"Investigate?"

He was silent for a moment, then he sighed. "Negative. Catalog. We'll start with an exterior sweep tomorrow. I want to run some detailed scans of the station itself. Try booting up the computer. See what the records say."

"I can check it out tonight while you do that. Doesn't sound like a two-person job, looking at the screens. Besides, it's not like I can interpret half that data."

"Fine," he agreed as they sped over the surface. The station was much closer now, and Nel realized it wasn't as tiny as she'd originally thought. Easily the breadth of the Bakjeeri spaceport and twice the length, it crouched like an architectural arachnid, teeth sunk into the meat of the asteroid itself. She brought up the map, glancing between the two. "You wanted to get in via the transport corridors—is there another way?"

"Not unless I want an emergency override. And I'd rather do all the scans before I go meddling with the systems."

"Understood. Where do you want to park, then?"

"Just outside the main structure. There's a set of access doors where we'll enter, once I determine the structure's integrity."

The area he indicated on her helm was mercifully flat, if hemmed in by the remnants of an ancient crater's edge. Their transport eased to a stop and Dar hopped off. Wordlessly he began unpacking their little cargo bin. Nods and gestures were all that passed between them while the vacuum-sealed and compact equipment transformed into a serviceable, if Spartan, high-tech campsite. The process took the better part of the afternoon, leaving no time to scout the area.

Dar drowned himself in duty and screens and analytics, but she would have nothing to do until they actually accessed the physical mine. Though its location in the vacuum of space was less than ideal, in Nel's opinion, something about the lifestyle in general appealed to her. It was akin to her early days shovelbumming as a contract archaeologist—fall in with a crew of strangers who very quickly became family, complete with the arguments and dysfunction. Traveling from site to site, each place bled into the next in a blur of inclement weather, beer, and increasingly unbelievable anecdotes. Maybe she made a better space explorer than she thought.

"This is horrific." It was only hours later that Dar finally broke their tense silence, hunched inside the tissue-thin tent walls. Nel fought back a laugh. This was the most undignified she had ever seen him and frankly, she was enjoying the fuck out of it. It was cold, despite the sturdy modular shelter they had erected. The technology seemed to be a more elaborate—if smaller—version of the shield they used on Samsara. It afforded pressurized atmosphere and a small generator to charge their atmosuits, but little in the way of warmth beyond keeping it livable.

"It's camping," she answered, "and damn high-tech camping at that."

His brow arched and she caught a glimpse of the pretentiousness he usually boasted. "Maybe this is high-tech for a fucking plebeian dirt-brained Earthling," he almost spat the last word, "but this is positively primeval."

"Your ancestors did this all the time, you know," Nel remarked.

"And yours shit in their fucking water source. There's a reason why we progress, Bently. Do all terrestrial humans get sentimental when camping?"

"Maybe archies do—archaeologists. There's something honest about a campfire." She chuckled and stretched out in front of the single warmer glowing between them. "Even a shitty fake one."

"Hey, without that warmer and these shields you'd be nothing more than an icicle with a bad attitude." He rolled his shoulders and stretched before positioning himself gingerly on his own sleeping cot. "You know, I think I get it more now. Conceptually."

"What's that? Space? 'Cause I'm lost on that. My wee brain blinks at the stars and says 'oo pretty,' then just short circuits back to butts."

"Okay, maybe I rescind my statement a bit." He paused and his face settled into that other look, the one Nel could never quite place but that always made her hackles stand up. "I meant you and Lin. I thought she was slumming it, honestly. But she could never resist a total mess of a person."

"Asshole. I assumed she was trying to tick off your parents."

"Like they'd care. They loved the idea, initially—you look good on paper, you know."

Nel flipped over onto her side, the picture of an expectant child ready for a campfire story. "Your parents think I'm cool, eh? Go on."

"Vain."

"Dude, everyone up here either thinks I'm a fuck-wit or like, a terrorist so I'll take what compliments I can get. Especially from my girl—ex's parents."

"My father didn't want Lin focusing on relationships right now, but my mom knows how wartime stuff goes. Everything is hot: firefights, topics, coworkers, enemies. Like with their marriage, she thought disparate backgrounds might be good for us. Thought you and Lin could help ease the tensions between Earth and IDH when we finally went public."

"Disparate," Nel muttered. "Understatement of the fucking century. Were they supportive of you and Paul?"

His face pinched from discomfort to sorrow. "They never knew about him."

"Seriously? Like half of everyone who I've talked to knew about you two. And you're like IDH royalty or some shit. Surely your every dalliance was splashed across the space tabloids."

"Do you just slap the word 'space' in front of everything we do instead of learning the proper words?"

"Duh. Told you," she tapped her temple, "short circuits right back to butts. And putting 'space' in front of shit reminds me not to get too used to all of this."

"Would that be so bad? If you got used to this life? Thousands of others have over the years. You're far from the first person who reluctantly joined our ranks for a pretty face."

She shuddered, unwilling to follow all the subsequent trains of thought that could leave from that particular mental station. "Back to you and Paul."

He rolled his eyes but didn't push it. "We went to no lengths to hide our relationship, but nor did we make it public. I kept my professional life separate and my highest priority. A choice I will deeply regret for the rest of my life, thank you for asking."

"Sorry." She lapsed into silence for an awkward moment, then remarked, "I think it's really cool that everyone's alright with the gay up here. Or at least, some factions are. Were your parents?"

"They were fine with it." He frowned. "As touching as this all is, I'm getting some sleep. First thing tomorrow you get to go exploring, but don't wander tonight, alright? And keep your comm on vibrate in case there's a system message. I don't like surprises."

"Sir, yessir. Sleep tight."

"Don't let the asteroid mites bite."

"Asteroid mites?" she whispered with a grimace. Surely he was joking. *He's gotta be.* Her skin crawled with the idea of sleeping with open comms, the faint not-quite-present sound of static. But she shut her mouth and kept the line open. They needed to know the second shit hit the fan. Even if her only warning was a scream.

Whether it was due to Dar's threat about alien bugs or the sheer amount of space above her, Nel didn't sleep. The small hours of the night spun past, her left hand gripping the base of her tether, the right's mag clamped to the stone beside her cot. She couldn't even bring herself to shut her eyes for more than a few moments. Each time she did, she felt the asteroid spinning, untethered, beneath them, felt the lack of gravity coaxing her from the surface and out, out, out.

"Please!"

She shot upright, whirling to stare at her companion. Dar slept like he existed—meticulous and rigid. And, apparently, deeply. *I must have just drifted off.* She shoved the voices from her mind and set about making rehydrated coffee. If she couldn't sleep, she needed to counter the inevitable crash.

It was only a few minutes later that Dar stirred, rising wordlessly to shove a slim vial into his port. They sat in silence, Nel nursing the worst cup of coffee she'd ever had while he hunched over his wrist computer reading missives.

His eyes flicked to the digital time readout as it flipped to 0600. "Shall we?"

"Guess so." Nel tugged her atmosuit over its thinner electric cousin and settled into her borrowed power chair. Exploring the surface for an hour the day before had been one thing. Exploring a mine was something else entirely. She was suddenly furious at herself for dragging her feet—well, foot—about getting integrated. Surely that would be easier if she insisted on getting into shit. Arnav might be up for the paralympics, but she sure as hell wasn't skilled for a covert mission with only a few test runs under her belt.

Donning a helmet, she followed Dar's stiff shoulders through the portal in their shield. He was right—without the warmer, the airlock was frigid. After just a few seconds her hands were already shaking with cold. *Suit: warm.*

Her wrist flashed a notice. She had four hours with that power usage. She glanced at the map again, common sense trying to claw its way from beneath the big rock under which she frequently shoved it. Winning the battle for the moment, she dismissed the warning.

"I'm going to go around the side, where the maps showed that airlock. And yesterday's anomaly."

"Keep in contact. I think we're safe to enter, but wait for my confirmation."

"Yep. Good luck." Whatever camaraderie they had established last night had shriveled in the cold, perhaps, or been overtaken by their two warring flavors of anxiety.

The station's dull, scuffed material was only a few shades darker than the surface of the asteroid itself. Add to that the acquired texture from being pummeled and abraded by debris over the decade it had sat there. *And wherever else it could have been stationed.* Her map flickered. She peered at the glowing lines arrayed across her helmet. *What now?* As far as she could tell, the image was unaltered. Like most of the paired or fully integrated tech, it drew its power from her body and the battery pack of her external suit. So why was it malfunctioning? Drawing up outside one of the mine's struts, she double-checked her heading. Just 200 meters to go. "Almost at airlock 31. Anything yet?"

"All readings show it's completely dead. The entire thing's shut down, but these places don't have quite as many systems in place to make that difficult. Some of them don't even have a long-term human hab. It's more than possible this place was just decommissioned."

"So why would someone go here?" Nel asked.

"I refuse to speculate until we have evidence. Trying to keep my mind open."

"Yeah, well, I have a bad feeling about this. If we find people who—more victims," she forced herself through the thoughts that accompanied the words, "it's someone else's turn to deal."

"I need to focus," he bit back.

"Whatever." Another turn and 120 meters later, she drew up at the airlock. "I think I found our anomaly."

"Oh?"

"It's a ship. Or shuttle, I guess. Whatever you call these things. Docked at the airlock."

"One of the station's?"

"How should I know?"

"Lord, you're useless."

"Hey, you invited me. Not my fault you didn't bother to read my incredibly short resume." She tried to compare it to the various crafts she'd been in. "If I had to guess, it looks the most like Bavin's ship."

"*Thunder-bump?*" he scoffed, though whether his attitude was directed at her or the colorful pilot and his ship, she couldn't tell.

"Yeah. But maybe bigger? Or just more living space, maybe. I might have found a way in."

"Careful. These scans look normal, but I don't trust anything out here."

She didn't bother to answer, just pressed the digital lockpick into the door's port. Emilio had given her a crash course on the simple tech Dar trusted her to use, and it was no more complicated than the average Trimble GPS. It processed. She scanned the surface around her. The yawning black above was heavy. As if it stared back at her.

The lockpick chimed. The door slid open. "Going in, okay?"

Dar didn't answer for a moment, and she let him think in peace. She stepped into the dark, glancing at the open cockpit. It was empty. Satisfied no space-zombies were going to lurch from the pilot's seat, she continued toward the rear of the craft. It was there that the craft attached to the station itself. The ship was certainly bigger than Bavin's, and either newer or simply in better condition. Sure enough, the ship's airlock doors stood open, revealing the dark and deserted corridor leading down into the mine's bowels. "Entering the mine."

"We don't know what's down there."

She frowned at the strain in his voice. *So the hotshot pilot is scared of, what, the dark?* Nel eyed the opening before her. It was impossible to feel anything through the insulating layers of her space suit. Still, she swore the base breathed at her.

"Dr. Bently—"

"You do your thing. I'll just take video feed and pictures, alright? It'll probably just turn out to be the most boring Go-Pro tour of some abandoned mine. And I won't press a single button. Even big red ones. Promise."

"Fine, but I'm putting the feed up on my screen."

She flipped her middle finger up to the tiny lens at the crown of her helmet.

"Fuck you, Bently."

"Your sister already did," Nel quipped.

"Keep the comms clear and Lord above: Do. Not. Touch. Anything." Apparently her tactic worked: the fear in his voice was replaced by hostility.

She chuckled and set off into the cloying black. The map was little help. What Nel assumed was poor labeling turned out to be accuracy—much of the station was little more than a series of vacant storage bunkers. It took an hour to get to the small, round wart of a building that served, apparently, as the habitation unit. Resisting the urge to break their uncomfortable silence for even more uncomfortable conversation, she just set a new waypoint at the room's entrance and moved to unlock the door.

"Did you see the registration for the ship?"

She frowned. "No, where was I supposed to look? The glove compartment?"

"Ships aren't integrated with electrogloves," he muttered, as confused as he was annoyed, apparently.

"Never mind. No. I didn't. Thing was pretty dusty. I'll do a proper vid scan on my way out, if you'd like."

"I should be able to get the details once I connect to the system."

"You're still not in?" She peered through the dim light. Reinforced windows ringed the ceiling of the room, and the dome itself appeared to be the mechanical iris of a massive door. Perhaps that's where the transport rigs would attach when relocating the station.

"I'm working on it," Dar snapped back a second later after letting loose a string of what sounded like muttered curse words. "It's almost like the whole place was just...gutted. Digitally speaking. There's nothing. Not even an operating system to connect with."

"Could you boot one up?"

"Not without losing most of the data we're looking for. If there's any left at all."

"Guess we're back to Earth-style reconnaissance."

"I don't know why you sound so pleased. It's not like you excelled at that either."

"Better than you, bud." She hummed across the room, making sure to move her head slowly enough for the video feed to register what she was looking at. This place seemed lifeless in every sense of the word. No ambient energy, no flickering stasis lights. Not even the distant rumble of a generator. The entirety of the hall—Hab Center—was not much larger than *Recursive*'s cantina. While it was difficult to imagine drifting for decades in the darkness, confined to what amounted to a cabin erected on the surface of a sunless asteroid was almost comforting. Tucked into the curve of the hall, being able to see the other side of her tiny domain made the vacuous maw outside seem just that much smaller. As she moved through, the wrist comm blinked a warning:

Battery Power Low.

"Dar, my suit's fucky." A second later she felt a chill as the suit's thermoregulator went out. "Just lost my temp control."

"That should be one of the last things to go. How much power do you have?"

"Third of a battery. It was charged when we left the camp. I swear I double-checked."

"Abort. This is too dangerous and too important to risk destroying data or one more casualty."

In that order, too, I bet, she mentally grumbled. A tingle swept across her skin, followed by an echoing, gentle squeeze. Warmth returned. Her electrosuit readout flickered, returning to its previous display:

General Power: 87%
Battery use: Minimal.
ΔT: 109°C
Internal Temperature: 36°C

"Never mind. I guess it's fine. Back to normal."

"Your connection to the outer suit's power pack must be imperfect. Keep an eye on it. If it happens again, head back immediately. We're only working with what we were able to scrounge from IDH. I intended to have a fully stocked ship but..."

"You crashed it?"

"You shot my extraction plan to hell."

"Pretty sure that was all your sister."

"She was always good at ruining my plans."

Veering quickly from the topic of Lin, Nel updated, "Almost through the living quarters. Where do you want me next?"

"Gross. Where are you on this map? I can't make sense of this."

She snorted and glanced around at the signs before confirming on her own map display. "Looks like your choices are the systems room, across from where I came in, some place called 'Shaft Overlook,' which is in the main mine portion directly to my left—198° to be precise. And I guess the mess of storage facilities. Though from what I could tell on my way in, those are probably mostly empty."

He was quiet for a moment, then his voice crackled back through her helmet. "I guess Systems, but seriously, don't touch anything unless I ask. I'd really rather be down there myself."

"Wanna switch? This whole explorer thing is cool, but if you're game to sneak through a bunch of cold, dark tunnels, be my guest."

"You could never in a million years do what I'm doing up here. Not without blowing us all up."

"My explosion survival track record is actually pretty good," she commented, "but whatever. Heading to Systems. Anything I should keep an eye out for? See if anything's unplugged?"

"Just be my eyes, alright?"

"'Kay. Opening the door now." She jetted to the huge reinforced door. The path to it was clear, though the place was devoid of any clutter or signs of recent life. She clipped the lockpick into place and waited. The screen cycled between processing and displaying a "NO SIGNAL" message. "Spoke too soon. It's not even registering that there's a door at all."

"Told you—the entire station system is dead."

"Well, then let's just confirm that and move on. This place gives me the creeps."

"Try the manual override. Center of the door. Big lever. Can't miss it." His tone was strained with annoyance again.

Nel was starting to wish, just as much as he, that their places were switched. She hated being micromanaged and hated even more when it was necessary. She drew closer to the door and glared at the heavy red lever several inches above her grasping gloved fingers. "Can't reach it either," she muttered before carefully unclipping her belt and gliding upright onto her single leg.

The lever resisted, then slammed down. The doors shuddered, dust blooming outward and drifting in the lack of gravity. With a groan and a shove, she pushed the left side open just far enough to permit the width of her chair. She hesitated, peering against the utter darkness ahead. Even the shaft of pale starlight filtering from the ring of windows behind her did nothing to illuminate what lay beyond. She eased forward into the dark. Each scuff of her boots echoed long and soft as she moved deeper into the room. "There's atmosphere, at least some of it," she relayed. "I can hear."

"Impossible."

"I thought you couldn't get any reading with the systems down."

"Right, but I'm monitoring your suit."

She glanced down at her wrist. Sure enough, the display—still flickering between low battery warnings and normal readouts—showed external conditions as being just barely above pure vacuum, the temperature a balmy -74 degrees Celsius. "But I can hear—"

The comm cut out and a message blinked into being above her wrist.

Switching off audio-comm. Whatever you're hearing isn't outside your suit.

Teeth clenched against the thought of the sound being inside her suit, inside her head, she typed back:

Roger. I'll keep an eye and ear out. You still receiving the video feed?

I am.

Panting breath. The hissing pulse of her blood in her ears. The pop and gurgle of her empty stomach. But no echoing footsteps. She crept forward. Her light bounced over the arc of a rough, low-tech version of the senti-comp stations she had come to recognize.

They ever use Senti-comp tech out here?

Waste a mind like that on something as automated as asteroid mining? Never. Why?

Look at this.

She turned in a slow, careful circle. The bank of computers and system controls arced along the far wall. Massive cables snaked from the hole ripped in its base, winding haphazardly to the command chair.

The sound was back, a susurration of footsteps, of shuffling feet, not one, not a pair, not even a hundred, but thousands. Nel whirled, looking for the source, half expecting to see the entire crew of the mining station lurching out of the dark.

It took her a moment to register what she was seeing: a length of black hair. Vacant brown eyes staring from a moon-pallid face. And the surname *Nalawangsa* emblazoned across the suit breast.

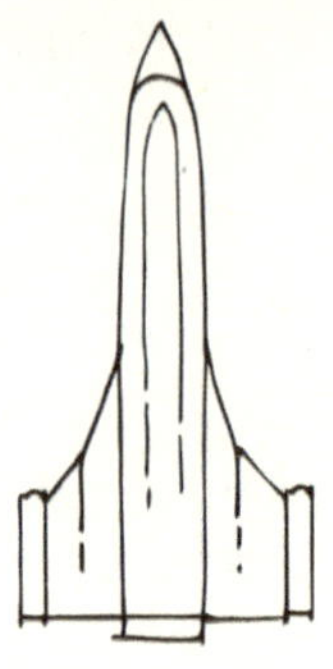

ELEVEN

"Fuck, is that a body—?"

Nel slammed her hand over the camera's lens. Her breath shuddered from her lungs. No amount of her electrosuit's squeezing calmed her nerves. The ship docked at the mine years ago. Well before Nel had ever set eyes on either of the Nalawangsas. And she had seen enough to know the body splayed across the command center floor was too broad to be Lin's, and the face too angular. *It's not her.*

BENTLY!

A second later his voice popped in her comms: "Bently? What's going on? I lost the feed."

She kept her shaking hand over the lens. The body might not have been Dar's sister, but they were someone in his family. "Sorry. I'm okay. There's a body down here. I was trying to audio you and I must have turned the feed off instead. Still a bit shaken."

"I take it back. I have no idea what Lin saw in you."

"Apparently, very little," she muttered, hating that he could hear the tremble in her voice. She tried the counting exercise. It took two counts to seven for her mind to be clear enough to recall how to manually cut the video feed. "Give me a minute." *Suit: access video feed.*

Accessed. Command?

"When you get the feed back, I'm going to patch *The Recursive* in."

"What button is that?" she asked, pretending to look. "Never mind. My luck, I'll unseal my suit. I'm just gonna take photos instead, alright? I still have my wrist cam."

"Goddammit, Bently."

Suit: shutdown remote access video feed.

The recording light blinked off on her helmet. She snapped a few dozen images, then drew up beside him. Engaging both her chair and her own mag-locks, she slipped from the seat to kneel beside him. His hair was long, braided like Lin often kept hers. She didn't know how to do a full suit scan, like a medic would, or even if her space suit was outfitted for such a thing, but she peered at the display on his wrist. It was dead. Apparently, just like the station itself, the ship, and his body.

She knelt beside him, peering at the features. That he was related to the Nalawangsa family was unquestionable. He looked perhaps a generation older than either Lin or Dar, with the pointed caveat about wealth and the youthful gleam brought by cryo. He looked like he could have been sleeping, aside from the eyes. As if someone had just powered him down into oblivion. Nel angled her head, frowning as she brightened her helm's beam. It wasn't a black braid snaking from the base of his scalp. A massive cable was embedded into a clunky-looking biomechanical port grafted, not onto his wrist or clavicle, like many she had seen, but onto the entire length of his cervical vertebrae, branching up to cup his occipital.

A perverse notion flickered through her thoughts: if they powered the station back on, would he wake? Taking in the sickly color of his skin, the ruptured vessels apparent under his half-open lids, and the instinctual sense she had about death that he was simply not there anymore, she shuddered. Polyana had an entire bank of memory and processing units to come to terms with being awoken to a putrefied shell. Nel didn't want to consider what it would feel like—if it were even possible—to simply turn a man back into being.

"Please."

Nel jerked upright, light scanning through the drifting darkness, catching only dust drifting in the lack of gravity. She jabbed her suit's speaker. "Who's there?"

This time, when the sound came, it was everywhere. Not just shuddering through the dusty darkness, wavering through the speakers in her helmet. It thrummed through her suit, vibrating in her very bones. It pulsed in her veins, a microsecond out of sync with her own blood. Whoever—whatever—was speaking wasn't just inside the station, inside her suit, but inside her.

"You unmade us!"

She fought her churning stomach and scanned the darkness between glances at the unknown Nalawangsa. *I don't trust this.* Moreover, something in the animal part of her brain didn't trust the body before her. He may have just been a flesh shell jacked into a dead mining station, but in her limited experience of this strange world and stranger technology, nothing good came from connecting oneself to a massive computer. *No offense, Phil.*

Bently? What's going on? Your audio just went out too.

He knew about the voices—had seen evidence that they were real with his own eyes. It didn't change the pinch of insanity that came with hearing voices that no one else could. She told herself she'd tell him back at camp. When they were safe.

I'm fine, just some weird suit malfunctioning stuff. I'm going to record the deposition of this person and get out of here.

Screw the body.

He'd regret those words later, when she broke the news to him about who, exactly, was sprawled across the Systems lab floor.

It'll just take a minute. Promise. He might hold our answers.

It took twelve. First close to a hundred photographs and a closed-circuit video of the man and the surrounding equipment. She didn't know what was relevant, so she noted everything.

The cable was the tricky part. Even with the added grip of her gloves, she couldn't manage to remove it from the back of his skull. Not that she particularly wanted to do so. After another halfhearted attempt at wrenching the wire free, she settled for severing the cable itself a few centimeters from the nape of his neck. It parted with difficulty.

Next was the horrible process of levering an utterly frozen body off the floor. Weightlessness was one thing, but maneuvering wasn't easy. She cracked a smile, remembering her dad's catch phrase when moving anything remotely tricky: "It's not heavy, just awkward." She doubted very much that he ever imagined his daughter contending with this scenario.

Extracting a reflective space blanket from her chair's pack, she shook it out and tucked it under one elbow to keep it from drifting away. *Man, keeping track of my trowel on sites was hard enough with gravity helping.*

She pulled the tool in question from her belt and eyed the man for a final time before squeezing her eyes shut. "I'm so sorry, sir."

Then she wedged her trowel beneath the thick, slick surface of his suit and scraped his frozen form off the floor like a freezer-burned burger. She lurched forward to prevent the body from floating out of reach, then wrapped the blanket fully around him. The tether anchored to her belt went around his chest and waist. She secured it with a trucker's knot. A flimsy metallic shroud and a cable were as dignified as she could manage, but at least Dar would learn of his kin's passing from her mouth, and not from the image of his frozen body being towed behind a hovering wheelchair. "Alright, sir. Let's get you home. Well. Back to family."

Headed back, she relayed to Dar.

I'm bringing him with me.

Him? You get an ID?

"Oof," she muttered, pondering her answer as she settled back into her chair and clipped the belt over her lap.

Working on it.

The journey back through the base and ship took twice as long, but at least gravity—or lack thereof—was in her favor. It was time enough to run through the few names Lin had shared with her and the others she'd learned about during her invasive, clingy phase of space-Googling her hookup's surname. Age was the tricky factor, but Nel was fairly certain Lin had spoken with their parents recently enough to rule out Brigadir Jenderal Santoso Nalawangsa himself. If they had their timeline right. *Dar's going to have to ID him.* Nel's gray matter fluttered with memories of a different body, a different disposition. A different man.

Dar was waiting just outside their camp, pacing, when she arrived.

"What the fuck?" he snarled through their comms, apparently too angry to handle text communication when she was just a meter away. He eyed the body, but made no move to help her. "What happened? And what's with your suit? We can't be out here if your suit keeps malfunctioning."

I'm pretty sure it's me that's malfunctioning. She hummed to the airlock of their camp and guided the body inside. She only half listened to Dar's litany of complaints as she settled the shrouded remains onto the floor of the airlock.

"—and you still haven't explained why you feel it's necessary to bring a dead stranger in here with us!"

One. Two. She drew a slow breath. *Three.* Another breath. She reached five, and felt collected enough to speak. "Dar, I don't think he's a stranger. And I'm done for today."

"I think we're done for good! This is too dangerous—" He stopped. "What do you mean?"

"Come in here where we can talk without these fucking garbage bags around us," she insisted, pinching the sleeve of her space suit. The sounds from before still sang through her body, but under the surface. It wasn't shock that made her calm as she tethered the body in place. It was surrender. Certainty. When she laid eyes on the familiar cut to the man's face and the distinctive uniform and badge, something slid into place behind her eyes. "We'll regroup. Make sure we don't miss anything."

Dar faltered, then nodded. His mouth opened, then he fired off a quick voice-to-text message before trudging back toward the mining base.

Her wrist flashed.

I'm going to gather the equipment.

She didn't answer. Inside their camp area, the temperature seemed to have dropped. Or her suit battery was failing in earnest. Her shaking fingers fumbled over the knob to turn up the warmer. She set their rehydrator to prepare two cups of tea and perched on the edge of her cot. The vibrating light of the warmer drew her gaze, humming the way her thoughts did each time she closed her eyes.

She was still seated that way, chin in hand and staring into the deep red glow, half an hour later when Dar returned and wordlessly sloughed off his space suit. He peered at the two metal cups of tepid tea and set them both to reheat. One set of long fingers rose to grip the back of his neck, rubbing absently as he stared at her. "What happened out there, Bently?"

She blinked, forcing herself back to reality. "I don't know. I have no idea how he died—though I did find him connected to the system. Maybe whatever blew the computer out took him with it. Or he took it."

"I meant with you. You took off into that base too soon. With a malfunctioning suit. You went too far—fuck, you don't even know what you're looking at half the time! You could have blundered into anything! And for some absurd reason, I let you!"

Her focus narrowed on him, realization popping like a bubble. "Dar, we're okay. We're both fine. We're a glorified refugee ship—of course we have shoddy equipment. Of course we don't have enough resources or help or time. I'm no stranger to pushing cheap tools to their limits. Half the time I'm the cheap fucking tool, honestly. We're both okay. Sit down. Drink your tea."

He did as she asked. After his second sip, he cleared his throat. "There's a body in our airlock, Bently. Why are you so calm? And nice. You're never nice."

She frowned. She wasn't calm. Not strictly speaking. She ground the heel of one hand over her eyes. "I'm just too fucking tired. This is nothing new. Death, darkness, and more questions than answers. Maybe for once we're on my turf." She took a long pull from her tea, wishing, suddenly, her mother had thought to pack whiskey. Dar would need it by the end of this. She needed it now. "Dar, I believe the person I found is someone you know."

"What do you mean?"

She fidgeted with her wrist comm as she quickly swiped to the images of the man's suit breast and wrist comm. When she was sure there was nothing else in frame, she reached across the warmer between them. "Do you know who this is?"

Dar's mouth worked, then he swallowed. "I do. That is the commendation, rank, and personal integration number of Jenderal Mansur Nalawangsa."

The rigid way he spoke, the overly formal words, jabbed certainty into Nel's gut. Family. Dar's gaze slid to the warmer and she withdrew the pictures. "Your relation?"

"Ayah's brother." He was very still, as if someone had told his suit to pause him completely. "I ought to scan his remains. Or his suit." He did not look up, his eyes wide and distant. "Did he have a suit?"

"Just an electrosuit and those officer's robes. The cold preserved him, for the most part."

Dar looked up to where the covered body lay beside the cargo bin in their airlock. He would have looked dejected were it not for the blaze in his eyes. "Could you tell what happened?"

Nel glanced up from the cooker. "No. I'm not a medic, though. The suit didn't have enough power for me to scan, even if I knew how."

"But you were sure he was gone."

"I was, yes." She hesitated. "I know death is different for everyone. And for every person you lose. It was always important to me to see them. To affirm, I guess, that they were gone. That they had transitioned to something else, whatever we might choose to believe that something is." She paused, watching his face. "Would you like to look at him?"

His glance was knife-blade sharp. "I've never seen a dead body."

Her brows rose, and she hoped in the dim light of the station's lee, he wouldn't notice. "You didn't see Paul?"

He winced. "I heard what happened. And when he was brought up for burial, I was told it might be distressing."

"I imagine it would have been. Especially if you hadn't been close to death before. Your uncle though, he doesn't look much different from life, except for his eyes."

"You think I should?"

She shrugged. "It's your choice. I find that proximity to death, to those who we loved, who passed, is healing. Not everyone feels that way, though. There's no shame in either."

He set aside his empty cup and tottered to the airlock. Nel watched him stare as the space came to pressure and atmosphere. He was swaying. She unfolded her temporary crutch and followed after him as quietly as possible. When the airlock opened, she limped through first, propping her crutch on the wall before lowering herself to crouch beside the body. Dar tottered down beside her.

"Do you want to be alone?" She almost missed the headshake under the bulk of his suit. She folded the edge of the space blanket, taking care to leave her tethers in place. "I'll stay right here, at his feet. In case you need anything."

Dar reached out, then hesitated. "Can I?"

"Of course. When you're ready." Nel recalled all the bodies she had seen, all the remains she had discovered while digging. It didn't matter that you were ready or that you weren't. It was always earth-shattering. It was always profound.

He drew the sheet down, exposing his uncle's pale face, the stiff, knotted muscles of his shoulders. There was nothing to be done about how the cold had pulled back his eyelids or filled the space below them with hoarfrost and haze. At least the dark fabric of his suit concealed most of the lividity, and whatever had killed him left no obvious wounds.

Dar stared. She watched as he took in the body, watched as the dread and fear eased from his face, replaced with sorrow and curiosity. His hand brushed the hard skin, fingers skimming the seam between stiff hair and conduits at the base of Mansur's skull. "Are they always so pale?"

"Depends. His blood settled when his heart stopped. His back will appear bruised. But he looks quite good. Peaceful."

Dar nodded. "He looks like he was just…turned off." His hands still shook and he faltered twice trying to recover the body. He met her eyes, his own wide and bloodshot and utterly overwhelmed.

"I've got it." Nel pressed a hand to Dar's arm. "I'll get him taken care of. First thing tomorrow, we'll bring him back. We can go from there."

"There's so much equipment," Dar worried, "I don't know if the trailer has room—"

"We'll make room, Dar." When he met her eyes she held them, hand gripping his wrist with every ounce of her strength. There was a wildness in his face that she knew intimately, though, like most of her feelings, she'd never thought to name it. "That's what we do for the dead, Dar. We make room."

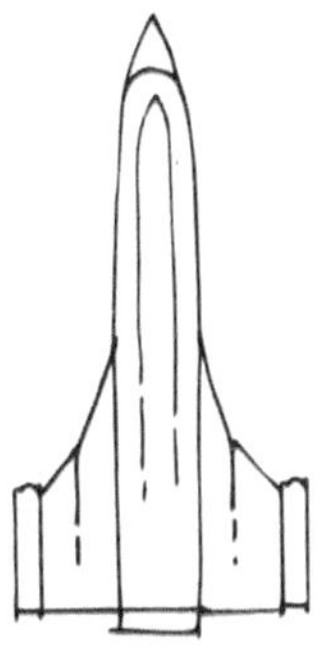

TWELVE

It took the better part of the morning to pack up camp. It would have gone quicker, surely, if Dar had helped, but when Nel rose early that morning, he was already suited up and glaring at the equipment jacked into Morphose-131. Nel left him to it, and instead turned her attention to how to pack the already precariously stacked crates and boxes. It was an unspoken agreement that they would leave as soon as the asteroid's rotation brought them within view of *The Recursive.* Nel noted the recorded version for mission termination: malfunctioning suits and possible biohazard. The real reason, she knew, was Dar's shaking hands and shattered resolve.

They might not have gleaned the information they really wanted from the asteroid or its ghost-town base, but the cases were loaded with samples from its surface and carefully shielded data cards from each of Dar's failed attempts at turning the place on. *At least we know there's very little data for us to miss.*

Nel ratcheted down another set of straps, glancing at the horizon. Part of her expected the return of a prodigal sun, hoping it had saved some warmth for them. The sky above remained sullen and hungry. With the most expensive and important crates secured—minus whatever pieces Dar used for his last-minute attempt at controlling this pear-shaped mission—Nel turned her attention to the camp itself. She had already written off the shelter. There was no way she was going to fold it all by herself, not before the narrow window for their launch from the surface. Frankly, they didn't have the space. Not without leaving someone behind.

By the time Dar trudged back, equipment stowed and ready for transport, Nel waited beside the depressurized camp. He glanced at what was left, but made no move to argue. "Powerpacks and solar generators?"

She nodded. "Everything but the walls, really. You can do a last sweep, though."

Again, the almost imperceptible headshake. His gaze slid over the cargo transport, pausing on the covered form at the very top. "You found a body bag."

"There were some in the emergency packs. I left room over on this side for that shit." She jerked her chin at the cases in his hands. "I can strap them down."

He stepped around the side himself and loaded the rest. With a last glance at the base, he held out an arm to help her up. Then they were skimming back across the craggy surface.

They didn't speak as she secured the cargo or during the elaborate pre-flight checks. She watched his hands as they moved over the instruments, trying to gauge whether this was reservation or a caldera waiting to blow. He cranked down on the engines, the shuttle shuddering beneath them as they waited to be within trajectory of the ship. *The Recursive* appeared over the edge, a gray, blocky form among the asteroid field. The shuttle lurched into the air and, at long last, Morphose-131 fell away beneath them.

Nel didn't mind comfortable silence. Preferred it, really, to conversation, especially when it came to chipper students or a U-Hauler hookup. There was nothing comfortable about this. Perhaps they were close, perhaps they weren't, but whatever Dar felt about his uncle was complicated.

The Recursive grew larger as they curved around its bulk and into the docking stations within the hollow body of the main cylinder. Another shuttle scooted in just before, bearing protein from the vats on *The Yarmouth* or further laboratory equipment from *Chéngnuò*.

Dar drew back on the yoke and let the shuttle hover for a moment while the first docked. "Bently."

"Dar."

"We need to go through this evidence, to learn what really happened down there. No one is to know of this until we can give them a solid answer that's not going to scare the shit out of most of the people relying on us."

Nel grimaced. "Respectfully, I disagree. People already know you aren't coming clean. People notice bodies. People notice that we're still out here, conserving fuel. They're going to talk, they're going to speculate. I know you don't have answers, but like you said—you need help. You have thousands of people out here. Let them help us. And not for nothing, but you need to grieve."

He didn't answer.

She leaned on the arms of her chair, eyes narrowed on him. "So what're you going to do?"

"If I knew I wouldn't be here, I'd be making it happen."

"Well, take your time, make your peace, and then figure out how you're going to save these fucking people."

He didn't respond, just slid the brake clear and coasted forward into the next available dock. They thudded into place and finished the final checks before powering down. The shuttle's air writhed as it combined with the ship's, and Nel released her helmet with a deep sigh of gratitude. She was limping toward the ship when she realized the officer still hadn't moved from his pilot's seat.

She didn't like the man, but she liked the look in his eyes even less. "Dar—"

"I'm fine," he snapped, dissolving into hurried motion as he rose and checked the cargo. He drew up instructions on his tablet, probably making sure it would be unloaded later, when most of the ship was asleep.

The *clap-thud* of mag-boots sounded from the gangway, followed by a gentle Chilean voice. "That was quick. How'd it go?"

Nel turned to see Emilio, dressed in a full suit of his own, helmet under one muscled arm. "Hey. It went." She glanced at the bustling hangar behind him. "We'll explain more later, though."

Emilio's gaze slid over her to Dar, who hadn't turned or spoken. The pilot's eyes were huge, nostrils flared as he heaved in breath. His gaze was fixed on his uncle's covered remains.

"I'm glad you both made it back." Emilio stepped onto the shuttle, dark brows furrowed. He stopped when he saw the body bag. "Who—"

Nel cleared her throat. "His uncle."

Emilio lowered his eyes and pressed a hand to Dar's shoulder. "If you need anything—"

Dar whirled, hands snaking out to grip the other man by the thick collar of his electrosuit.

Nel was about to shove between them to stop whatever machismo-laden fight was about to break out but froze when, instead, Dar's mouth collided with Emilio's. The Founder's officer's eyes widened, then slid shut, one hand rising to grip Dar's forearm.

Envy and confusion warred in Nel's heart. She looked away. It was rude to stare and the specter of Lin's lips haunted the cavern in her chest. Whatever Dar needed, he couldn't get from her. She shouldered her pack, laden with most of their data—data she could barely decipher—and made for the elevator. There would be planning, analysis, and surely a healthy dose of fear. But right now they needed time, even if it was carved from the bones of one more body.

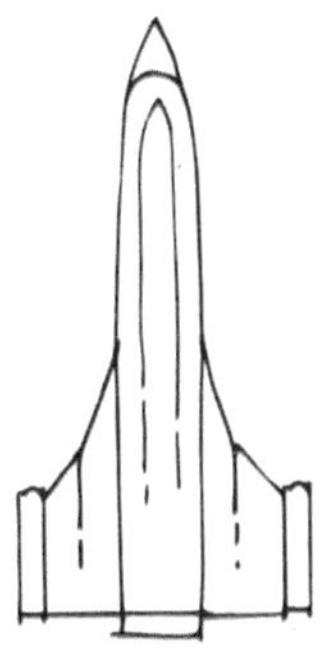

THIRTEEN

Nel's muscles ached with the echo of no gravity and the tug of mag-boots. She showered until the ration-warning chimed, staying beneath the stream until it dribbled unceremoniously off. Residual grief stung—hers and Dar's and her mother's and maybe even Lin's. Distracted frustration simmered in her brain, neurons firing seemingly just to remember the burn. Nel stared at the door to their apartment, knowing her mom was about to return from her shift and would be worried. Slumping down at the counter with Mindi and a cup of tea was probably what Zach would recommend. Talking it out until the feelings shriveled in the recycled air.

She pressed a hand against the walls. The ship was full of whirring, whispers of gasses, synthetic and organic gurgles beneath the printed plastic of the walls. It wasn't quite rhythmic enough for white noise, not loud enough to fully distract her whirling thoughts. Nel's body longed to move, to pace, to escape the encroaching press of claustrophobia. If she moved enough, emotions couldn't find her. Neither could the sounds. Even if they were real.

Fuck, Bently, mope much? Unwilling to face the events of the last few days just yet, she made her way out of the apartment block. It was only as the elevator hissed shut behind her that she realized she had no destination. Flexing her grip on her crutch, she headed out to the cantina. It was a familiar route, but she found her eyes lingering on the signs, as one might point helpfully to who she used to be.

Pockets of *The Recursive* never slept, but they were within its bowels, the same systems that kept the ship's innards burbling and rumbling. The cantina, however, was deserted. The last shift— usually hers—had cleaned and packed away everything for the early morning. Low orange evening lights cast the battered tables and chairs into bronze.

A tap of her wrist allowed her passage into the storage rooms and she perused the unlit shelves. After a few attempts and far more than necessary whining, her hand found a dusty bottle. With a gleeful chuckle, she tottered back out into the dining area to examine her find. "Oof, Bently, how the mighty have fallen." It was screw top and, judging by the Latin on the mildewed label, intended for mass, but Nel's thoughts clamored loud enough to be prayers. *And,* she rationalized,

I've kissed enough Catholic girls that it's practically Communion.

She shuffled across the smooth floor to the outermost edge of the cantina windows. If the bulky shape of the ship had a prow, she guessed the gleaming curvature of the cantina overlook was as good a candidate as any. A twist of her hand cracked the seal and she let the top skitter across the table beside her. Apparently the PT really was working.

The wine was warm and thick. Bitterness washed over her tongue, matching the abrasive feeling in her chest. She wasn't a wino, but she downed another sip and another until her soul was muffled, edges sanded down to safe muddiness. It almost looked like sanity, from a distance. *Yeah, if you squint one eye and close the other.* Like the wine, eventually everything became palatable through attrition.

A tap of her index finger brought up the varied catalog of media aggregated from thousands of passengers. Had the data automatically synced? A flush creeped up her neck at the thought of what her computer might have uploaded to the space-cloud while she was unconscious. She scrolled through, too aimless to know what to search for.

"Slim pickings," she muttered before pausing on the entire Tegan and Sara discography with a grin. "Guess I'm not the only lesbian." The first chords of "Bad Ones" twinged, tinny and tenuous from her wrist and she leaned back. It was a remix, or cover, maybe. Not a very good one. But she found her chin bobbing.

"You know, they were never tough enough for me, when I was a baby gay," she remarked, eyes lidded. She addressed no one. Or refused to admit, even to the engulfing solitude of the sleeping spaceship, that a shadow shimmered on the edge of her vision, all gleaming grace and fathomless eyes. Now her shoulders rocked in time, solitude permitting feelings, even if it was just feeling the beat.

Another swig, soft and rich with tannins, rolled down her throat. She longed for someone to pass the bottle off to, or for slender hands to press a condensation-slicked bottle into hers. She was reminded, abruptly, of Emilio replacing Dar's mug, of the wordless knowledge of what someone needed without asking, without dismissal, without resentment. All the long days Lin pulled while racing across Earth, the nights Nel woke to find her still squinting at a screen so cluttered with jargon it could have been an alien language. She'd been so upset over not being able to help, she hadn't realized how she actually could. *I was a shitty girlfriend.* Sure, Lin had been working toward blowing up Nel's planet, but she hadn't known that at the time.

"Knock, knock," a low voice drifted from the shadowed cavern of the cantina.

For a second, Nel let herself pretend. Then she turned.

Jem hovered several paces away, flashing a rueful smile. "Am I interrupting?"

"Yeah, but I was about to start singing along and that would shatter these windows."

Jem chuckled and settled into the booth beside Nel, following her existential stare out to the darkness beyond the narrowly rescued acrylic. Their shared silence swelled against the tinny thread of music for a moment before Jem remarked, "You came back early."

Nel gave a single nod. There was no way she was breaching the classified nature of their mission, even after downing half a bottle of shitty merlot. "Guess there wasn't much left in the operating system or something for Dar to look through. Plus the suit I had was janky, so it was safer to bail."

Jem regarded her thoughtfully but didn't call her bluff. They were out of their usual utilitarian uniform, dressed instead in loose pants and a cropped leather binder dyed the same brilliant teal as their hair.

"Nice outfit," Nel offered awkwardly. "I miss having clothes that feel like me."

"You didn't pack anything?"

"Dar packed my shit, I guess. Or Emilio. So it's either B-movie space horror esthetic or sport lesbian college chic."

Jem snorted. "Is that what's got you in here moping and drinking a bottle of—" they lifted the bottle to frown at the label, "—yikes, is this any good?"

"Fuck no," Nel answered, punctuating the statement with another swig before offering it to the tech. "Misery loves company."

They gave a single solemn nod and took a long pull. "So fashion disasters and terrible booze aside, what brought on the pity party?"

"That isn't enough?" Nel joked, but found herself looking away from Jem's gentle curiosity. "I'm pretty far out of my element here. Like, I knew that, but I thought it was just the tech. Not the society."

"You're an anthropologist. You know how tools shape people."

"It feels a lot safer when you're on the other side of invention. Trusting each advancement is easy when you already know its effects. The sacrifices feel justified in hindsight. There's so much dark, scary shit out here and I can't shake the feeling that we're being watched. Toyed with, maybe. On top of it all I don't know how to help." She shrugged.

Jem splayed a dark hand across the smooth tabletop. "It's like the station, Nel. People come from all sorts of places out here. Honestly, we're all lost somehow. These weird airless corners of the universe. Walk in as one person, walk out as another."

"That how you left home?"

Jem's eyes flicked up. "You think just 'cause I'm trans that I must have had to run away from some shitty family?"

Nel grimaced and picked at the peeling wine label. "No. I just always wished I could do that. Disappear. When I traveled a lot for work I'd pretend for a bit, sometimes. New project, new persona."

Jem snorted. "How'd that go?"

"Left a trail of emotional casualties and companies where my trowel wasn't any good."

"Well, my family thinks I'm rad—my older brother and kid cousin are both trans too. I said it was easier up here, but that's only because there's more places to run. And," they returned to regarding the asteroid field, "wasn't them I was running from."

The conversation about credit and debts flooded back and Nel found her gaze sliding to the glinting metal visible under the hem of Jem's binder. Silver ports studded the gentle swell of the tech's belly. "But you don't hide those."

Jem met her gaze when it rose again. "Running ain't the same thing as hiding. I haven't lived this life for as long as I have just to be ashamed of something else."

Nel stared, searching for a counter argument that wasn't based in her own fear. Instead, she mouthed wordlessly before licking her lips. "I don't think I know how not to be ashamed. Not of being gay, exactly."

"Of just being you?"

She nodded, energy sparking up her nerves at the truth. It had been a long time since she had been seen. Maybe she never had been. Tepid wine made everything fuzzy, most of all her reason. "You're a good listener. Or talker. Whatever."

"Maybe you're not as different from us space aliens as you thought," they teased. The music lapsed for a static-filled second, then the thrumming guitar of Julien Baker rose in the space between them.

"Well, someone's taste in queer-longing songs is familiar enough."

Jem just smiled in response. Their eyes were bright and warm, almost burgundy under the turquoise curls cascading from the top of their head. She enjoyed Jem's humor and appreciated their kindness. She admired their strength and how they molded their body to fit themselves best. Now she saw the delicate lines that made their lips look like plump citrus and the brown freckles smattered across their cheeks and jaw.

Without breaking eye contact with Jem's mouth, Nel tipped back the bottle in an attempt to wet her suddenly dry throat. Desire was smothered under her exhaustion and fury and the ever-present threat of Lin. But with another person's lips hovering inches from her own, she realized how fucking starved she was for contact. For touch.

"I'm not much for attachments, you know," Jem remarked. "Heard you weren't either."

"How old are you again?" Nel interjected, gaze scanning their smooth features.

Jem laughed, a small curl forming at the edge of their mouth. "Old enough—circadial and otherwise."

Conscience soothed, at least until morning, Nel ran a shaking hand down the bright leather of their binder, feeling where muscle bunched under the stiff material. *No attachments sounds kind of nice.* Her fingers hesitated where flesh ended and metal began. *Touch,* she reminded herself. *Grip. Kiss.* But her hands and lips faltered. As if her sexual fluency was severed along with her leg.

"You good?"

"I, ah..." Nel sat back, blinking in confusion. "It's like I forgot the steps."

"Maybe you're just waiting for a certain partner," Jem didn't withdraw, their face just as welcoming as ever, "and maybe I was wrong about what you needed."

"This is what I need, I just—" Nel scrambled to recover the moment and her pitiful pride, but every time she tried to picture hooking up, her brain replaced Jem's curls and quiet surety with a long braid and eyes filled with danger. Still, clumsy sex seemed better than slinking, embarrassed, back to her room wine-drunk. She flopped back with a frustrated sigh. "Fuck, I'm a mess."

"Yeah, kind of," Jem answered. "But that's pretty normal for being a human."

"Do you think she's happy? That she got under my skin so bad I can't hook up with a hot stranger even after she tried to blow up my planet?"

"Stranger? C'mon, I think we're at least buddies," Jem joked. "Honestly, I don't know the Nalawangsas, and what I do know tells me I don't wanna know more. But she's hot and evil so, probably happy about screwing over any hope you have at a normal love life."

"Ouch," Nel muttered.

"Hey, I won't yuck your yum if hot and evil is your kink, but it ain't mine."

"I didn't think it was, but I guess things change. And speaking of changing," Nel segued awkwardly, "let's find a subject that doesn't showcase how sad and pathetic I am."

"If sex is off the table, we can just hang out, that's good. Or go back to mine?"

Nel polished off the wine with a grimace. It had passed the point of acquired taste and become almost cloying. *This is going to be one hell of a bad hangover.* She drew a breath and turned back to Jem. "If my awkwardness hasn't been a total turn off, yeah, let's go back to yours."

Jem's apartment was within one of the outermost house blocks, close to the medical bays in case of an all-hands emergency. It wasn't a long walk, and Jem had the decency to stop to let Nel rest—and not do anything so cringy as try and hold her hand.

"You lived on ships before this, yeah?" Nel asked.

"Most of my life, honestly. There aren't many places—aside from asteroids—that aren't technically ships or stations out here. Some are better than others though," they added ruefully, rattling off a few names. "If you ever have a choice, avoid them. Oh, and especially Natasha-Qe-Wallace."

Nel snorted. "Sounds like a celeb's name."

"Casino station, mostly caters to the very powerful. People like you and me, though? Never see beyond the first few levels, even as the help. Did a three-term stint there patching up wrestlers after rigged fights when I was earning medic credits." They slowed and tapped a panel beside a narrow door. "Here we are."

The bunk was a single tiny room, but their years living on various ships had served well, apparently. Everything was carefully organized, with screens to hide the mess that came with living in a small space.

"Shoes off, if you don't mind."

Nel obeyed, limping in as she scanned the room. "Wow, you really like turquoise, huh?"

Jem laughed, sliding the door shut behind them and toeing their own shoes off. "Yeah, kind of the one constant. Plus, it looks good on me."

Right, flirting, Nel reminded herself. "It really does," she tried, clearing the nervousness from her throat. "You always look so luminous."

"Luminous is a new one. Stop trying so hard." Jem grinned, nodding to the cabinet. "I only have kombucha and plain soda pop, but you're welcome to either."

"Think I'm good, but ah," Nel stepped closer, barreling through her uncertainty, "I wouldn't mind trying something else."

Jem didn't answer, not with words. Their hands slid around Nel's back and up, sliding along the sides of her spine until they gripped her shoulders. Their hands were strong, like an archaeologist's, but smooth, and Nel's head tipped back as they rubbed circles into the meat under her shoulder blades. She hummed, letting her eyes lid for a moment before reaching out to reciprocate. They felt good in her arms—solid and full.

"How are you with different anatomy?" Jem asked, leaning back enough to meet her eyes.

"Enthusiastic but perhaps not terribly experienced," Nel hazarded with a shrug. "I figure it's like anyone new—ask what they like and go from there."

"Works for me." Jem closed the gap between them then, trailing kisses along Nel's jaw. "I'm pretty equal-opportunity myself."

Nel opened her mouth to respond, only to find lips on hers, certain and steady, and her tongue decided it would much rather swirl itself around Jem's than remember how to speak. Warmth trickled through her body, slow to awaken, but building in her center until all she could feel was heat and the insistent press of another person's body. Jem backed toward the bed, towing Nel after them until they both flopped onto the thin mattress. A muscled arm held Nel against them as one of their solid thighs wedged itself between hers, pushing, pressing, grinding until Nel thought she might melt.

The binder stayed on, but with a merciless shimmy of Jem's hips they shed their pants and boxers. Nel's hands snaked around to grab a palmful of warm, silky skin as she moaned into their open mouth. They reared back, grinning, and tugged pointedly at Nel's shirt.

Impatient. Confident. Certain. Nel's shredded soul needed Jem's easy acceptance and arm's-length intimacy to forget the ghost that kept slipping into the space between them.

"Hold up." The mattress let out a loud creak in protest as Jem rolled over to grab something out of a drawer under the bunk. "Hope you don't mind protection—we both get around."

Nel watched, curious, as they carefully rubbed what looked like thick lube over themselves. "Never seen that before, I'll be honest."

"Like the liquid gloves we use for surgery. Works as a barrier that fits no matter what bits someone has. Plus," they leaned over, slick fingers reaching for Nel, "It's real fun to apply."

Pleasure spiked through Nel as their fingers swept across all of her most sensitive places. Her breath escaped in a shuddering groan and she found her hands gripping Jem's generous ass just to anchor herself to the real world.

They tumbled into one another, all grabbing hands and seeking fingers and breath and groans. It was nice to lose herself in someone again, not a stranger, where Nel had left most of her terrible feelings in a desperate bid to forget them forever, but a friend. A friend who didn't make demands of her heart she couldn't answer, or worse, demands of her own she desperately wished someone else would meet. Jem came first, the sensation sending delightful flickers across their face and under Nel's fingers wrapped around them. Their panting breath turned the sterile recycled air beautifully organic and warm and soft. They basked in the afterglow for only a moment before rolling on top of Nel, eyes bright with inspiration. Her own climax, minutes later, was hard and brief and a bitter relief.

Jem's eyes were still pleasure-dark when they settled beside Nel and offered a glass of water. Nel drained it wordlessly, before flopping back on the cot, smile languid. For a guttering, glorious moment, her thoughts were quiet. "You have to be up early?"

Jem nodded, stretching with a soft groan. "Stay as long as you want, though, I'm a quiet riser."

Nel snorted. "Me too. Years of sneaking out will do that, I suppose."

Jem's chuckle joined hers. "Probably the only time you don't make a hell of a scene."

Nel flicked their arm playfully. They weren't wrong. As much as habit urged her to dress and get out, out, out, before the heady tang even dried from her hands, she forced herself into stillness. Jem wasn't a cage.

Still, sleep refused to come.

Nel lay on her side, back warmed by Jem's bare skin. She'd never been much into cuddling, but right now she enjoyed the sensation. Their breath was the soft, even rhythm of sleep, dark fingers occasionally twitching where they rested on Nel's hip. Around them, the ship's humming shuddered, then halted as another blackout swept through. Nel's chest tightened, counting the seconds. Five thousand two hundred and six seconds. The humming swelled again and with it, Nel's disappointment. Beyond the steel and aluminum and acrylic, across the sizzling of space, Lin hunted her.

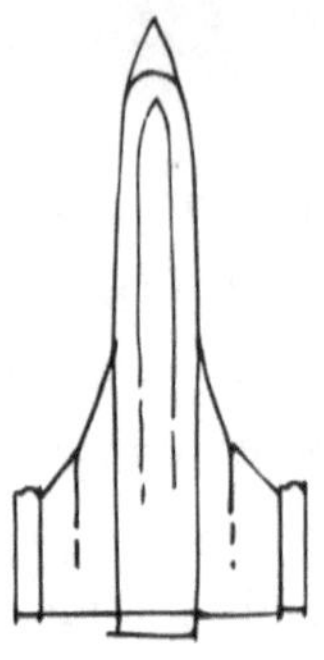

FOURTEEN

Mealworms really weren't bad when you got over the shape. Nel grabbed a few from the bucket before she dumped it into the grinder and popped them into her mouth.

Big-rig shot her a look that clearly said "you're lucky we can't dock that from your rations," but a second later he clapped her on the shoulder. "You've been here since 0600. Take fifteen, 'k?"

She flashed double thumbs-up and wheeled into the stock room. The midmorning lull was just beginning, and it'd be another few minutes before the insect powder was ready to be sealed or set aside for the lunch menu.

"Hey, loser." Lee slouched along the stock shelves, sticking his finger in a jar of something and tasting it before grimacing and putting it back.

Nel flipped Lee off and made a point to wheel all the way around to avoid passing him. "Hey, fucko. Thought you were on sick leave."

"Nah, just a personal day. Teska was getting their shoulder mechanism replaced. Hopefully this one doesn't fuckin' grind, ya know?"

"Yuck." Nel shuddered with a grimace. "They recover okay?"

"Yeah, thankfully. I'm makin' their favorite peanut noods tonight." Lee shoved another pallet of preserved gelatin onto his cart with an assured nod. Lee's single redeeming quality seemed to be his devotion to Teska. Even if half a dozen other names lay beneath the semi-opaque ink covering most of his skin. He dug in one ear, regarding the mostly empty shelf thoughtfully, then headed back toward the kitchen. His hygiene, however, left everything to be desired.

"Oh, Bent," he called, turning abruptly. "What's this about the new trajectory? Your shitbrained handler got another bad idea?"

New trajectory? Apprehension chilled her nerves. "Not a clue. And he's not my handler. Probably just a resource hunt again."

"Well I don't care what he is," Lee sneered. "We keep robbin' desolate rocks instead of stopping at a proper fueler, we gonna starve out here."

She watched the door swing wide behind him, wishing she could ignore the sickening dread in her gut as easily as she ignored Lee's body odor.

"Airlock jump be faster than hunger." The soft voice drifted from the dark, all-elbows figure hunched at the battered card table in their break corner.

"Hey, Zeda," she answered, pulling up beside him. The scrawny man was bent over a half-finished puzzle, one pale pink piece held in his scarred fingertips.

A flimsy shelf held a cloth checkerboard, two versions of Red Five that, between them, had enough pieces, and a mancala board. Checkers bored Nel, and she didn't understand the rules of the space-invented Red Five. Mancala was fine, but she refused to touch it after she caught Teska testing how many of the glittering glass pieces they could shove in a single nostril.

"Made some headway since yesterday," she noted, twisting her head to try to see the picture. The box was torn and stained, but she made out an island lighthouse.

"I like the ones with the Nubbles," he remarked, trying the piece above a finished portion of waves. It didn't fit.

"Nubbles?" Nel asked, tugging out an apple she'd scrounged on her way through the shelves earlier.

"The towers by the ocean. That's what they're called, right?" He pointed to the faded words on the side of the box: *Nubble Sunrise.*

Nel's laugh barked in the echoing room. "That's the name of that particular lighthouse. Nubble Light. It's in Maine..." She trailed off. "We used to go every summer."

His untamed brows arched. "Lighthouse. They're pretty."

She hummed in response. "Their light warned ships of the rocks at night or in bad weather. I suppose you folks don't really need things like that out here. All the radio and scanning and all that."

"Some deep places have beacons. Same. Kind of." He tested the pink piece in a new spot, smiling as it slid perfectly between a rocky edge and a wisp of clouds.

A silent moment passed while she watched, enjoying her apple and the man's unassuming silence. Of all her coworkers, she liked Big-rig and Zeda the most. Rig was honest and straightforward. *Zeda is…*she glanced at his gentle, fixated expression. Zeda was Zeda. Not all there, but whatever he said he meant and whatever he meant he did. It was a welcome difference from Dar's snide duplicity and her own shitty temper.

"You ever visit one? A beacon?"

He stilled, though she couldn't decide if it was out of discomfort or trying to place the next piece—a soft gray-blue one. "Seen 'em. From a distance. Raised by Marcassian monks. Toured a lot."

Nel didn't know what the hell a Marcassian monk was or if she should be impressed or sympathetic. "Oh wow. What brought you here?"

This time, she knew it was discomfort that stalled his movements. A rare flicker of eye contact punctuated the finality of his broken sentences.

"Left for my dedicate's decade: travel, observation, and prayer with strangers' gods. Never made it back."

Something close to curiosity, close to fear, shuddered in Nel's chest. Praying to others' gods was a beautiful way to describe anthropology, in her mind. "That sounds a bit like my journey," she offered softly.

His mouth twitched. "IDH does not pray to gods. It kills them." He handed her a piece. "Break's up. Your turn."

The piece was colorless, white against the tan-gone-sallow of her hand. Marcassian monks. Secret trajectories. Nagging hunger. She set the piece down before the clammy clench of her palm warped the cardboard. Prayer never came easily to her, not the carefully constructed prayers of western Christianity, at least. Still, murdered gods or not, she couldn't put another name to the longing, wordless refrain humming in her bones.

Later, Lee's accusation spun in her head with the insistent discomfort of inaction. Usually, she'd find the nearest single body and fight or fuck until she forgot why she was running in the first place. She'd had fun with Jem, and their friendship was one Nel appreciated more than ever. *It just makes me miss her more.* Too angry at the idea of missing someone to even take care of her desire herself, Nel flopped onto her bed and dragged her personal computer over. A tap lit her screen again and her fingers faltered across the illuminated holographic keys.

Unsurprisingly, her search through the digital Nalawangsa family tree turned up just as little as it had on Earth. IDH may have been a drop in the bucket when it came to all the different factions in the known universe, but there was no denying that the Nalawangsa name held power within the Institute. The likelihood that Dar's uncle was simply a coincidence was laughable. Despite the nagging in her head, Nel couldn't get the pieces to fit in a way that made sense. *Probably because there are dozens of pieces we don't have yet.*

Furious at herself for not seeing the big picture, and at Harris and IDH and countless others, she settled into her chair and was halfway to Dar's room before her judgment kicked in. She wasn't even sure if he was home. He was a man grieving. And she was about to complicate his grieving process. Like Emilio, Dar lived in the singles section a few decks away. It was late, but she knew he rarely slept. The faint green light outside the door showed the room was, indeed, occupied. *I should have sent a message.* But then she might chicken out.

Before she lost the will to fuck up his night, she pressed his doorbell, announcing, "It's Bently."

The light on the lintel blinked and the door slid open. "Come in," he called. "We were just having a drink."

"We?" she asked, moving out of the entryway.

Sure enough, Emilio sat at one end of the couch, beer dangling from his tan hand. The other one rested on Dar's ankles, which were propped in his lap. Dar himself was stretched across the length of the couch. His face was wan, and the shadows under his eyes were deeper than usual.

"Evening," he greeted.

"Hey, I can come back—"

"Stop being awkward," Emilio murmured.

"I'd offer you a seat but," Dar slurred, gesturing to her chair, "well."

"Fuck off."

"And if you want something to drink I'm sorry, but you'll have to get it yourself. The room started spinning about twenty minutes ago."

Nel's brows rose and she noted the tube clipped into the port on his forearm. "Thanks, I'm good though. I just wanted to talk to you about something."

He frowned. "I'm not really working right now."

"First time for everything," she joked, though it felt flat even to her. "It's not really about work. I mean, it is, technically. But it's mostly about the voices. And your uncle."

His glassy eyes brightened, but his pupils were still overlarge. *What the hell did you mainline, Dar?* "Go on."

"There's something that's been bugging me since I found him. I don't think my suit was malfunctioning. I think that there was," she shrugged, feeling more and more like a nutjob as she continued, "something there. You said it wasn't coming from outside my suit but we did safety tests like, a zillion times during prep."

"Safety tests don't always emulate the extreme conditions—"

"They were begging."

Emilio turned to stare at her, eyes widened slightly. "Pardon?"

"The voices, or whatever the fuck I'm hearing. They said please, clear as day and louder than it's ever been. And then when I asked who was there, they said 'you unmade us.'" She heaved a sigh as both men just stared at her. "Look, this shit is creepy, and I'm not a superstitious person, but outside of a fucking space seance, I really don't know what to do here."

"We never should have gone—" Dar snapped.

"Do you have a video feed?" Emilio interrupted Dar's burgeoning rant. "It might help pinpoint the nature of this."

"Fiddle-fingers over there accidentally shut it off in panic," Dar muttered.

It was all she could do not to smack him. "Actually I do. I recorded the whole thing, like any forensic anthropologist would do. I took one look at the body and knew they were your family, if not exactly who. So I covered the lens and pretended until I could break the news properly. I meant to tell you sooner, but seeing as your grief is the only kind worth halting this investigation..." She trailed off, losing the desire to fight even as she bared her teeth. Snark wasn't helpful and she'd been a hypocrite to keep secrets.

Dar blinked at her and put out a hand to steady himself. "You recorded it?"

Emilio sat forward, gesturing to the table. "Mind if I—"

"Go ahead," Dar sighed. "If I stare at the screen too long I might vomit, though."

"Computer: access closed-circuit suit feed from EVA to Morphose-131 for personnel: Dr. Bently, Annelise."

A portal appeared in the air between them, projected from the slim beady mechanical eye embedded in his table. Video footage flickered into being and Nel leaned forward. The halls of the mine shuddered, grainy, the only hint of actual color present in the wavering readouts of her suit. Footage-Nel fumbled with the manual door latch. Embarrassment flashed through Nel's gut. At least Dar was too distracted to mock her out loud.

"What are we looking for?" Emilio asked.

"I'll know it when I see it. It started just before I saw the body." She peered closer, eyes aching against the glowing blue of the screen. It didn't matter, she didn't want to miss it. "There." She jabbed her finger at the image.

The screen shuddered, image warping into static, then back, then again.

"Probably residual radiation messing with the system," Dar remarked.

Mansur's body was prone on the floor, somehow made more horrendous by the poor video quality. It lasted only a moment, and then the image turned to black. "That's my hand over the lens. Is there audio?"

Emilio nodded. "Computer: volume 11, rewind ten seconds, play."

The tinny atmospheric sounds of the mine emanated for a moment. Then, hideously loud, another voice cut in, dozens of voices overlaid, speaking in thunderous unison, shapes blurring the image in time with the word. "Please!"

"Computer: pause," Dar barked. It was not static. Grainy, translucent hands grabbed at Nel's helm, at her hands, squeezing her wrists as her suit's readouts flickered with electrical anomalies. More shapes seemed to reach toward his uncle's body. Dar's dark eyes bore into the stilled security footage, brows drawing together in thought, or perhaps condemnation. "I hope that answers your question, Bently, because I have some of my own now."

She watched Dar wobble into the kitchenette and snap another vial into his arm. She waited until he was safely deposited on the cushions before asking, "Dar—if I'm not crazy and not talking to God, what did I hear? What are those? And why am I the only one who's hearing it?"

Dar's face twisted, morphing from a furious frown to something like a smile, but with too many edges. A new, deep crease cut between his brows.

She was starting to think this journey might make it a permanent addition to his otherwise cryo-young features. "Is there more footage?"

"Not that you should see," she admitted honestly. "It's mostly of his disposition. And I didn't hear much after that." She cleared her throat. "Look, there's a fuck-ton we don't know, which becomes more obvious by the second, but I think we need to work with what we do know."

"Precious little that it is," Emilio murmured, watching Dar's expressions flicker.

"I know we don't have access to audio feeds outside this voyage or those you bought off the black market or whatever. But there's got to be something. You said your uncle's ship showed up here after leaving Samsara. Is there any way to determine where it came from before that? Don't you have to report your routes to air traffic control?"

"Of course, every trip's trajectories are registered, but pilots can change course afterward. He was high ranking enough to bypass that, even. Obviously Philos combed through every trajectory when the event first occurred."

"Well fuck you too," Nel scoffed, wishing she hadn't bothered to visit at all, let alone discuss this with him. "Look, when we were on Earth, I looked up your family. It was invasive and rude and I probably should have asked Lin, but I saw your uncle's name. That's how I knew about him. It referenced a missing person's case and some lawsuit, but the links were all dead. We have so few leads, and he's obviously involved—"

"Don't you dare!" Dar roared, surging off the couch to tower over her.

"You asked me for help, this is me helping," she reminded, hands out in an attempt to placate him.

"No, you're babbling. You wandered off like a fucking child on that rock with a shitty suit. For all I know you fell and hit your head. Goodness knows you've done that more than once. I'm aware that when your understanding of the universe is tiny, everything seems connected, but this honestly could be coincidence. Maybe you're seeing connections that aren't there just because you want answers." His pupils were wide, and the fine ends of his hair trembled as his body shook, swaying over her.

Nel lurched to her feet, jabbing him in the chest with one gnarled finger. "You're the one who found the fucking connection in the first place! We are stuck up here with no equipment, no fuel, and like, maybe two half-cocked plans. We're all involved, you pompous alien twat!"

Emilio's hand was firm on her shoulder, his other one on Dar's as he pushed them apart. Nel sputtered into silence and Dar staggered over to his couch where he collapsed in a heap of long limbs and mutters.

"I think we should all work separately for a bit," the Los Pobledores leader remarked. "We each have our own theories, many of them good and just as many will prove to be dead ends. Until we can function as a team, there is no point in trying to work as one." He gestured to the door. "Nel, I want to speak with you, if you'll just give me a moment?"

She scowled and rolled out into the hall without another word to either Emilio or the inebriated jackass. It took a minute for Emilio to emerge behind her. His gentle features were lined with fatigue and frustration.

Guilt jabbed at Nel's brain and she dredged accountability from the sludge of her remaining pride. "I get it—that wasn't the right time. I could have been more patient."

"Bad timing maybe, but you were right." He sighed, rubbing a hand over his face. His warm brown skin looked sallow under the phosphorescence, and his brown gaze roved over the bulges and dips of the apartment walls as if he could find their answers wedged somewhere between the recycled modular pieces.

She blinked. "I'm right?"

"People can change a lot," Emilio offered. "People can become so different they are strangers in the place of friends. Or family."

Nel's frayed focus caught on the expression on Emilio's face. It was sorrow and empathy and something far deeper than rage. *Who did you lose? Was it your brother?*

"Mansur Nalawangsa is involved, though we don't know how. But we now have a much narrower search sector. Dar isn't going to be helpful, not until he recovers—and sobers—but I think you and I can bumble along without his genius to guide us." His tone was annoyed and tender at once, and he scratched the few days' growth of beard on his chin. "I'm going to talk to the trajectory specialists on *The Yarmouth* to see if they can narrow down the places he could have physically flown from, given his craft. Maybe someone knows how to search for video anomalies matching what you saw."

Inertia dragged at Nel's frayed spirits. "We need specialists. Even with an entire team it took IDH weeks to fuck around with Earth."

Emilio shot her a tired wink. "Maybe because half the team was actively trying not to fuck with Earth. Let's focus on just one step, eh?"

Nel nodded, relief uncurling at having some plan, even if it was tentative. "Can I help with any of that?"

"I meant what I said about working separately. I think, while our skills complement each other our methods and personalities could use," his smile warmed with wry humor, "space."

"Fair enough." *How much of that is because you two are hooking up, though?* Nel wondered. She was wise enough to know it was absolutely none of her business.

"Perhaps you could go through the feed of your examination again. Might turn up something.

Even more questions could lead us to a breakthrough, at this point."

"Wait." Nel glanced to be sure Dar's door was shut, then continued, "Could you point me in the direction of the morgue?"

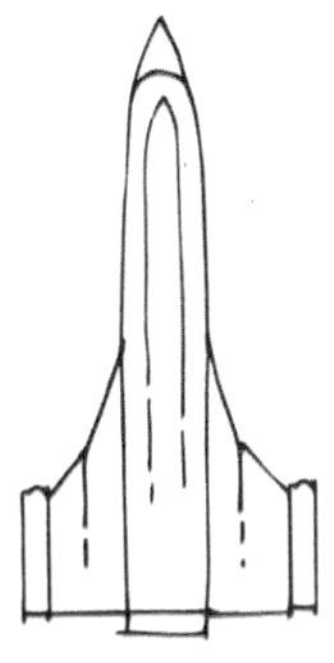

FIFTEEN

Death was no stranger to Nel. It was pervasive and familiar as family. She pulled up outside the morgue door and pressed her wrist to the scanner. After a second of digital conversation with the security system, the door opened. Like most morgues, it was cold and the smell of chemicals almost outweighed that of decomposition. Her brain had long begun to associate the acrid, sickly-sweet smell of formalin with decay, however, and she was abruptly grateful she had been too grumpy that morning to eat anything of substance.

"Can I help you?" A head popped out from the administrative office doorway.

"Hey." Nel offered a wave. "I'm Dr. Bently, anthropologist. I'm following up on some research for a project."

"Of course! Dr. Morchek." The man stepped from the office, wiping what looked like raspberry jam from his hands. At least, Nel hoped it was jam. They shook, and then he nodded to the room from

217

which he'd emerged. "Come in, come in. I was just going over some of my own notes with lunch."

She glanced around the empty space before following him into the smaller room. It was the same sterile gray, with only a few photographs sticky-tacked to the wall beside the holographic screen. Like most of the technology on *The Recursive*, it showed wear, lines jittering through the display from faulty projectors.

Nel squinted at one of the photos, a selfie with another young person in front of towering basalt columns and black sand. "You've been to Iceland?"

"I have! My sibling and I visited during my study of the primitive death practices on Earth. Do they still embalm?"

Nel flinched at the remark, but nodded. "At least a lot of Western cultures do, last I checked."

"The environmental impacts alone..." Morchek tutted and polished off the rest of his jam and toast with a smack of his lips. "What can I help you with? You said you were doing research?"

"Yeah. About a week ago a body was delivered. Found frozen during a, ah," she scrambled to remember what their cover story had been, "resource scouting mission."

"Oh, yes, of course. Pity that. Exposure in space is never a way to go."

"Have you performed an autopsy yet?"

Morchek's brows rose. "Cause of death was listed and I wasn't given orders to do so." He glanced at his screen. "I may have missed a memo—"

"No, no. We hit some snags on our end and just thought I'd request it personally. I'd like to be present. And assist, if possible."

He blinked, mouth opening once before glancing back at his screen. "I'll have to run that by—"

"I'm working with Komodor Muda Nalawangsa. It's a classified project, which is why it hasn't shown up on the main service distribution boards. I can get another notice if you need." She didn't waver, though asking Dar if they could cut apart his uncle wasn't high on her list of priorities. "Unless your clearance level—"

"No, no, that won't be necessary. Every examination is protected information. Are you familiar with our methodology?"

"I'll need a brief orientation with the tech, and I'm happy to accommodate your schedule, of course. I'm here more in a research capacity."

He blinked again, and she watched the desire to pull rank war with curiosity. "I just finished a routine exam—all the technology in the galaxy and we can't stall age. The rest of the afternoon is free, if you are."

"Perfect. Thanks again." Her nerves fired at the dual relief and anxiety that came from knowing there wasn't enough death to make him busy, or to give her time to prepare.

Morchek strode briskly to the wall studded with a single round hatch, about a meter across. The rest of the wall held a wide array of gleaming tools, many of which, Nel was relieved to see, were familiar. Many others weren't, however. The mortician typed a security code into the holographic keyboard and brought up an array of diagnostic screens. "If you're accustomed to terrestrial technology, you'll be pleased with the speed of our testing equipment—I'm afraid most of us have been appalled at the dismal quality."

Nel snorted. Usually, she was thrilled by the impact of even the smallest advance in technology on her work. Morchek's tone made it hard not to snark back. "Who knows, maybe you'll learn something too."

He flashed a grin, seemingly unaware—or unfazed—by her attitude, and pointed to the data on the main screen. "These the correct remains?"

She scanned the information, glancing briefly at the grainy photograph from the intake, before nodding.

Morchek tapped a button and stepped back. Whatever lay behind the hatch whirred and shuddered. A few seconds later the red light above blinked to green. The mortician cracked a lever and rolled the door aside. Mansur's remains glided from the cylinder, coming to a silent halt between them.

He looks slippery. Nel shoved aside her first observation and watched as Morchek lowered the platform so she might better see. "He's in good condition. What are your preservation methods?"

"Indeed. The low temperatures of many space-related deaths often initiate preservation, however we also use a cocktail similar to that used during cryo. This film," his gloved fingers pinched the translucent layer coating the body, "retains any surficial evidence."

"Explains why he looks, ah…" She faltered.

"Buttered?"

"I was going to say shiny." She let herself relax a bit. Sanctity and respect were of utmost importance when dealing with the dead, but the sanity of those who handled remains was a close second. Dark humor was a balm on a bruised psyche. "Mind if I do the recording?"

He gestured for her to continue and began setting up an array of equipment.

A shaking breath steadied her and she tapped the record button on her comm. Now she could slip into the reserved, analytical facet of her brain. "This is Dr. Nel Bently. The time is currently 1408. This is the morgue on *The Recursive* ship. I am observing the autopsy of Jenderal Mansur Nalawangsa, performed by Dr. Morchek, resident onboard mortician. Records show the deceased was a fifty-eight-year-old cis-gendered, multi-racial man. From my initial assessment, I concur. His remains were found by myself within the technical room of a mining base on Morphose-131 and positively identified by Komodor Muda Dar

Nalawangsa, nephew of the deceased." She caught Morchek's eye and, ignoring his bald nosiness, gestured for him to begin.

The covering came first, peeled away in a cruel mimicry of a newborn's caul. Each section Dr. Morchek dropped into its own barcoded vial to be examined later for surficial evidence. Nel got her first proper look at the nebulae of lividity across his flesh. He had died on his back, it seemed, or had hardly been moved at all. *He died hooked up.* She clenched her teeth. It wasn't a time for assumptions. Remembering the recording, she stammered out her observation and followed Dr. Morchek's careful gaze as he peered at Mansur's face. He glanced at Nel, fingers hovering over the obvious biomechanism at the back of the skull. "There is no discoloration that would indicate suffocation. Nor ligature marks. Of course, his eyes are too damaged for much examination."

"Could he have frozen to death? If he were asleep during a system's failure?"

Morchek hummed thoughtfully, lifting one of the hands and showing her the fingertips. "There aren't signs of frostbite, which would likely occur if he was exposed long enough to kill him. Space is a tricky place, however. So many unique ways to die." His tone was neutral, as if he were commenting on a genre of music he didn't find particularly interesting. He continued down the body, pausing to explain each finding. Or, more often, what he didn't find.

"From my external examination," he concluded, straightening with a soft sigh, "I find no evidence of foul play or sudden violent death. There is no sign of external trauma."

"Scalpel?" Nel asked.

"Troglodyte," Morchek scoffed, raising a heavy, wide ring at the foot of the exam table. "To-BI. Total Biomedical Imaging. Scans the entirety of the remains through every current imaging system. Helps us determine damage to any tissue, including neurosystems without damaging them further."

Nel watched as the ring slid along the table's length, its results spreading incrementally across the screen over the table. Morchek regarded the images, face unreadable beyond distant curiosity. "You said he was found within the base?"

"Yes, he was." She tried to pick at her cuticles through the gloves for a moment, wondering how much she could share before the mortician realized something was seriously up. "He was in the computing room. Why do you ask?"

"His tissues are almost completely intact. No sign of internal damage. It's as if he just ceased."

Her gut clenched and her jaw followed suit against the surge of bile in her throat. Fixating on the readouts helped. She knew enough to identify the different systems, each glowing in a different shade. Beyond that, it was a holographic mystery. As much as the evidence seemed to indicate a natural cause, a gentle death as he slipped into the unknown, she would bet Dirt-o-mancer that someone ended him. *Or something.* It was odd, for Nel, not to have the autopsy consist mainly of dissection. As much as her stomach was relieved not to see the jellied pools of coagulated blood or smell the inevitable scent of decay, she feared their high-tech approach would miss something. As if only by sinking her hands into the viscera itself, could she understand the truth.

"Dr. Bently?"

She blinked and looked up at Morchek. "Sorry, what?"

"I asked if you would mind helping take samples."

"Right." She took the proffered tool, a delicate hybrid between a biopsy needle and pipette. Silence expanded around them, broken only by one or the other's occasional narration. They moved down the list, biopsying each organ and tissue. Its mass was recorded, and Nel slid each sample into a labeled vial for the toxicology panel. Perhaps there, an answer could be found.

"That'll be the last of them," Morchek said, setting aside the pipette and dropping a vial of liver tissue into the rack. A robotic courier appeared a moment later to transport the vials to the lab. "All that's left is checking his augment and the neural scan."

"Right." She followed his motions, clipping the synthetic jelly-like material until the entire ventral side of the body was gently wrapped. One of Morchek's pianist's fingers depressed the control on the table and it whirred softly, gripping the remains and rotating them until he was prone.

"We are now beginning the neurological and biomechanical portions of the examination." Morchek recited his preamble, gaze raking the device before them. "There is what appears to be a biomechanical augment on his occipital. This alters the usual methodology."

Nel's teeth ground together as she watched him lift the severed cables in one gentle, curious hand. Her pounding heart was certain simply touching it, looking at it, even, would end him. Maybe all of them. Instead, she swallowed her terror and asked, "You called it an augment. Is this something that's familiar to you?"

"It is not. I've seen many biomechanical devices over my years, from the primitive pacemakers and turn-of-the century wetware to fully functional lumbar-to-foot prostheses. I couldn't say I'm familiar with most, but I can usually identify their function."

"And this one?" she prodded.

One gloved thumb slid over the cable's frayed end and Morchek looked over at her. "I'm not sure if I fully understand what we're looking at here, if I'm honest. It calls to mind the early synth-syn hookups. It was a last hope for many in a vegetative state. A similar—if far more rudimentary—device was used in an attempt to replicate the patient's synaptic data, a poor copy familiar enough for the family to say their goodbyes or for the patient to express final wishes, if a will wasn't present. There was a fad—briefly—of uploading the replica to personal computers. A little time capsule of their loved one. Takes a huge amount of power, however, and most can't afford the expenditure, and the results when the highly complicated files inevitably became corrupted were…" he peered closer at the device, "unnerving."

As blunt as Morchek was, she appreciated his encyclopedic knowledge. But the concept still made Nel's skin crawl. When she was younger and felt invincible, the thought of any disabling event was enough to start her screaming to pull the plug. Now, her relationship with her body was far more complicated.

"Let's begin with the external exam. Would you care to start?"

Nel narrated as her gloved hands probed the metal surface. Unlike before, Morchek's interjections were fewer and less assured. The device appeared fused to Mansur's skin and had been long enough for the surrounding tissue to scar, but not so long that the scar tissue was white. It was puffy, pink. "The biomechanical device cups the deceased's occipital, with several electrodes and feeds descending externally in an insulated cable. Its origin and function are unknown to both Dr. Morchek and myself. It was connected to several cables when the remains were discovered, which were severed to retrieve the body."

Morchek adjusted the scanner and peered at the image. Metal was a cold, dull gray against the technicolor biological material. Hard, unyielding lines indicated where inorganic matter intersected with organic.

"Look." Nel pointed to the back half of the skull. Instead of the intricate, wavering sutures of the cranial bones, there were angled outlines of the hexagonal device. "He swapped the whole thing out."

The mortician hummed in agreement. "Correction: the biomechanical apparatus at the base of the skull is not adhered to the occipital. Rather it appears to have replaced it."

"Judging by the scar tissues, the procedure took place between a year and two months prior to death, wouldn't you say? Ah, that would be in circadial time."

"I concur. Due to potential cryosleep, the actual time frame is unknown. Apply the neuro-scan feeds, will you?"

Rereading the instructions, she untangled the mass of electrodes hanging from the scanner ring. Her hands shook as she clipped them to the wires Morchek indicated at the base of the skull. "Does cryo speed up or slow healing?"

"A bit of both," he admitted. "It hastens it, in that the body only has healing to focus on, instead of the superfluous activity of living, interacting, and so forth. Of course, cryo slows all biological processes, so it is, technically, slower. I suppose a better way of thinking is that cryosleep, or cryostasis in a medical setting, streamlines the process. Beginning analysis of neurological tissue." Morchek reached to set the machine to cycle through its scans.

"Wait—" She bit back the words, but it was too late.

Morchek's steady pale eyes settled on her. "Yes?"

"I, ah..." The man already had a chip on his shoulder. What was one more reason for disdain? "I'm afraid. Of hooking him up again. Afraid of what it might do."

"Afraid of..." He trailed off, hands folding before him in the picture of saintly condescension. "Dr. Bently, while our technology may appear incredibly advanced to one such as yourself, I assure you that not even we can reverse death. We are not about to wake the dead."

There was no use in attempting to hide her sneer. Curated academic language was as much a security blanket as her F-bombs. "Dr. Morchek, while my society may appear primitive to one such as yourself, I assure you that not even I think you're capable of miracles. I'm referring, instead, to the classified events that took place during the mission on Earth. I believe you had neither joined our team nor received the appropriate clearance level to be privy to the details."

His mouth opened, but instead of speaking, after a second of floundering, he settled into a delighted smile. "Of course. Forgive my assumptions, Dr. Bently. I admit they may have been premature. What is this danger to which you refer?"

Classic bully. Just needed some of his own medicine. "Over the duration of the mission a series of deaths occurred directly associated with biomechanical augmentations. I suggest we use aural and electronic containment. Assuming, of course," she met his gaze, "your incredibly advanced technology is capable."

His grin widened and he dipped his head, an obvious, wordless "touche." A few taps on the system settings and the air surrounding the body wavered, then cleared. A tiny green light now blinked on each of his ear-comms. "Upon the advisement of Dr. Bently, I have switched on the electromagnetic containment fields and primed the morgue system for potential containment breach. Shall we proceed?"

Nel fumbled her earphones into place, but hesitated over their settings. *What if you heard them again?* What if the burning, disembodied voices returned? What if this time, instead of pleading, screaming, condemning, they had answers? Shoving the scientific curiosity from her mind, she flicked on the noise cancellation. "Proceed."

The image juddered again. Overlaying the crisp white of skeletal structures and the faint gold of lymphatic systems, worming around the fractal lace of blood vessels and purple sarcomeres were neurons. They showed teal on the readouts.

"Oh my," Morchek breathed.

Don't like that. "What is it?"

"The beauty of the human body is second only to our desire to understand it. To improve upon it," he explained, tracing the lines like a lover. The image flickered in the wake of his fingers. "But I have never seen anything this extensive. This level of augmentation makes our technology look like, well," he tossed her a teasing, arrogant wink, "yours."

Nel was too distracted by the implications of his observation to rise to the bait. "Those are organic structures. So he didn't replace his whole neurosystem. Just connected to it?"

"Indeed. If it's not broken, why fix it."

Nel tilted her head, recalling the numerous MRIs she'd undergone throughout her accident-prone adolescence. "The neurons—is it just the readout or are they damaged? The color isn't as vibrant."

"Perceptive. The entirety of his neuro system has been cauterized. I've seen similar damage when I did a rotation at one of the high-security prison stations. My initial likening to the synth-synapses wasn't entirely misplaced—the connections are the same. This doesn't appear to have copied him so much as burned through him." Morchek enhanced the image, looking back and forth between the scan and the molecular results on the adjacent screen. "The damage is on a molecular level. Maybe even quantum."

She didn't really want the answer, but she asked anyway. "Did it kill him?"

"I can't be certain. It's almost as if he were—" He shook his head, searching for the right word.

"Erased." Nel didn't have the intimate knowledge Morchek did, nor had she studied biomechanics as long as Jem, but she knew whatever had been done to Mansur was linked to the device on Samsara, to its doomsday twin on Earth.

"I believe we're finished then," Morchek remarked, beginning to tidy up and prepare the body once more for storage. "I hope this addresses some of your research questions, Dr. Bently."

"I'm afraid not." The lie was a whisper. Her eyes fixed on the readouts, tracing the digital spider silk branching through his gray matter. They'd gone so long without answers, without enough data for even the least educated guess. Now, an answer glowered back at her from the screen, all merciless honesty and baleful irony. It wasn't the answer she wanted. It wasn't even an answer she understood or could explain, though she knew soon she'd be forced to do just that. "This concludes the medical autopsy of one Mansur Nalawangsa." She hesitated, finger hovering over the recording button. "Cause of death, unknown."

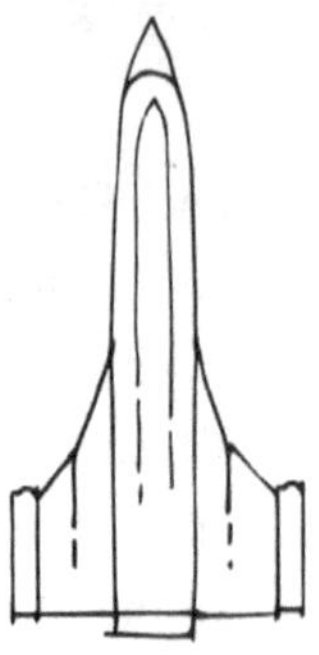

SIXTEEN

The apartment was still when Nel returned from her kitchen shift late the next afternoon. She groaned and forced herself through a half-hearted round of exercises before slipping into the deserted kitchen. Her mom had set out muffins and a clean mug filled with powdered decaf. Avoiding the muffins, she popped the coffee into the hydrator and watched the stream of steaming water hiss into the mug. Decaf was the greatest of all sins, but her sleep was too filled with rotting corpses and sizzling, sentient static to justify caffeine. Her fake coffee was barely ready when her comm flashed a reminder.

Right. Therapy. If there ever was a time for it, she supposed finding a body qualified. Glad her mother wasn't within earshot, Nel put together another cup and settled onto the couch in time to accept the incoming call from Zach. "Evening."

"Good evening, archaeology princess!" He smiled. In the background she heard rich music and someone talking.

"Is this a bad time—?"

"Just working from my cabin, one moment." His finger loomed as he tapped something near the camera lens. Silence fell and he sat back to smile at her. "Noise cancellation. I'm having dinner with friends after this, but right now you're my priority. How've you been?"

"Thanks." She rattled off her PT progress and lied about the improvement in her sleeping habits.

"Last time we spoke you mentioned having trouble moving on from your relationship with Lin. Did you want to talk more about that?"

No. "I think I had a bit of a breakthrough. I hooked up with someone a little while ago." The idea of casual sex being a breakthrough for her was laughable, but she had to tell him something— anything—other than the sickening dread building in her gut.

"If I recall, hookups were your way of avoiding intimacy before you met Lin. Do you feel like your relationship with sex has changed since?"

"Damn," she laughed humorlessly. "Little close to the mark there, Zach."

His smile was broad but kind. "That's not a bad thing, Nel. Reconnecting with sex and intimate— physically, at least—relationships in the way that makes you feel most comfortable is good, as long as everyone's having a good time. Do you think this hookup will become something more?"

She shook her head. "No. But I stayed most of the night." *Awake, wondering what would happen if Lin caught up to us.* The sound of her voice was overloud in the small room and she faltered into silence, trying to figure out how to phrase what had been weaseling through her mind since she set eyes on Dar's uncle. "It was...nice. I guess. They're a friend. And funny. And kind. No strings though. Think I have enough strings to untangle right now, so to speak."

"That's good that you're identifying what you're able to handle before you become overwhelmed." He hesitated, peering through the pixels. "I hear something in your voice. Any other episodes?"

It wasn't the classified nature of their ragtag investigation that twisted her words. "No. I think it was stress and maybe some fear."

"Of course. There's a lot to be concerned about. Are you safe?"

"As much as any of us are. This isn't that type of crisis." Forcing the annoyance from her voice, she added, "Thank you, though. I'm just, I'm working on something. With Dar and Emilio. Not sure what I can share. This is confidential?"

"You know that. Unless I learn that you or someone else is in immediate danger. Share how you're feeling, if you'd like. That's really my biggest concern."

"I'm okay, but worried, I guess. And tired. So tired," she repeated.

He leaned closer. "Physically or otherwise?"

She drew a long breath and glanced at the apartment door. Outside, the soft sounds of their neighbors preparing for supper reached through the thin modular plastic and metal. "Otherwise. Dar kind of stalled out. And I don't know enough about this world to get him going again. But there was a bit of a development. Maybe."

Zach's thin brows rose.

"I was part of the EVA to that asteroid."

"The resource mission?"

"Is that what they called it?" She scoffed. Frustration sizzled up, erasing her caution. "We didn't find any resources. We found an empty base and like, no data. And a body." Somehow the body sitting in the dark of their morgue weighed far more than his simple mass of bones and flesh.

Zachariah leaned forward. "This would be the man reported dead from your ship when you docked?"

How'd you know about that? "Yeah. I thought they were keeping that quiet. Did they disclose his name?"

"'Quiet' just means it wasn't broadcast. Death was attributed to technical failure on the mine. I looked into what you were registered for since we last spoke to try to identify what might be happening. As your psychologist. Nothing more."

She winced. "Sorry I never made those appointments—"

"That's something we'll just have to work on. And as for your other question, and his name: no. I imagine they're waiting to notify the family."

"Maybe. Probably also trying to figure out what happened to him. Well it's Dar's uncle. The man we found. Dar was pretty shaken."

"Peace be upon him." Zachariah bowed his head. "And I imagine you were also affected?"

She shook her head. "I didn't know him. Dar and I had, I don't know. A nice moment?" She stopped. Explaining what had passed between Dar, the body, and herself seemed like breaking some confidence Dar had placed in her. "It was sacred. As it should be."

"It sounds like something doesn't sit right with you. You're equivocating."

"I guess it doesn't." Her frown deepened. "We've been up here for weeks—months, almost. And we're barely even running anymore. There's no fuel to speak of, and our resources are dwindling. It was risky to dock at that station, and I doubt we'll do it again, even if Dar does need to make some trade or whatever. I get grief. Really, I do. And it's not like there's a ticking bomb this time. But I haven't heard shit from him. We're sitting ducks in a shrinking pond and I'm getting tired of waiting for Dar to say it's okay for us to fucking fly."

Zach nodded thoughtfully, twirling a lock of his hair as he considered her words. "If I recall, it took a while to get you back into work after your injury. Maybe he needs someone to remind him that while he could step back, the mission itself must continue. If you truly think there's something to this that can't wait."

"Do you think I'm just being a bitch?"

"I don't have the information you do or the experience. But if your heart is saying this, then you should trust it." He was quiet for a moment. "We're about at the end of our session. Is there anything else you want to discuss, or maybe make a note to talk about next time?"

"Thanks. Not really. I think I—" She straightened, the nagging in her chest only growing. "I'll talk to Emilio about it. He might have more insight." *Considering they're fucking.* "And I mean it. Thank you. For listening to my bullshit. I'm sorry it's not always easy."

"Nel, I've said it before, but I'm your friend first."

"You too," she answered, with a small wave. "See you later. Have a good dinner."

They signed off, and she was left with a blank screen and a sour stomach. Lying never sat well with her, though she did it by omission countless times. Often it didn't feel like lying, but instead not knowing the right words. Not knowing if the proper words existed at all. Admitting the voices were real meant admitting how not safe they all were. Admitting they were utterly fucked. *Oh.*

Breakthroughs in therapy were great, she supposed, if you were living in a tiny apartment in Northampton and going through your first Real Breakup. They weren't great when you were struggling to find a radio signal that kept killing people only to discover that it was all around you, always, and there was nothing to be done.

The feeling she couldn't name was dread.

"You're doing well."

Nel glared at the floor. Jem meant well. She knew that. She knew the medic deserved gratitude not snark, but the words spat from her mouth before she could think better of them. "Yeah, for a fucking baby."

Jem shrugged. "Then do better."

This time Nel glared properly. "I'm trying. As hard. As I can."

"Then quit your bitching." Jem's full mouth quirked up at one corner.

"Quit picking on a cripple."

"Quit being an asshole to a friend who's just trying to help."

The burn of anger was familiar, and for a moment, drowned out the burn of movement, of failure, of embarrassment. They were right. She was being an asshole. But fuck, if that wasn't the only thing she was still good at. Breathe in, step. Breathe out, step. By the time she reached the window at the end of the hall, she was drenched in sweat and her body shuddered with the effort of simply standing.

Jem, mercifully, said nothing when Nel slumped down into the waiting wheelchair.

She rubbed at her thigh where the ill-fitting prosthetic's sleeve covered her skin. It was red where the silicone had bunched and chaffed. "This thing doesn't fit."

"No. Close as we can get, though. Try this." Jem produced a tube from their medic bag.

Nel peered at it. "Anti-itch?" she asked.

"Light analgesic and anti-inflammatory." They sighed, the circles under their eyes extra ashy under the uneven lighting. "You'll get through this. Promise. It'll just suck for a while. I put a note in requisitions for silicone for a custom sleeve, you know. But a lot of our req list supplies are tied up in the system support."

Nel sighed. "Understandable. I mean, I'd like a new shiny one. Dar said I could have one with, like, a smart map program in it."

Jem stared at her for a moment before bursting into laughter. "That man's a nut." They glanced at their comm. "I've got another appointment, but I want you to do another few laps. Slow as you like, but do them, alright?"

Nel grimaced but nodded.

"I'll check the security feeds later, make sure you actually did," they threatened, though their eyes were soft.

Nel flashed a halfhearted smile. "You free later? I thought we could watch some shitty terrestrial movies and get drunk."

"Yeah, should be. I'll message when I'm free."

She watched the medic grab their bag and head back toward the main infirmary. Her thoughts were an unwilling astronaut on an untethered EVA in the roiling cosmos of her mind. She drew a breath, took a step. Exhaled and took another. Her heart hurt, thrumming faster than this steady pace warranted. Another tug strained the anxiety-stretched neck of her A-shirt wide, as if it would help her skin expand enough to fit all of her feelings comfortably.

She glanced down and demanded her left toes wiggle. It was a futile prayer to the past. So many events over the past few years divided her life into chunks of "before" and "after." Before her injury. Before Samsara. Before Lin. But as much as she wished that was the same for the body she had just cataloged, there was some part of her that was no longer surprised enough to mark before or after. Horrified, but not surprised.

Heaving an angry sigh she eyed the prosthetic. Her prosthetic. *My leg.* Buzzing filled the plush layer of fat and sensation between her skin and bunching muscle. A real-not-real ripple that rushed up her thigh and flanks to flicker into her gray matter. She hated it. It was invasive and unavoidable and reminded her of the mental pitching as she looked into the void of space or succumbed to cryosleep. Of the emotions pressing at her sides to the point of rupture. She hated how different every other step felt. Hated that the reverberation of her foot hitting the hard floor of the spaceship's corridor felt so utterly different when it traveled up titanium and circuitry, instead of through the heavy wet weight of flesh.

And she hated how relieved she felt every time it took her weight.

She was Nel. Dr. Bently. A woman who could dig test pit after test pit. A woman who took off into space for a booty call. She could conquer anything.

Except, apparently, a missing limb. Her hands clenched on the rail along the hall, palm sweaty. The recycled air chilled her brow and the space between her shoulder blades where sweat beaded at the effort of simply walking.

For all her talk, she was rarely at home anywhere. Her body had been the exception. Made in the image of her father, with a few sprinkles of her mother's DNA, there was nothing she knew like her own flesh, nowhere her legs couldn't climb, no place her hands wouldn't grasp. Soil from four continents and three planets had collected under her filed nails. Rocks of every color had scraped skin from her palms. She knew each billow of her lungs and thrum of her confused, furious heart. There was no place her legs could not carry her.

Until now.

Drifting in a ship through a minefield of danger, asteroids, and death, the only place she could go was up and down the main corridor.

Her comm buzzed, but she dismissed it angrily when she saw it was Dar. Three silent weeks had passed since Emilio insisted they work alone. She had spent most of her hours working in the kitchen, head down in sullen silence. Other than Dr. Morchek's pointedly curious emails and a few late-night propositions from Jem, no one had contacted her. The second buzz went ignored as well. Was it embarrassment over how she had acted or anger at how he had? *Or I'm just tired of letting everything be on his terms.*

A voice, loud and strained with annoyance, boomed over the only-for-emergencies PA system. "Dr. Bently, please report to the bridge."

She flopped back into her chair, waffling between procrastinating PT or seeing the prick. This time it was her personal comm that crackled with Dar's acerbic voice.

"I know you're listening. And it's not like you're busy. Ever."

"Fuck off, Dar," she muttered to herself, not actually answering him.

"Fine. Don't join me in exploring this fuel ship Emilio tracked down. It's not like I enjoy your company anyway."

She was at the end of the hall and slamming her hand on the button to open the door before the last words were even out of Dar's mouth. Her map might have been rudimentary, but it helped narrow down where the bridge certainly wasn't and after the better part of ten minutes, she was deep in the upper decks, following helpful signs and strips of colored lights. A set of massive doors awaited her when she rounded the final bend, a panel blinking expectantly beside. She frowned at it, then tried pressing her palm to it.

"Stop molesting the ident scanner and just come in," Dar snapped through the comm. A second later the door opened, revealing another set. No sooner had the first closed behind her than the second opened. *Extra security.* The thought of needing it, especially on a refugee ship with few resources and even fewer allies made her skin crawl.

"So what's this about a ship?" Nel asked, wheeling onto the bridge. The words died on her tongue. It wasn't the gleaming lights and holographic screens that stalled her speech. Instead, her eyes fixed on the massive ship blotting out half their sky. She knew what the other refugee ships looked like. She often glimpsed *The Yarmouth* from the generation gym. This was at least twenty times that size, depending on how far it extended past the cockpit windows. "Holy shit."

"Knew that would get you. We're refueling. Thought you might want to check it out," Dar suggested. She couldn't tear her eyes away from the sight. The smattering of stars were almost entirely blocked by the freighter's belly. At least, Nel assumed it was a freighter. It lacked the gleaming sleekness inherent in IDH cruisers, or the portholes and aesthetics of some of the smaller private ships she saw when they docked on *Odyssey*. Aside from the gaping bay at one end, it didn't appear to have anything that could be a weapon. *And I really hope that big hole isn't a cannon.* "Refueling?"

It was a wonder his eyes weren't stuck facing the back of his skull, with the number of times he rolled them at her. "You think we power this thing on our canned farts?"

"I don't fucking know, it's as plausible as any of your other space tech."

He opened his mouth to argue, but Emilio appeared from behind a holoscreen with a wry grin. "She's not wrong. Maybe something to look into, conserve resources and all that."

"Shut up," Dar muttered.

"Emilio," Nel glanced at the ship, half expecting the yawning black hole to blink at her, "is this a good idea? Because it seems like very much not a good idea."

His voice pitched low, hard to catch over the trilling and clacking of the surrounding tech. "If you recall I was looking into something that might help or shed light on our situation."

A dark gleam in his eyes dared her to point out all the security issues with the idea. Her gut clenched harder at the realization that he didn't mean their low food and fuel supplies. "This is where we ended up?"

"Indeed." He leaned over one of the smaller trajectory screens and tapped a few gleaming buttons. Her comm buzzed a moment later and a tiny map appeared above her wrist. Her gaze traced the spider-threads of the Jenderal's journey. The ship looming in their sky to Samsara. Several unnamed points among their same asteroid field. *And from there to Morphose.*

"And you think these people will, ah…" she frowned, searching for vague enough words, "have enough spare resources?"

Dar jerked a curt nod at her. "It's not unheard of for haulers to take pity on the marooned." Turning to another person whose augmentations made Grettatron's look like low-budget film prosthetics—and sent a shudder of horror through Nel—he asked, "Did you hail?"

"Yessir. It's 201-Q12L5, registered as *V Drugoye Mesto.* We sent a general contact signal to them as soon as we were close enough. No response."

"What's that?" Nel asked.

Emilio lowered his voice so as not to interrupt the flow of jargon. "Just a neutral greeting between our two systems. A digital 'do you copy?' If any part of their system was still online, we'd receive something. It's automatic. Conveys the craft's metadata, status, manifests and itineraries. Everything."

"But you got nothing? Is there another way to find that stuff? Or scan to see if there's people—wait, you said all systems. Is there life support?"

"Manual connection could tell us the details," Dar mused, turning to scroll through a stream of miniscule words on his personal comm screen. "As for life support, it could be—even if something tripped it there's a backup switch that flips automatically when the signal is broken—"

"Too much science," Nel interrupted. "So it's impossible to turn off, essentially."

"Inconvenient would be more accurate."

"Komodor Muda, we're within full scanning range."

"Go ahead." Dar's eyes were fixed, not on the scan, but on the ship itself. His gaze roved over it like he looked upon the body of a new lover.

Nel made a face and peered at the glowing screen. Instead of the intricate heat signatures and radiation blooms reflected off their shielding, the entire ship was a solid block of gold. "Is that hot or cold?"

"Damn it all to hell," the tech snarled. "Well, that tells us one thing: it's an older model in the Civilian line. Registered pilot flew for a mining co-op."

"How can you tell?" Nel asked, wheeling closer. "Thing's all lit up."

"Full hull shielding. In newer ships they just cover the cargo areas. More efficient, you know? But before that, they used to make the entire ship out of insulating ore, in case they were hauling anything radioactive. Every single wall was thicker than my leg. Took huge amounts of fuel to get them going."

Nel jabbed her finger at the screen, ignoring his glare when her finger sent ripples through the photons. "Can't you look up what this could be in some base data...base?"

Dar didn't dignify her pun with acknowledgment, but the tightness around his mouth indicated it registered. "A lot of them keep imperfect records and update them infrequently. It's rather what I was gambling on, coming out here. I knew that whatever people we might encounter wouldn't have heard the news just yet."

I'm not sure I even know what the fucking news is. "Cool. Can you tell if it's occupied?"

"Nope, all the shielding against the radiation and vacuum block anything slight enough to be body heat. Wish they'd respond though."

"Maybe their comms are down. They could have switched off all audio, given what's been happening," Nel posited.

Dar waved a hand at her. "Mother of God! Who's in charge here?"

Nel leaned back in her chair, arms crossing. "Well? Tell me all you know, O Wise Captain."

"Think this warrants an EVA. Best case, the place is fine and we refuel and go on our merry way."

"And worst case?" Nel asked, trying in utter vain not to picture what that might mean. The roiling in her stomach said radio security wasn't the reason no one responded. *Please, not another body.* To her displeasure, even Emilio didn't answer.

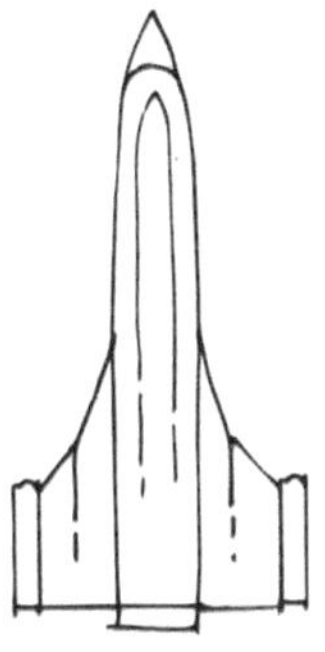

SEVENTEEN

Nel shoved her one leg through the suit's, frowning at the length of electromesh dangling beneath her. She rolled it over her biomechanical limb, surprised with how well the stiff cloth stretched and clung to the different curves. Try as she might, her life would never be the same. But when she drew back and examined it, it wasn't because of the limb left pulverized in the Chilean desert. And maybe, someday, that'd be okay.

"Need a hand?" Dar asked.

"No, just a leg."

"God, that joke is just never funny."

"It's okay, I always think I'm funny enough for everyone. Just happy to add one more terrible joke to my repertoire." She wove upright and snagged the waiting space suit with her free hand. "Round two."

These, at least, were modular enough so various pieces could be altered or removed completely without compromising the integrity of the suit itself. At least, that's what she hoped. She donned her helm and checked the seal.

Suit: power on.

A ripple spread through her inner layer, the outer one quickly pressurizing. Dar's angry muttering at his wrist display was now transmitted through the soft hiss of her helmet's comm. Her body warmed as the suit responded to her heightened nerves. She scanned the suit's readouts:

PRESSURE: NORMAL
TEMP: NORMAL RANGE
BIOFEEDBACK: HEIGHTENED
AUX SYSTEMS: CLOSED
GLOVE: NON-COMBAT

Other than her propulsion belt, which was at half-battery, everything looked normal enough. *All the tech in the world and people still forget to charge shit.*

"Ready, Bently?"

She glanced behind them. "I thought there were more of us?" The idea that she and Dar would make up the entirety of the scouting mission did not sit well. They were wholly unprepared for the brain-dead mine and its single casualty. Everything about this too-silent ship made her stomach seize with apprehension. Or maybe it was the sad apple she had scrounged from the kitchen that morning.

"We'll meet the rest down below. Got a good group, I think. Varied skill sets."

So who is gonna be the big guns of this heist? The rest of her speculation faded as she tucked her crutch into place and followed Dar across the anteroom to the elevator. The sheer size of their own ship didn't really hit her until they were shooting downward, the elevator carrying them farther and farther from any illusion of gravity.

Minutes later, they disgorged into the zero-gravity cylinder. The rest of their team waited there. Sure enough, there was a mountain of a person carrying a massive gun. The reinforced suit seemed more at risk of rupturing due to their substantial muscles than from the vacuum of space. They were in quiet conversation with a slender man bearing a medical doctor's badge on his suit.

"This is Dr. Bently, everyone. Bently, this is Dr. Morchek—"

"We've met, actually," Nel explained, offering the mortician a wave.

Dar shot her a concerned look but continued with his introductions. "Officer Lem is our munitions personnel." Dar indicated the large person, then held his hand out to the short, wide woman equipped with a sturdy hovering harness wrapped around her much smaller lower half. "And Kapten Markham: it's a true honor. I've been inspired by your techniques since I was a boy."

The Kapten's grin was broad even through the tinted helm. She floated a bit higher and grasped

Dar's gloved hand. "Always great to meet a fellow pilot. Gonna help me check out the nav systems?"

"Sure am," Dar responded, voice almost vibrating through the comms.

Holy shit, is the asshole starstruck? Nel didn't know Kapten Markham from Adam, but clearly she was someone due respect.

The elevator opened behind them and the final member of their odd group entered. She was a bit taller than Nel, with dark skin and bright green eyes. Instead of a gun, she bore an augmented prosthetic arm with several attached gadgets that looked like wrenches on steroids. A large case rested under her other arm.

Dar turned and gave the woman a curt nod. "Afternoon, Casey. Thanks for joining us."

"Silent ship in the middle of an asteroid field? You bet your ass I'm here. So what's the plan?"

"This is the passenger dock beside their refueling port. From here, as long as there appears to be no emergency, we'll spread out, gather what information we can."

"Roger that," Lem answered, voice surprisingly high.

Nel reached out to steady herself, before realizing there was little risk with zero-G. Still, it made her feel more in control. The doors rumbled open, or, at least, the vibrating of the rail in her hand made her imagine they rumbled.

It was dark inside the docking port. Nel might not have been able to feel the air or smell it, but she sensed the stillness. The same way she knew when a placid lake was cold without touching its surface. Whatever happened here was over. They just had to figure out what that was.

Readouts blinked on each of their suit's wrists:

ATMOSPHERE CONDUCIVE TO HOMO SAPIENS

She frowned. If other lifeforms were so rare, why the specificity? Were the teachers really all that different? She supposed sentient sound wouldn't really need to breathe. Shoving the brain-breaking thought from her head, she followed the others into the blackness. The hall was narrow, but after a few turns, widened into a sort of utilitarian foyer, with several large corridors leading into the ship's bowels.

"Everyone has their maps?"

Murmurs of assent drifted through the comms. With each operative's voice, a different colored dot blinked on the periphery of her helm.

"Alright, please keep comms clear, except for observations and so forth. We all have canceling devices in our helmets, but let's not be reckless. You hear a weird noise, shut it down. I think all of these suits are programmed with simultaneous voice-to-text, so we should be fine either way. Move out, people."

A thrill of adrenaline shot through Nel. Danger. Finally, a reason for her body to burn, for her heart to hammer against her ribs, for her mind to race. *Fuck, I've missed this.* Dr. Morchek took a right, followed by the mechanic. Kapten Markham nudged Lem and nodded toward the bulk of the ship. They disappeared, leaving Dar and Nel alone. "So..."

"Crew quarters and residential stuff for you, I think. I'm checking out the computer systems before joining Kapten Markham on the bridge."

"Gotcha." She pulled up the map—a luxury she would never take for granted again—and oriented herself. After a second she felt Dar staring a hole through her shoulder. "Yeah?"

"So if we, ah..." He frowned at his own map, pinching and dragging it. After a pause he tilted his head. "We're where again?"

Her brows went up. "Komodor Muda Dar Nalawangsa, are you unable to read a map?"

"I'm just not familiar with these ships—"

"That's why you have the map. And yours," she reached over and tapped an icon on his screen, "is upside down."

His face remained a neutral mask of ignorance. "It looks the same. And I still don't know where we are."

"Well, we came in here and took two lefts and a right, which would put us...here." She pointed. His slow blink was the opposite of reassuring. "Okay, I'm sorry, I'm not trying to be mean, but dude, you can pilot a fucking starship but can't read a map? How is that possible?"

"Because I usually have an entire team of navigators and a senti-comp doing the map bit for me!" he ground out. "What skills I have as a pilot are my reflexes, my intimate understanding of how these machines work and nerves of steel. None of which," he spat, "you can get from a map."

"I see." She tried not to laugh, really, she did. "You gonna be okay to get to the computers?"

He glared at the map.

"Here." She reached over and tapped a few commands. Within the first few days of the Samsari dig, she'd learned most of the more useful aspects of IDH's mapping programs. Dar's map blinked, then she saw the faint haze of lights appear on his helmet's glass.

"Oh. Oh, this is fantastic. It'll show me the whole way there?"

"Yep. Just double tap on your computer screen to switch your waypoint."

"Thanks, Bently." He flashed what might have been a genuine smile and jetted off down the hall with all his usual confidence.

Nel was alone. Seemingly. This ship was huge. And while it looked deserted, there was no way to know for sure. *And people are the scariest factor of all.* No matter what Dar said, her heart pounded. Just because news hadn't reached this far didn't mean their enemies hadn't. And even if these people hadn't received an IDH-Most Wanted poster on their holoscreens or whatever, that didn't make them friendly. Nel's time in CRM had brought her to more than a few rural areas, each boasting an array of colorful characters. She flexed her hand within its electroglove. At the end of the day, it didn't matter if you were in Sci-Fi Sector 42 or West Virginia. Backwaters were backwaters.

Her own map led her through a winding maze of narrow corridors until she emerged into a broad hall. Though there seemed to be no power, she noted extinguished lines like *Recursive*'s along the floor, and signs marking the way to various places, though the letters were Cyrillic.

Ahead, a large doorway opened into a cavernous room. "I'm almost at the atrium, I think," she relayed to the rest of the team. After a second glance at the map displayed on her helm, she continued. "Approaching from port-aft. Still no signs of anyone."

"I've made it to the medical bay," Dr. Morchek informed them. Even his unimpressed tone softened with relief when he continued, "No signs of emergency treatment or quarantine of any kind. I'm going to analyze their medical log and compare the physical inventory, but so far I'd guess that whatever occurred is non-pathogenetic in nature."

Silence reigned as Nel continued down the twisting main corridor aiming for the larger series of central crew common rooms. Dar's communication came through in mostly written bullet points, punctuated only by brief discussions with Markham. Nel emerged into the dim cantina, flashlight beam ghosting across the tables. Plates and utensils drifted through the air, along with clumps of long-spoiled food. Nel was doubly glad she'd opted to keep her helm on. "Got signs of people. I'm in the cantina. Everything's just floating."

"A breach?"

Nel checked her wrist display. It took her a second to decipher the readout. "Looks like I still have atmosphere here, at least. What about you?"

"Ditto. Cursory scan says all the life support systems were still running, at least until they ran out of juice. There's some electric damage—a surge, maybe. But just the grav's out," Casey barked back.

"Here too. Looks like they were in the middle of a meal. Plates, forks, and your grandmother's pot roast all still here."

"This is why we seal mess halls from anything remotely mechanical," Dar muttered. "Because it's a damned mess."

Nel ignored his tirade and moved through the atrium. Her flashlight glinted off forks and spinning ladles. She froze as it caught a smear of red across one wall. "Blood."

The word cut off Dar's tangent. *He must be nervous to babble so much.*

"Where?"

"Wall. Smear of it. Starboard side of the atrium. Floor too."

"Positive it's blood?"

"I sure ain't tasting it."

"No, I wouldn't suggest you do so, Bently, however your glove has an analysis port for a reason," Dar reminded.

"Right. One sec." She propelled herself across the room to the smear. It was small, not enough for loss of life, she didn't think. She snapped a picture; then, using the tip of her trowel, she peeled a sliver off and tipped it into the port. It whirred, a tiny circle indicating it was processing the data. While it contemplated, she moved toward the kitchen.

"False alarm," she called with a chuckle. "It's fucking barbecue sauce. Sorry folks. No bloodshed here."

The kitchen itself was trashed, though she couldn't tell for sure if it was due to the sudden gravity failure or something else. Dar's initial examination of the ship indicated there hadn't been any crash.

"I got nothing here as well," Dr. Morchek's voice crackled through her speakers. Perhaps it was the comm, but his voice sounded strained. "Whoever was here left in a hurry."

"Or not at all," Casey muttered.

"We don't know that," she answered. Nel had her share of pessimism, but Casey was beginning to grate on her nerves. She moved through the mess hall and into a corridor. Ahead, her beam bounced through the darkness of what looked like an even larger room. "Body count is only as high as the number of skulls." It was an oversimplification but conveyed her point just fine. "So far we don't even have one."

"Only one shuttle launched," Dar explained. "And no matter how much people liked each other, you're not cramming the entire crew of a hauler this size, let alone with all their families, into one shuttle."

"You got their records?" Lem's soft voice cut through the comms.

"Sure did," Casey answered, before rattling off a few key points. "Looks like their last stop was a routine pickup from a Mercassian station. Before that they dropped a load at Ka Chain. Seems routine too. Don't know what brought them out here though."

"Crew is freelance, right?" Nel offered. "Could be a job."

A high, barking laugh answered her through the comms. "Gotta be rich motherfuckers coming way out here. Only job they gonna find is poor twats like us without a credit to our names—"

"If you could all keep the chatter down, I'm doing a full system diagnostic scan."

Data, abbreviated beyond Nel's understanding, flickered along the side of her helm's glass as the scan's results flooded in. Others, in the colors matching their operatives' speech indicator, appeared and disappeared as each prodded the ship's systems into wakefulness. It was distracting, even without meaning.

Suit: dismiss non-emergency readouts.

Routine readouts dismissed.

She had done this countless times—stood in the aftermath of human spaces and dredged a hypothetical narrative from far, far less. *This is no different from any other site.* Nel turned down the voice channels next, until they were little more than a lofi background murmur. She forced a long inhale through her nose and stepped into the center of the mess hall. She had no idea what happened here, but that didn't matter. Her job was to determine what the crew had been doing just before It happened.

Things weren't exactly right where they'd been left, but she had to start somewhere. Dented tables. Dinged plastic flooring. Doors dangling open without gravity to guide them. It was mealtime. Dozens of dirty plates drifted through the darkness. Some, with the heaviest smears of food, now sported colorful arrays of mold. The chill and recycled air made judging time from that alone impossible.

Using her propulsion belt, Nel moved toward the kitchen entry. Stacks of pallets told her they were prepping for another meal. Perhaps, like on *The Recursive*, mealtimes were staggered to avoid overcrowding and overwhelming the staff. The cooktops were seared black, whatever had been cooking baked into unrecognizable, carbonized heaps. Chopping knives dangled on the ends of their safety tethers. Whatever it was had happened fast. What was so terrifying that you left the stove on?

A peek into the storage rooms sent a thrill of excitement up her spine. Their shelves were packed full. Food was spoiled here too, but a quick sampling of what she could recognize returned unremarkable results. *Probably not poisoning, then.* Nel tagged several shelf-stable racks for the collection crew that would sweep through if the ship was deemed safe and fully abandoned. Even if they found no answers, at least this whole effort wouldn't be entirely in vain.

Retreating to the mess hall, she froze. Across the room stood a massive, open doorway. Like the rest of the ship, it was dark. She swallowed hard. Shadows moved in the darkness, in the depths that were blacker than black. Under the swooshing of her blood, and the ragged billow of her breath, the whispers waited. No words, really. None she could decipher. The lizard part of her brain knew, without a doubt, that the space beyond that doorway was not empty.

Her wrist buzzed. "Bently, do you copy?"

Prying her panic-clenched jaw open, she rasped, "Yeah. Copy."

"Found anything?"

"Supplies. Not much else." She glanced at her readouts, noting Dr. Morchek's latest update registered no signs of life. Beside it, a bitchy blinking told her the battery on her propulsion belt was already drained. At least the zero-G and corrugated walls enabled her to pull herself along most of the corridors. "I'm entering another big room. Judging by the map it's..." she glanced down, then back at the corridor number to confirm, "the ship's Aft Atrium. Whatever that is."

"Used for residential cargo, recreation, or gathering in case of emergency."

"Gotcha." *In case of emergency.* What had once referred to sliced digits and bee stings or—on one particularly bloody occasion—a machete to the scapula, now meant planet-altering mechanics and massive detonators. *And missing limbs.* "Entering."

She glided into the room, grasping a handle by the open door to swing herself down toward the floor of the room. Most of the ships she had been on while traveling with IDH could have easily fit into the cavernous space. Various colors smeared the surfaces here too. "Another glob of stuff here. Looks like trash and food or something."

"Probably spoiled resources. Everything not tied down will eventually drift into stasis in anti-grav. Anything of note?"

Items drifted past, small ones: tablets, a guitar, and what looked suspiciously like a Lego set. *Families?* Nel's chest clenched at the thought. If she were the praying kind, she'd bow her head and beg not to find children. "I'll take some pics. Bunch of personal effects too. Toys."

"Fuck," Dar muttered.

"Did you find out how many people were last on board?" she asked, skirting the topic of kids as she tried to get a better visual of the shadowed depths.

"Usually these things have about 300 staff, plus family." He paused. "Their last report was four months before they went dark. All systems were good, passenger count at 378. One of the logs about a month before they went dark mentions a child born to the family of a lead mechanic. Surname Damascus. Last log mentions a stop at the edge of the asteroid field. They rescued a marooned pilot." Dar's voice was hard, harder than it should have been, tight with uncomfortable certainty. "The pilot's ship launched less than two weeks later, along with a single escape vessel."

Maybe it was something simple—a gas leak, or someone pushed the wrong big flashing button. It didn't explain the dread still tapping her on the shoulder, or the nagging susurration pulling her attention to the center of the cavernous room. The sound almost had form, it was so constant, so pressing, so present. It plucked the strings of dread within her chest until their song was closer to grief.

Scorch marks covered half the walls, pitted and black as if they had been burned not just by fire, but something corrosive. Fractals emanated from the largest swaths of char, and Nel recognized they had a shape. *Intention.* She snapped another series of photos, the flash sending tracers across her vision and illuminating the space with merciless clarity. Above, hovering in what must have been the center of the room, was a mass of trash. She pushed off gently from the floor to get a better look, letting her own momentum carry her closer. Her archaeologist's eyes picked out recognizable details: the mass floating in the center of the atrium must be a conglomerate of food.

She was within a few meters of it now and asked, "They send any distress signals?"

"None. Why?"

"Food, belongings, burners still on. They left in a hell of a hurry. Something was really dis-fucking-stressing." Her flashlight's beam crossed its surface. Shards of bone glistened between globs of gray-brown fat. Shreds of spare clothing and chucks of slippery purple meat. *Oh no.* Screaming, she twisted, trying to claw herself onto a different trajectory.

"Bently!"

"They didn't leave at all." She groaned through her comm, one hand pounding uselessly at her propulsion belt. The curve of a human orbital arch jutted from the pulpy surface, cradling a lidless, ruptured eyeball. A second before she collided with the mass of spoiled human flesh her brain registered one thing: their eyes had been blue. Nel vomited into her space suit.

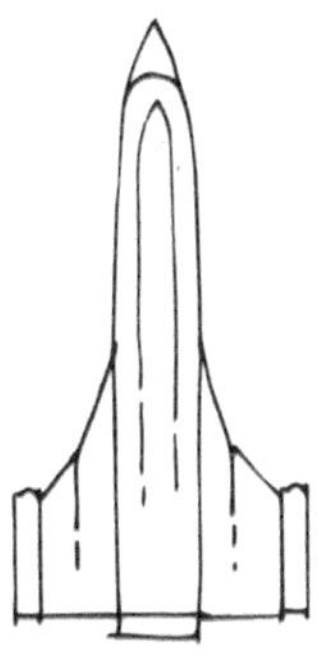

EIGHTEEN

"I'm helping," Nel insisted, wiping out her helmet for a fourth time. Her hands wouldn't stop shaking. Markham and Casey were still in the bowels of the ship, their patient blessedly mechanical. Lem was already on their way to the atrium with the first load of body bags and cataloging equipment. The rest of *The Recursive* rotated above them, blissfully unaware of what they had found. "I've experience with human remains. I did a stint with a mass grave site." *Those bodies were decades old and you were only there to bone the field director at the time.* She growled, shoving the memory away. "I know what I'm looking at."

"And clearly you still don't have the stomach for it." Dr. Morchek secured another vacuum-packed stack of body bags onto the hover cart with an utter lack of expression. "We've got it from here."

"You didn't see what I did."

"I've seen the dead before, Dr. Bently. In all manner of indignity."

She stood, giving her helmet a reluctant sniff. She could still smell the bite of bile through the cloying antiseptic. "If you walk in there and don't feel ill, then you're a damn monster. I'd like to help. I need," she cleared her suddenly tight throat, "I need to help. I found them, after all."

"Bently, they're gone, you can't help," Dar insisted. "They're bodies."

"Bodies. Just bodies?" She sneered as she stalked toward him. "We care for our dead! When was the last time you lost someone?" Nel snapped, before she could think better of the words.

Dar's face lit with fury, an utter blaze of grief and righteousness. "You irresponsible, ignorant bitch—"

She barreled on, too angry to apologize and too guilty to back down. "You people are utterly fucked. I get that out here you've got nothing to do but stare at the black void outside and contemplate doom, but I don't believe that for one second you actually believe that bullshit. There are people in there. Even if they don't look like it anymore. I don't know what happens when we croak any more than you do, but I do know that those bodies, as you put it, are all that's left of 378 living, breathing people. Their cooks, their medics. Their techs and mechanics. For fuck's sake, the month-old baby. Now you can pretend I'm a squeamish girlie who can't handle the ugly job we're about to do, but the only thing my vomiting tells me is that I still have a fucking heart." She glared back and crossed her arms. "I know you lost Paul and your uncle, and what I said was shitty. But you aren't my commanding officer. Out here, you aren't anyone's. I'm going back there and doing what's right. And neither you nor Dr. Morchek can do a fucking thing to stop me."

She shoved her helmet back on and tapped her comm without looking back. "If any of you are capable of pulling your massive heads from your assholes, there's actual work to be done."

Thankfully, neither were fast enough to catch up with her during the long winding journey back to the gruesome scene. She couldn't handle the awkwardness, and it gave her a few minutes to quietly sob. Dar was lucky enough to remain on *The Recursive.* His residual authority at least made logistics easier.

At the atrium entrance, she gripped her recharged propulsion belt's controls and hummed out toward the center of the room. This time she was prepared, technically, for the sight of almost four hundred human corpses fused and melted beyond recognition of anything other than once-alive. Flashlight beams cut gouges of visceral red through the mechanical twilight. She drew up at some arbitrary spot, one her subconscious chose perhaps because it looked the least human. This time, her stomach had nothing left to lose.

A minute later Dr. Morchek paused at the mouth of the atrium, peering against the darkness. In the dim light, his orbital scanning device glowed a faint pink. "Holy Mary full of grace." The doctor drew closer. "I do see some skeletal fragments but many—most, I'd argue—are destroyed. It's almost as if they were..."

"Melted?" she hazarded.

"But while the flesh itself is damaged, it's not burned. Or cauterized. Or even corroded. Simply altered."

"Transformed." She whispered it to herself, not daring to voice it over the comms. Whatever it was she had heard in the darkness, she refused to give it more life than it had already claimed.

"Forgive me, Dr. Bently. I was callous earlier. This is horrific."

Dar's leaden voice cut through the apology. "I have a transport team here. They're headed your way to move individuals to our morgue. Should I prep the other ships?"

Nel glanced over at Dr. Morchek. "Is there any hope of actually cataloging them?"

"Not physically, I fear. Genetically, if we spend weeks on it. Komodor Muda, have them wait. We'll radio when we have extricated...when we're ready."

Nel eyed the contraption attached to the brow of his helm. "Your ocular scanner gadget, how deeply does it penetrate?"

"It's made for the depth of a single body—albeit large ones included. But this mass must be hundreds of meters across."

"About two-fifty, actually."

He looked up. "Is that a suit augmentation or biomech?"

"Um, it's the grid on my helm's glass, if that's what you mean. You don't have one?"

"Mine's optimized for surgical and triage. I think the forensic and field medic suits have something similar though."

"Huh," she muttered. It was inane, and hardly a topic she particularly cared about. Which made it the perfect distraction from what they were about to do. Stealing herself, she reached toward the surface of the flesh. "You know, at first I thought the suits were a fucking nightmare—way too tight, creepy when they talk in your head, material has a weird texture. But the more I use them and see all the custom things, they're kinda neat. Wouldn't mind a coat or something though, somehow still feel naked."

Morchek snorted. "Why do you think all the officers and surgeons wear robes and lab coats?"

"Figured it was for dramatic effect."

"Maybe in Nalawangsa's case—"

"You know I can hear you, right?" Dar snapped.

They both lapsed into awkward silence, but Nel chuckled weakly. Over the next few hours she and Dr. Morchek extracted, pried, ripped what identifiable pieces they could from the mass, photographing, cataloging, and scanning them before each piece was sealed and settled into a body bag. Already the bags brimmed with viscera and shattered bones. They spoke or they didn't, the silence in between growing longer as their energy faded.

It was past midnight when Nel crumpled onto a seat beside the service elevator exit on *The Recursive*'s topmost deck. She dropped her head in her hands. The smell of her puke still remained and, with her helmet off, the pervasive stench that must have filled the atrium emanated from her space suit. Her stomach no longer seemed to care and even the edges of her pounding heart were crisp with apathy. "I don't know if I can do this anymore," she muttered.

"How many are left?" The bench creaked as Emilio settled beside her. He looked as exhausted as she felt, helping the transport teams ferry bodies through service halls and maintenance shafts while Dar figured out how to explain this to the rest of the fleet.

"That was the last of them. I just mean...all of this."

He was silent for a moment, then looked down at his clasped hands. "You don't have to. No one asked you to do this, and no one would fault you for refusing."

She snorted. "I'm pretty sure Dar did ask and would most certainly fault me for anything he could."

"Dar didn't see what you did. Most of us didn't. And won't. I spent years trying to scare you off our land and know better than most that if something's enough to shake you, it's bad."

She tried a smile, but judging by the unwavering concern on his features, it wasn't convincing. "All those people. Reduced to—to that." The last word came out more of a moan than a proper word. "Losing my dad was the worst thing that happened to me. And then Mikey. And then Paul—though I didn't know him—those images are gonna loop in this brain of mine forever. Same with Gretta and Moe and probably a bunch of other stuff that doesn't even register as trauma anymore by comparison. But today?"

Another officer, someone from the relief team whose name Nel couldn't recall, staggered out of the elevator and began the laborious process of removing their suit. Nel shook her head. The mere thought of what she saw sent another jerk through her guts. Maybe her stomach did still care. "What turns every single person on that boat into something I can't even recognize?"

"Not every single person," the new officer rasped.

Nel's head snapped up. "What?"

"Got another body. 'Cept this one's still breathing."

She grabbed her crutch and lurched upright, but Emilio pressed a firm hand against her shoulder.

"Chair," he suggested, dragging hers from the personal effects cubicle along the wall of the decon room. "And home."

"Emilio—"

"No." He slipped into Spanish and his tone grew tired. "Whoever they are will undergo a hundred medical tests and be swarmed with questions, if they're even conscious at all. You going up there now won't be helpful for the mission, for them, or even you, Bently. You need to go home. To your mother. You need to eat, though you won't want to, then rest. And," his face wrinkled in distaste, "for the love of God, bathe."

"Don't think I'll ever be able to bathe enough, honestly." Her laugh was a habit, the muscle pathway dangerously too close to a sob. She dragged a sweaty hand through her matted hair and bit back the rest of her feelings. "Okay. In the morning though."

His hand rested on hers for a beat, squeezed. Then he stepped back with a nod and let her pass. "In the morning."

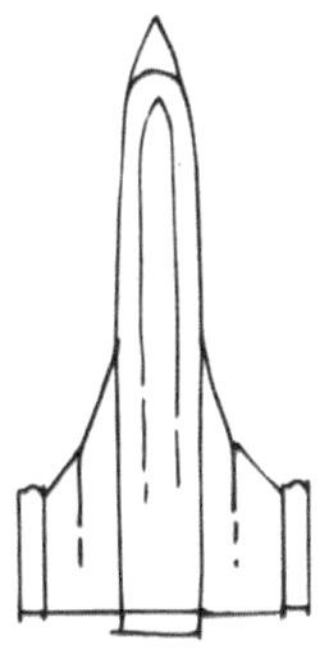

NINETEEN

Only the kitchenette light illuminated the apartment. Every few seconds it flickered, guttering as their limited energy supplies were reprioritized. Nel slumped, head hanging, on the couch where she'd collapsed three hours earlier. She had unfastened the top button on her electrosuit but couldn't bring herself to do more. Even without her atmo helm, whispers persisted. She no longer knew whether they came from the surrounding air, her own terrors, or her heart's longing for the terrible, twisted, beautiful woman hunting them across the stars. Their hold was filled with bodies; their plans were filled with holes. After years of being in over her head, she longed to drown.

"Hey, honey," Mindi chirped from the doorway as she returned from her resource management shift. She glanced up, slipping off her shoes, and paused. "Anna?"

Words wouldn't squeeze through the emotions clogging Nel's every pore. She swallowed, then swallowed again, but could only drag her gaze as far as her mother's hands.

Mindi's bag dropped to the floor. Wordlessly, she set the rehydrator to make tea, then disappeared into Nel's room, returning a moment later with a stack of clean clothes and Nel's toiletry kit. Only after the clothes and kit were deposited in the bathroom did she crouch down beside her daughter. "I'm making tea. Let's get this off, then into the shower with you."

Nel didn't have the will to nod.

Mindi was all business, unclipping what she could of the electrosuit and undoing the straps on Nel's boots. Freed from the worst of it, Nel dragged herself out of the sweat-stiff fabric, too exhausted to even care about the appalling gym-bag stench of anxiety, decomp, and vomit. She staggered into the bathroom, tugging her leg's wires off with reckless apathy before rolling the silicone down and stripping away her tank and boxers. She held them over the chute to the incinerator for a moment, swaying, but four changes of clothes weren't enough to permit destroying this pair. Groaning, she dropped them into the laundry receptacle instead and lurched into the shower.

She'd been good about using the cleanser during their rationing, but some stenches warranted actual hot water. Whatever the next few days brought, she would meet it smelling not like a body bag. Every emotion was distant, reaching her psyche from what felt like lightyears away. Gratitude for the bars helping her stay upright. For the blistering heat of precious water. For the faint sounds of her mother in the next room. For the fact that, for now, none of them were tucked into the black stillness of the morgue.

Water poured over her sweaty hair and shoulders as she washed one-handed. She managed in the gym or during PT, but she wasn't about to risk concussion number whatever balancing in the shower. Clean of sweat and soap, she allowed herself the luxury of a moment under the hot water, surrendering to the pounding heat and muffling steam. Her eyes traced the swirls in the recycled plastic of the wall, picking out shapes that almost looked like Lin's features.

"I'll let you finish washing." The memory of Lin's voice was as haunting as Mikey's ghost and far more insidious. At least his voice never bugged her in the shower. Frustrated, she pressed her aching hands into the colorful play of bruises blooming from her ill-fitting suit. She sank into the pain until it surrounded her. Until she couldn't tell where the physical burn ended and the emotional inferno began.

A tinny beep cut through the miasma of steam and feelings, a reminder that water rations still existed, even if normalcy never would again. Muscle memory dragged her through drying, dressing, but she only got as far as the doorway to their living area before her will stalled again.

Mindi simply looked up and pointed to the waiting chair. "Tea's ready."

The words mobilized Nel enough to take the seat and cup her water-pruned hands around the warm plastic. Gradually, she became aware Mindi was speaking. Soft, almost a murmur, staring at her own tea.

"...and it's funny, because she really does act just like the woman at the library back home, though they look nothing alike. Thankfully she's on leave for the next two days. At least we're not busy. Oh, I meant to tell you, one of the transport guys had a cousin who worked with you, apparently. Small world..."

Nel listened. The words were preciously meaningless. The stories gossipy and inane. Tension in her jaw eased, her shoulders settled a tad lower. Every time Nel well and truly lost her shit, Mindi slid a cup of tea over and begin a gentle litany of unimportant small talk until Nel felt grounded enough to speak. Mindi's latest update on the member of her book club who started a fling with a much younger man, petered into quiet.

It began with a sip, then a second. Nel's voice was a disused door, grinding open. The words tumbled from behind Nel's precarious mental barricades. It was too late to bite them back. "Mikey was beaten to death, Mom. I don't think I ever told you that. Beaten and left on the side of the road. And Lin was there. Then we lost my friend Paul. I think he was my friend. He could have been, at least. He died right in front of me. And he tried to—" She glanced up, finally looking her mother in the eye. Her jaw snapped shut. Mindi didn't need to hear about Paul's desperate attempt to strangle her, how his skin ruptured and melted in Samsara's poisonous atmosphere. "What did they tell you about that ship? About what we were doing?"

"It was out of commission. Abandoned after some technical failure. So we were salvaging what we could." She eyed her daughter.

Nel squeezed her eyes shut. While Dar hadn't strictly said things were confidential, it went without saying that starting a panic was ill-advised. *Except if I don't tell my mom, I'm gonna be the one panicking.* A shuddering exhalation wrenched confessions from her chest. "It wasn't a resource mission. We were following some evidence from that asteroid a few weeks back. It wasn't abandoned. There was—maybe it's related to what happened on Samsara, on Earth. I can't see how it's not. Feels like everything is out here. I—" Her resolve faltered.

"Anna, you don't have to protect me, you know."

Nel's heart ached with the kindness. They could pretend it was Mindi she was protecting. Pretend it wasn't her own terror hooking the words in her chest. "There were remains.

Hundreds. That's what we were doing. Examining them. Making sure there was no infection. Cataloging them so they might be identified and put to rest somewhere."

"Oh, honey." Mindi's warm, soft hand rested on hers. "That's hard work."

"Yeah," she rasped. "And I've seen a lot of terrible things, but what happened to those people—" She stopped herself. The nightmares were for her and Dr. Morchek and the rest of their transport team. Not her mother. But the images already crept into the safety of this room on the tail of her confession. Burning flickered in the bowels of her dissociation. It ignited a groan that grew and grew until it tumbled from her mouth.

"Honey?"

"I'm done with this!" Nel slammed her hand onto the counter with a roar. "Dar! Lin! This entire fucking world. They march in and take and take and take with all these pretty promises of technology and altruism and oh-so-fancy eco-fascist bullshit. You know the resources we burn just by running? The energy we're spending on a mystery I don't even really want to solve anymore? The sounds and voices and memories that follow me around like fucking flies—"

Mindi reached across the counter, knowing better than to actually touch her inferno of a daughter. But her gaze settled on Nel like a firm hand.

One. Nel tried to draw a steadying breath, really, truly, she did. *Two.* The gentle scent of rose in her mother's perfume was sickly sweet, like the decomp underscoring the bile-tartness that still seared her nostrils. The decades-old admission tumbled from her mouth like clotted blood and soil. "I'm not okay. I haven't been okay for a while. And even though she caused half of it, I can't help but think everything would be fixed if she were here now."

"I thought you'd be here." Dar's low voice yanked Nel from her fitful, horror-infused dreams. Nel lurched to her feet, forgetting she only had one. She staggered, caught herself on the edge of her chair, and swayed there for a moment as she regained her bearings. The tiny, dark space wasn't hers, but the meditation room off of the intensive medical unit.

Upon discovering her kitchen shifts were canceled for the next week, Nel had parked herself outside the survivor's observation window to wait out the quarantine period. The doctors had placed him in a medically induced coma for the interim. She had fallen asleep watching expressions flicker across his unconscious face. Echoes of fear and pain and once, briefly, a smile.

A yawn yanked her jaw open, sending pangs through her twisted, aching muscles.

"How'd you sleep?"

She didn't answer.

Dar reached toward her, as if about to pat her shoulder. Maybe it was the awkwardness, or the utter futility of a comforting gesture in the face of what they had experienced, but he dropped his hand before it ever touched her. "I can't sleep much either. Not without a port full of sedatives, at least. I imagine what you saw sticks in the mind."

"What do you want?"

"He's awake." Dar's voice sounded ages older. What they experienced seemingly reversed every extra minute cryo bought. He frowned through the open door, hands clasped, white-knuckled, behind his rigid back. "He'll be alright."

"If I've learned anything since IDH got its claws in me, it's this: nothing is certain, most of all whether any of us will be alright. He might live, and I hope he does, but with what he might have seen?" She straightened and began the process of assembling her leg. "Who knows if he'll ever be okay."

He watched as she got settled and unlocked her wheels. At least he didn't argue. "The medics are with him now. But we can go in next. If you want."

"Of course I want," she muttered.

"On one hand I hope we can learn enough to know for sure if we gotta be worried. For their sake, though…" He slid open the meditation room door and led the way out into the corridor.

A gaggle of medics and various personnel bustled outside the boy's room. Dar's shoulders rolled back as he donned his "person of great import and authority" mask. Nel rolled her eyes but appreciated the speed at which everyone got out of their way.

Nel couldn't tear her gaze away from the thin, ashen face. A short mop of dishwater-brown hair, skin an even, almost matching tan. A face dotted with acne and pockmarks. Now that he was awake, eyes wide and movements uncertain, she realized how young he really was. *Just a kid.* "What's happening with the ship? We destroying it?"

"Hardly. Waste of fuel and our guns are far too small to make a dent. Changed its status as a refueling station, though. It'll just be set adrift. Most ghost ships are. Just waiting for the requisitions staff to handle all the resources, now that the pathogen tests are negative. It's a damn nightmare. By this time tomorrow, we'll be moving on."

Nel didn't really care about the ship, beyond dread-tinged curiosity. Her focus hung, heavy with the hundreds of remains now under their care and the weight of a single nervous teenager. She half listened, running her chapped fingers over the display beside the door.

Alexander Petre Damascus, he/they
Age: 14 Circ. (21.8)

Bloodtype: A+

Allergies: latex, butrephanim

"Hell of a name. Wonder what he goes by."

A doctor emerged from the quarantine chamber and caught sight of them. He tugged his mask down, nodding to them both. "Komodor Muda, Dr. Bently."

"Is he stable?" Nel asked, really one of the only medical questions she knew enough to ask.

The doctor sighed, reaching over to darken the window for privacy now that the boy was awake. "Bit malnourished, and his labs show signs of prolonged stress, but otherwise, completely healthy."

Nel glanced from the darkened window to the doctor, then back again. *How is that possible?* Though lone survivors were typically the first suspects, her gut told her that wasn't the case, at least not the whole story. Maybe it was the haunted expression behind his eyes, or the fitful sleep, even while sedated.

"Cleared for questioning?" Dar asked. When the doctor nodded, he gestured for Nel to go first. "I think one person at a time is probably wise."

She balked. "Me? I don't know kids."

"You're the least mature adult I know."

"Point. And your bedside manner is shit." Anxiety bloomed in her stomach. She wasn't very good with kids, or trauma, or really anything involving the normal range of complex human emotions. But for this kid—as alone and adrift as she—she'd try her damnedest. She pressed the door alert and, when the light beside it turned green, she entered.

Pale, wide eyes fixed on her. The cot made even his gangly limbs seem small. Nel stopped just inside the doorway to give an awkward wave and smile. "Hey."

"You're not a doctor." He frowned.

"Not that kind at least. I'm Nel. Mind if I come in?"

"Sure."

She rolled closer and when the door had shut behind her, she locked her wheels before leaning back. She hoped it gave her a relaxed air, but based on the wary expression on his face, it didn't help. "Do you go by Alex or…?"

"Xand. He/they."

"Xand," she repeated. "Nice. And I, ah, use she/her. It's nice to meet you. How're you doing?"

His eyes lidded and he looked away. "Fine."

"Yeah, and I'm the pope," she scoffed. *Shit, bad start.* Maybe they could bond over her juvenile attitude. "I always feel like shit when I wake up out of cryo—even on a good day. This is probably super overwhelming."

He glanced back at her, a hint of curiosity in his eyes. "Who are you? You said you weren't that kind of doctor. So what, are you some sort of therapist?"

She snorted, crossed her arms. "God no. I've barely gotten used to having a shrink of my own and am in no position to offer that sort of advice. I'm an archaeologist, actually. From Earth. I was part of the team that found your ship."

He flinched, gaze boring into the spot where his hands fisted in his sheets. "Thanks, I guess."

She let him have a moment, then nodded. "Kind of hard to thank people when you feel like they didn't really save you at all, huh?" She patted her foreshortened right thigh. "I was so pissed when I woke up without my leg. Like, thanks for saving only part of me, jerks. I'm glad you're here. And that you made it. But it's okay if you're not on the same page right now."

His eyes narrowed. "You sure you're not a therapist?" When she nodded, he continued, eyes still fixed on his lap. "I, ah, I can't remember it. If that's why they sent you in here. I can't hardly remember anything."

Nel tilted her head, torn between asking every half-baked question rattling around in her brain and just letting the kid talk. "I always get a bit of amnesia with cryo."

"Well, I don't," he snapped, then looked up guiltily. "Sorry."

She opened her arms. "Have at it. If there's one thing I get, of all the human feelings, it's being fucking pissed. It's sort of my default."

"You swear a lot."

It was her turn to wince. "Yeah, sorry. I can try to stop, but goodness knows even my mother couldn't break me of it."

Something that, on a face less carved with trauma and grief, might have been called a smile, appeared at the corner of his thin mouth. "It's okay. Everyone else treats me like a kid."

"Kids are people too, I've learned. Is it okay if I ask about what you do remember?"

He lifted one shoulder in an awkward shrug.

That's not a no. "Do you know why you were in cryo?"

A head shake.

"Do you remember that week? The manifest says you picked up a passenger."

Again, the head shake, this time hard, stiff. Under the thin sheet, his chest rose with quickening breaths. His narrow nose flared. Even if he didn't consciously remember, his body did. *Whoever came on board did something.* Whether it was a horrific attack or just some tragic accident, however, it was impossible to tell.

"I remember my dad," he whispered. "He was shouting something."

"Your dad's an engineer, is that right?"

"Was, yeah." He met her eyes, his own as watery and blue as an ocean, and just as furious. "I know they're dead."

"Someone told you that?"

"No, I just..." He lifted one shoulder again, hunched over as if still seeking to protect himself. "I just know. I dreamed of them, you know. In cryo. All of them. They were speaking, but no sound came out. Just blood. They kept rotting. Falling apart, but still alive. Aware. And I—" He hunched forward, shoulders heaving in panicked gasps.

"Hey, deep breaths. In through the nose. Breath in for the count of seven. Hold it." Nel leaned forward, moving her chair to the side of his bed. Patting his shoulder probably did nothing, but it was all she could offer. He still trembled under her uncertain palm, but his breathing slowed. "There you go."

"Why seven?" he rasped after a moment.

She mimicked his shrug. "Don't know. Just like the number. You know, I have bad dreams. In cryo, too, but just in general. I lost a couple friends recently in some pretty scary situations. It's really hard not to see it every time I close my eyes."

"I'm sorry," he offered.

"Me too. I know you don't remember much, but I have a friend who is helping figure out what happened to your ship. Do you think you'd be up for talking to him? He might have better questions."

"I guess." He sniffed and wiped his nose on the back of his hand.

Kids are so gross, Nel mentally concluded. Tapping her wrist, she activated the comm. "Dar? You can come in, if you want."

The door hummed open and Nel glanced back at the kid. "Xand, this is Dar. He might act like a total jerk, but he's here to—"

Xand's face contorted as a terrified scream ripped from his throat. He scrambled backward, as if he could crawl right through the wall and into the safety of the next room. His wide eyes were fixed in horror and accusation on Dar's bewildered face.

Medics swarmed through the door. "Out! Both of you!"

Nel unlocked her wheels, but before she could move someone jerked her from the room. A second later the door shut, silencing the boy's continued hysterics.

Dar stared at the darkened window. "What the fuck was that?"

"Dude, I've got no clue." Nel rubbed her neck. Whoever had yanked her into the hall did her sore muscles zero favors. "You're a raging asshole, but even I don't scream when I set eyes on your smarmy mug."

He didn't even snap back at her jab. Already the injury to his pride seemed to be fading in favor of solving this latest puzzle. After a moment, he glanced down at his uniform, stunned. "They were an IDH officer. Or dressed like one."

Nel faltered, not wanting to voice the other possibility. *Secrets get us nowhere.* She swallowed her apprehension and murmured, "Or they looked like you."

He shook his head, pinching the bridge of his nose.

"Dar, your uncle—"

"I know," he rasped back, head still shaking, eyes shut tight. "I know you're right, I knew it before we even set foot on that ship, I knew whatever this mess is, it leads back to him, back to us, back to my family and our fucking hubris."

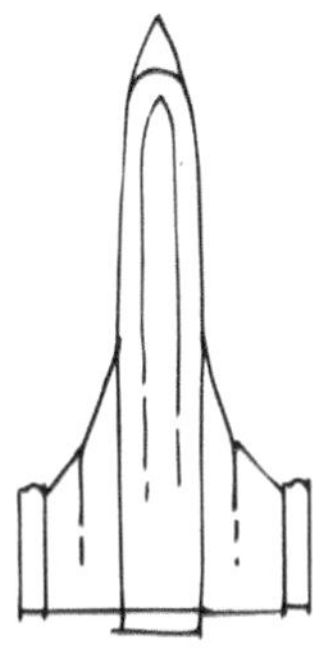

TWENTY

Dar increased the size of one of the screens and scrolled through. Stills of the security footage from the *Drugoye* common areas filled the air. Emilio snored softly on the couch while Dar pored over the data files. After countless attempts to get them to take a break, Mindi had relinquished her living room to their haphazard sleuthing and retreated to the rec room to read. Grainy pixels swam across the backs of Nel's eyelids each time she closed her eyes. She was starting to wish they'd taken her mother's advice.

"Take a look at this. The system was wiped, but the computer keeps a sequestered backup in case of total failure."

Nel glanced up from preparing her third cup of coffee. "Black box. We got those in our planes. Went through a kick in high school where I listened to a bunch of disaster recordings."

"Because that's normal." The pilot's gaze lingered on her, tinged with uneasiness before he continued, "I mean it this time, I think I found something." Dar tapped one of the timestamped stills. Blurry was a generous term, but Nel could make out the ship's dimly lit mess hall. A slender figure, all elbows and knees, bolted from the atrium, glancing furtively behind himself. A feed in what must have been a nearby corridor showed him look both ways before palming open a hatch and disappearing. A second later another figure appeared in the frame of the first feed, all billowing IDH robes. The image shuddered, then dissolved into static.

"That first person, was that Xand?" Nel asked.

"They appear to be. Boarding the emergency shuttle where we found his cryopod." Dar reversed the video a few frames to pause on the second person. "And it's hard to say whether the static was intentional tampering or simply accidental, or even corruption of the files after the fact."

Nel glanced between the paused frame and the unpredictable man glaring at the screen. "And what about that guy?"

Dar's jaw worked. "I couldn't say with certainty. But I'd bet my last credit it was—" He sighed. "He's not listed on the passenger manifest, nor are any other IDH officers."

"What about the new passenger—the guy who needed repairs or whatever?"

"They're listed as Yannis Papadopoulos."

She squinted at the screens. "That mean anything?"

"It's a Greek way of saying 'John Doe,'" Emilio mumbled, sitting up with a yawn. "How long was I down?"

"Just under an hour. You fell asleep watching the transcript populate not long after midnight." Dar's hand brushed over the other man's, though his attention remained on the glowing display before them.

"Anything?"

"Just confirmation of our more obvious suspicions."

Emilio stretched, rolling his neck and shoulders as he took in the stilled image. Like Nel, he looked between their mercurial leader and the unnamed officer before speaking softly. "Have you determined how he got from there to Morphose?" It was a quiet acknowledgement, gentle and firm, and one that allowed Dar not to name his uncle himself.

Wordless, Dar pulled up two seemingly identical scans of the massive refueler, zooming in to the bank of docks.

"I thought you couldn't read maps?" Nel teased.

Emilio glared a warning at her, but Dar let out a weak bark of a laugh. "Fuck off. This one is from just before...the event. And this," he gestured to the second schematic, "Is the one we conducted ourselves."

Nel peered closer, gaze flicking back and forth between the two versions until she noticed the tiny lump present on the first scan, but not the second.

"There. That Xand's shuttle or Papado-whatever's ship?"

"Papadopoulos. For an archaeologist you're pretty ethnocentric," Dar quipped.

"Most archaeologists are. The irony," Emilio noted, though his smile was kinder than the observation.

Nel flushed and tried the name again. "Sorry. Is that Papadopoulos's ship, then?"

"It is. Young Damascus's shuttle was set to launch when the ship's system failed. The same event that wiped the main computer and probably caused—" he grimaced, "probably killed everyone else."

"Lucky for us," Emilio jumped in, "you're required to submit a trajectory before uncoupling from a refueler. He could alter it the second he was clear, but it gives us a place to start."

"Manually altering trajectories in a ship this small is difficult." Dar brought up the submitted trajectory, but his next observation was lost as the corridor lights guttered and they were engulfed in darkness. Each machine beeped and shrilled for a moment until the emergency batteries took over. A suffocating moment later, and the backup lights flickered on, dim and inadequate.

Nel found her fingers were digging into Emilio's wiry forearm. "Blackout?"

"Unscheduled," Dar muttered, jabbing at his comm. "Stat-scan, report?"

"Picked something up behind *Drugoye*," a voice scratched back. "Patching to your personal computer, Komodor Muda."

"Debris?" Emilio asked.

Dar's wrist comm hummed and a blurry horizontal screen flickered in the air before him. His features did not change, but his dark eyes seemed to freeze at a certain point. The image juddered as his hands began to shake. "Bigger," he finally murmured. "And in formation."

Formation? Nel didn't understand half of what she saw blinking on the backwards screen. She was good at maps, but right now sectors and radar were all just a bit too overstimulating. And as much as Dar's face was unreadable, and Emilio seemed caught between annoyance and fear, Nel knew. The air around her crackled with it as if her very electromagnetic field responded to the woman barreling into their airspace.

"She's here."

Emilio's composure snapped. "Son of a—" He jerked to his feet and strode into the kitchenette to lean on the counter, nostrils flared with anger. "Carino, I told you this chase would come to an end—and a bloody one at that."

The pilot still hadn't moved. Ignoring Emilio, Nel took a slow breath. *One. Two.* Coherent words turned to ash in her mouth. Instead, she stared, wordless, at her scarred hands. Simmering fury gnawed its way up her long bones. Dar must have felt it too, because his gaze snapped to hers.

"I'm tired of running." Her words cracked through a brittle shell of fear. Something soft washed over her thoughts. It tasted of relief.

"Turn us all in, you lunatic?" Emilio protested.

She shook her head, looking between the two men. Both once her enemies, they were now the closest thing she had to friends in this feral excuse for a life. "Not all of us. Not the fleet, not *Recursive.*"

"Bently—"

"Just us." Dar's eyes widened, but a smile followed after, and it was his toothy grin, more arrogance than mirth. His lean hands clenched once before he glanced over at his lover. "Mil?"

"We turn ourselves in and what? Hope they let everyone else go? Those are Institute warships. We're fucked if they so much as fart in our direction. We have shields, but guns? *The Yarmouth* is days away and, I hope to God, not foolish enough to come help. The most we could do is fire some cannons, but those are built for asteroids and last I checked the Institute shield frequency—" He heaved a haggard sigh. "At best this is suicide. At worst it's a massacre."

"We won't be a trade," Dar answered, resignation twisting into calculation on his face. "We'll be a decoy."

The Los Pobledores general did not answer, not with words. Instead, he blinked, then let out a slow, soft breath. Straightening, Emilio gathered his things before slipping silently from Nel's apartment.

Dar allowed the rejection a single blink of acknowledgement before his red-eyed focus returned to the array of screens. The image of Mansur Nalawangsa and Xand's fleeing figure and the horrifying past seemed so distant now that a very mighty and present danger trained her reticle on their backs. Carefully saving as he went, Dar closed out of each of the windows until only the flickering radar feed was projected across Nel's living room. Static hissed as more ships blipped onto the radar.

Dar's eyes met Nel's across the chaos of blinking lights and screaming proximity alarms.

"I'm in, Dar. Make the call."

Then the man's fingers were flying, bringing up sector maps and system status bars before firing off half a dozen messages. "Kapten Cress? I presume they've sent the usual transmission."

"Yessir."

"Open a feed between my personal comm and their flagship."

"Sir?"

"I'm sending an updated logistics plan now. Once the trajectory is primed, Dr. Bently and I will board a shuttle. We will occupy their attention until you are clear of their fire. Order everyone to their rooms. Full lockdown. Suits on, every blast door sealed. I want every system prepared for full flight. You don't stop running until there's no fuel left." No answer came for a moment, beyond the voices clamoring in the background of the bridge. "Kapten?"

"We understand, ah..."

"Hail. Them," Dar ground out.

"*Lihifa,* this is *Recursive.* We copy." The kapten's voice echoed overloud through the room, before dropping to just include them. "All you, sir."

Inhaling sharply, Dar tapped his wrist. "What. Do. You. Want. Little sister?"

Stillness gripped Nel as she rolled on her leg, fastidious with each connection and taped wire. The silicone sleeve wasn't the emotional armor of her work boots. She was grateful that, if she had to face Lin again, her new leg would be concealed by the thick atmosuit. Even after fastening the layers of electromesh, however, she felt naked. She had gathered each piece of her gear and was digging through her bag when Mindi rushed through the door. She froze, taking in the glove on her daughter's hand and the thick fabric of the suit.

"It's fine, just a close call," Nel quickly lied. She could untangle the nightmare of explanations and damage control later. All she knew was her gut wasn't often wrong, and her gut said "go."

"Why are you dressed like that?" Mindi's voice was deadly quiet.

"I'm just doing some rounds with Dar. Make sure everything is in order."

Dar's voice buzzed over Nel's comm, too loud to be misheard. "Meet me at the aft shuttle bank in ten."

"Annelise Bently." Mindi glared.

"Mom, I have to. Everyone I have left is up here now. You're here." Nel dropped her helmet and grasped her mother's hands.

"And she's out there."

Nel tried not to think of the sheen of tears across her mother's eyes. She stared at the clips where her electrosuit integrated with her temporary connections. It was easier, even for her Earth brain, to focus on those than the dozens of emotions stampeding through her chest. "Look, if Lin's gonna blow me to kingdom come, I wanna look her in the eye when she does it."

"If you think she's going to kill anyone, I'd rather—" Mindi squeezed her eyes shut. "What are you planning to do about that? Because you should figure it out now. When she's in front of you for the first time since you last spoke, you best be prepared for all sense to leave your brain."

"I'll be fine," Nel protested.

"Anna, you left Earth on a rocket ship without reading any of the fine print for her. Don't you dare tell me what you will and won't do for a pretty lady."

A message popped up on her wrist:

T-1 min, Bently. You coming?

Nel swiped it away. She would make it if she ran. And she could now. "Mom—"

Mindi stepped from behind the counter and wrapped her arms around Nel's muscled shoulders. "These things seem so terribly flimsy when they're protecting your children, you know."

Nel squeezed, memorizing the exact way her mother's shoulders tucked against hers, the strange combination of soft and boney that came with age. "No matter what happens, you get orders from Dar or Emilio or me, or anyone else on this boat, you follow them. We've got some backup plans, but they tell you to run? You do it. We'll catch up."

Mindi gave one last squeeze before stepping away. "I know you. If there's anything you're good at, it's running. I love you."

"Love you too, Mom. See you soon, alright?" Nel backed toward the door, not even bothering to read Dar's next message. Instead, she let the door slide shut between her and Mindi, then turned to the cargo bay and broke into a limping jog.

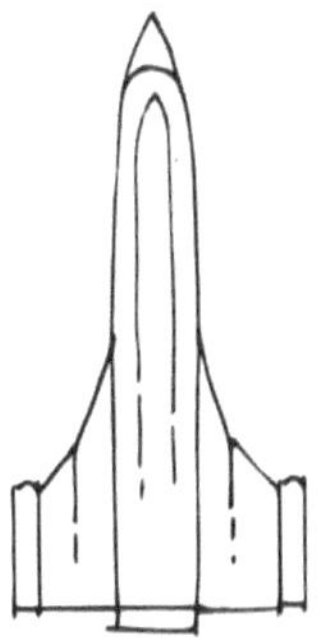

TWENTY-ONE

Dar was pacing in the docking bay when Nel arrived. His steps stilled as she approached, but neither spoke. They stared at one another for a beat. Lights flashed and orders flickered across dozens of screens. Nel followed Dar wordlessly onto the waiting shuttle and forced herself into the copilot seat. The space seemed a thousand times more claustrophobic than when they last flew together, hold laden with a single body and a thousand terrible secrets they had yet to uncover. She gripped the arms of her chair, blooms of condensation fogging the glass of her helm as she forced herself to take deep, even breaths.

Dar circled the shuttle a last time before sitting beside her. His motions were choreographed as he went through the pre-flight check, tapping, dialing, flipping. All but their running lights faded into darkness. Their shuttle's door was sliding shut when a hand blocked it with a metallic *thunk*.

Footfalls echoed in the stillness behind them, and a moment later Emilio settled into the nearest passenger seat. His Founders-issue suit was meticulous and dotted with weapons. Dar glanced back and reached a shaking hand out to brush Emilio's fingers.

"So do we have an actual plan, or is this an exercise in faith?"

Even Nel couldn't find the snark to respond.

Dar gripped the yoke. "Mostly the latter."

Emilio's chuckle was awkward, but it broke the sober terror hanging between the three. Laughter bubbled from Nel's chest, a tearful, joyous sound halfway to a sob. All the hope and fear of the last few months, last few years, tangled in a mass just below her throat. Emilio took Nel's wrist next, hand gentle as he set the timer on her comm. When *The Recursive* was clear, it would send a signal, one only they could feel. Timer set, he began to pull away, but she clasped his hand. "Thank you. For everything you've done. You didn't have to. I'm—" Her voice snagged on the crags of all the feelings she couldn't name.

His voice dropped into the low, rolling Chileno and he winked at her. "And you, gancho."

Beneath them, the engines sang to life, held in check for the order to launch.

Hangar doors ground shut outside, one after another, after another, until the only escape was a narrow square of darker black at the end of their taxiway. The shuttle decoupled and glided out, the hangar sealing shut behind them. Nel leaned forward to peer through the shuttle's cockpit windows. There was no sky. It had been entirely replaced with the steely gray hull of the warship they were to board. What had looked elegant and almost fragile from hundreds of thousands of meters away was vicious, the spire itself almost the entire length of the *Recursive*. Like a narwhal's horn, it made the ship look as alien as it did dangerous.

"*Recursive,* this is Shuttle 203. We're clear; over."

"Ten-four, 203. Countdown engaged. Godspeed; out."

Dar whispered the prayer back as the shuttle dropped from the hull, banking like a transferred electron between the valences of the two massive ships. The radio hissed out docking instructions as they neared the enemy hangar, but the details slid off Nel's thoughts. She traced the lines of their imminent doom, gaze lingering on the name painted over the blasted hull. Her fingers itched to launch every cannon until the sky was nothing but debris and corpses and fire, just she and Lin spinning in the vacuum. The way it always had been.

The forty minutes it took to dock passed in a blink, none of them willing to say more than murmured instructions. Dar glared at the comm, as if somehow they could see the lines of frustration on his face through the layers of reinforced glass and insulated hull. The shuttle touched down, air hissing and rippling as it mixed with the *Lihifa's* atmosphere.

"Welcome aboard, Shuttle 203. Please remain on board until your escort arrives. We look forward to putting this misunderstanding to rest. Out."

At the command, Emilio's face was rigid, Dar's a mask of carefully restrained dread.

Alright, Bently. Game face. She drew a breath in through her nose and held it for a count of seven. When she exhaled, it was in a rush and she leaned back against the network of cargo tie-downs.

"You good?" Emilio asked her, following the line her own eyes traced.

"Maybe she just wants to talk." Nel was unable to articulate exactly what she had heard in Lin's verbal salvo. It had been a long time since they saw each other. And it felt far, far longer.

"But you're still bringing a glove."

Nel smirked. "I learned my lesson about bringing a trowel to these things." It wasn't fully a lie, but the weight of Dirt-o-mancer still comforted her from the narrow pocket on her thigh.

They settled onto the docking track and inched into their bay between a massive hauler and some expensive phallic personal craft. Another loud *thunk* sounded and their shuttle's system died.

"Deadlock," Dar muttered.

"What about—"

"I'll figure it out then."

Nel's gut twisted. She had made a promise to her mother, one she wasn't keen on breaking. Walking into the certain doom of the ship's countdown in Chile was one thing. Her death, her terms. Everything about this was different. This was sickening, a coercion, a violation of her right to choose when and where she flipped life a final bird.

"I have a bad—"

"We all do, Mil," Dar whispered, a commiseration rather than interruption. "We have to try."

"Your door has been unsealed. Please exit with hands at your sides." When gloves were weapons, hands up was more a threat than a surrender.

Nel unbuckled and followed the men to the shuttle door. She let her arms settle at her sides, willing herself not to glance at the others for reassurance. *We're negotiating. Talking. Buying time. That's it.*

The door clanked open and brilliant light cascaded across the glass of their atmo helms. Nel winced, eyes watering. She had forgotten how dim *The Recursive*'s system had seemed at first, as they saved every last resource for their escape. *Suit: darken helm.* It helped, barely.

A dozen strangers waited outside. One, a brute of a woman with what looked like a cannon for an arm, stepped forward and slapped a disk onto the nape of their suits. Nel felt a drop in temperature.

The readouts on her helm flickered into stasis mode. Aside from basic life support, it was no more than a space-themed union suit. *You gonna figure this one out later too, Dar?*

"Hello, Kapten—"

"Save it," the man Dar addressed growled, before jerking his scowling face toward a large set of doors. "This way." The escort fell in around them. Nel itched to snark about the high-tech, low-style color scheme, or maybe remark how flattering it was that Lin felt they warranted that many guards. But her thoughts kept snagging on the fact that in a minute, or ten, she might set eyes on the woman herself.

The guards herded the trio through a series of doorways and broad, identical corridors. As the gravity grew perceptibly stronger, Nel's focus dedicated itself to minimizing her limp, attempting to muffle the obvious difference between her two footsteps. *Does that mean we're going out or in?* If only she had been paying more attention to Lin's tour of *Odyssey*, and not to how the electrosuit hugged the woman's body.

The room where they finally halted was a hybrid between a private office and a small computer lab. Projected screens lined the path to the enormous desk, which was bare save for a single ceramic mug, half empty. The screens, too, were blank, displaying only the flickering colorless haze of rest mode.

Nel's scan of their surroundings ended as she registered the lean, cryo-smooth features of the man seated before them. Months of speculation, countless nights imagining this moment, and she hadn't once considered it would be Harris sitting across from her. The shadow of Lin's betrayal was so dark, it erased the fact that she hadn't been the one leading the genocidal mission in the first place.

Adrenaline flashed, bringing the memory of burning flesh—her burning flesh. Her fury was too loud for her to immediately realize Harris was speaking. To her.

"...and Dr. Bently. I doubt you'll have much to contribute, but I appreciate the gesture, nonetheless." Harris's unreadable features settled into a benign smile. It made Nel's skin crawl. His dark eyes settled on Dar. "It's good to finally meet you in an official capacity, Dar."

"Komodor Muda Nalawangsa," Dar ground out.

As someone who constantly blew professional opportunities to hell with her anger, Nel smelled Dar's temper lightyears away.

"I believe you no longer have the privilege of a rank from the Institute," Harris noted.

"Let's just say I made a lateral move. The rank stays."

"If it's important to you," Harris compromised. For once, Dar wasn't the most punchable person in the room. "Now that we're all here, let's begin. I'm sure all of us would prefer this to be done with as soon as possible."

I'd prefer you done with as soon as possible. Nel forced herself to breathe through her nose. If they were all here, then where was Lin? Try as she might, reason warred with the single-minded fixation that brought her this far. Harris might be a monster, but he was a fair one. *Where is she?*

"We'll begin with terms. Ours," Emilio stated. Where Dar was a taut tripwire of tension and Nel a seething ball of undifferentiated hostility, Emilio was bedrock. Immovable and, at least to an outsider, impartial. "You've been looking for us under the belief that we're, what—the figureheads of some perceived rebellion?"

Harris's jaw flexed, but he did not meet the other man's eyes. He regarded Nel, a panther biding time as its prey inched ignorantly closer. At least this time, she walked into the trap with full intentions of tripping it. "I could pull up databanks of proven attacks on several IDH missions for each one of you and it still wouldn't be an exhaustive list. I promise you, your insurrection is quite more than mere perception."

The part of Nel that carefully curated her CV was dying to see the list of her more recent deeds, but she shoved it aside. *Focus.* Seeing Harris was an advantage she needed to take. At least they might get better answers without the confusion of personal drama.

Where is she?

"Terms," Emilo reminded. "You get us, for whatever sick retribution you've concocted and—"

"And what? In return we let your little ship go?" Harris was still smiling. He hadn't stopped since he first laid eyes on their ragtag group. "I can end each of your worlds with a word. I'd bring every last shred of reputation to the ground, Komodor Muda," he remarked, the title saccharine. "That ship filled with bodies? What will your family think when they learn you blew the life support of hundreds of people so your refugees could rob the dead?

"And Sepulveda. It doesn't matter what signals you send to scramble our tech or what self-righteous plan you've devised to outsmart my officers. You want to escape, go ahead." He gestured to the doorway behind them. "It's not sealed. Your suits are dampened. Your shuttle is deadlocked."

The smile widened. "And Dr. Bently. Since violence is the only thing you'll ever understand: every long-range missile in my fleet is trained on your defenseless hunk of steel. The squalling, desperate scum you've adopted as your new Earth? Whatever bedmate replaced Komodor Nalawangsa? Vaporized."

Nel missed the constricting warmth of her suit answering her fear. Humming rose in her bones. For a moment, she thought their countdown was up, that her suit was telling her they were in the clear. But the heavy dampener still weighed on her spine. A glance to her left told her if the other two felt it, they weren't showing it. "Where is she?"

Harris frowned with practiced confusion. "Who?"

Nel grimaced at the term. "Who do you think, asshole? Lin 'Your-fucking-lackey' Nalawangsa."

"Bently," Dar warned, "I think—"

Harris waved away Dar's interruption. "Oh, she's commanding the strike fleet. You know," he addressed Dar, "lateral move or not, I think she outranks you now. *Lihifa*'s guns are trained on your ship. Surrender yourselves all you want. It was never about you."

Dar shook his head, blinking furiously as he no doubt tried to salvage something from their shredded plan. "My uncle, he was a genius, but a terrible man. Why ally with an absolute megalomaniac and his electro-mechanical dream? Why go through the effort of double- and triple-crossing, of convincing IDH of the value of this project just to destroy humanity?"

"Komodor Muda Nalawangsa, you come from a very sheltered, privileged world. And despite your wealth and connections and arguable skills, your imagination is limited by that small world. It wasn't about destroying humanity. Only the terrestrial definition of it, with all its confusion and clamoring and flaws."

"What part of this mess fits into the Development of Humanity?" Nel snarled, "'Cause to my ignorant little brain here, that looks a lot more like the D stands for Destruction."

"I think adaptation falls under 'Development.' Mansur Nalawangsa saw the freedom of the Teachers and sought to elevate us. In the absence of our earthly limitations we will thrive out here, stretching farther and farther between the stars."

"It's fucking murder!"

"Bently," Emilio rumbled. "Enough."

"Let her. I'm sure she'd like an attempt at buying time for whatever plan of yours is about to fail." Harris waved for her to continue.

She gnawed on the half-formed retorts she desperately wanted to shout, resigning herself to a muttered, "Fuck you." Her tenuous hope was frayed beyond all recognition, and Emilio looked like he was ready to weep. Dar's eyes shone with the panic of someone whose meticulous strategy had gone pear-shaped without a single Plan B. The buzzing in her bones rose. It climbed the electrodes and marrow of her mismatched legs to simmer in her core, in her gut, between her ribs. With it, came the whispers. Distantly, she was aware of Emilio glancing down at his wrist, though with a damped suit she wasn't sure why. Could he hear them too?

"Now, unless Sepulveda wishes to add his own melodrama to this condemnation party, I think it's time we take you three into custody."

"Tell me where I went wrong." Emilio's head tilted, voice heavy with regret.

Stillness fell over the room as Harris's gaze inched up to meet that of the Los Pobledores leader. It was then that Nel realized it was for the first time. "Pardon?"

"Papa gave you everything—I gave you everything. It wasn't an easy life, but it doesn't warrant genocide as repayment." Emilio's voice dipped past its typical polite Chileno. His cadence spoke of familiarity, of the bittersweet intimacy of family.

The thought that nagged at the back of Nel's mind each time she looked at Harris returned full force. *Of course.* His features were familiar because she knew them. Their genetic scaffolding echoed Emilio's. *I lost my brother to IDH, you know.*

Shock was too visceral an emotion to cross Harris's sculpted features, but the spider-silk lines surrounding his eyes tightened to steel. "When did you figure it out?"

"I grew up watching you every day, even more so after Papa died. No amount of surgery or cryo sleep can erase the bones we share. You think I wouldn't recognize the way you move? The way you speak? The way your mind twists—"

The lights flickered. Harris froze, gaze dropping to the tiny data readout on his desk. A vein swelled below his left eye, pulsing. A static whine rose from the blank screens, crescendoing to a multifold scream:

"You unmade us."

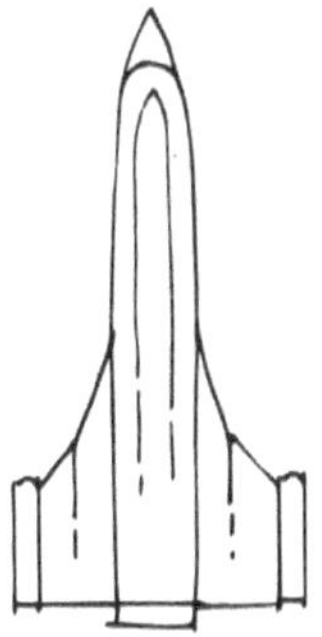

TWENTY-TWO

Chaos descended as the system flickered and died. Energy blasts erupted through the darkness and Dar dragged Nel to the ground. Through the ringing in her ears, Nel heard bone break. Emilio snarled something at his brother as the two fell to the floor in a fistfight. Some things, even among the stars, were universal.

"My glove, my glove, my glove," Dar hissed, fumbling at the disabling lump at the base of his neck.

Nel yanked her trowel from its pocket and grabbed Dar's hair to hold him still. She wedged the metal under the dampener and twisted. Another shove, and the thing popped free. A second's wrestling and her own dampener skittered across the floor. *Paired.*

Heat flooded her skin. Voices howled through her head.

"We gotta get to the shuttle." Vision in her left eye turned white as Dar's electroglove went off inches from her head. The guards dropped.

"Mil!"

"I'll catch up!" A hand rose from the tangle of limbs behind Harris's desk, and dropped with another sickening smack.

Nel aimed her shaking hand at the dim outline of the holographic screens.

Suit: Aim. Fire.

Confirm: Fire?

Suit: Confirm. Override safety confirmation.

Energy coursed through her body, exploding from her palm in a tickling inferno.

Fire.

The blast exploded into the computer bank. It erupted in a shower of sparks and the acrid smoke of melting electronics. They lunged to the door, Dar slamming the limp hand of one of the fallen guards onto the lower panel. The doors opened with a cheerful chime, and he turned. Emilio's face was battered, but he appeared to have the upper hand. Dar groaned.

"He's got this." Nel grabbed Dar's collar and shoved him through the door. "Run!"

The ship's corridors were like *Odyssey*'s: gently curved to maximize the effect of the artificial gravity and clear of clutter. Which made for a highly efficient spaceship or station, but a nightmare for finding cover during a firefight. They raced through the hall, Dar a pace behind her. Nel turned down a side corridor. Her boots lost traction and she went down in a pool of blood and lubricant. The body inches from her scrambling arms had burst from within, organic ribs and synthetic organs jutting outward from their plexus.

"The shuttle's the other way!"

"Too fucking late!" Nel snapped. Her only goal was to not get shot. *Or turned into meat-pudding.* Frankly, she'd settle for only getting a tiny bit shot. Judging by the thud and sizzle emanating from centimeters behind them, it was an unrealistic goal.

"Starboard!" he called to her. "Maintenance shaft."

"It's space, everything's fucking starboard!"

"That's not what—never mind." He snarled, grabbed the back of her jacket, and shoved her into a tube to her left. Then they were plummeting outward.

"Please tell me this isn't gonna launch us straight out into nothingness," she called over the rush of air.

"There's multiple airlocks between us and true vacuum." Still, she saw the pale sheen of his face and wished neither of them had dropped their atmo helms. Maybe they would have helped against the blasts too. *Or we'd be ripped apart by the suits instead.*

"Shit!"

Nel glanced down, squinting against the rush of air pummeling her smoke-burned eyes. Below, the lights along the shaft changed, flashing a sinister orange that probably meant they were about to die or something. "What's that?"

"Emergency stop panel—if someone's falling and their suit—never mind." He grimaced and grabbed her forearms to steady them both. "Engage your mag catch."

Suit: engage mag catch.

The added integration with her leg sure sped up the whole process, but it was still a conscious decision, translated from the more nebulous abstract images that usually comprised Nel's thoughts.

The suit dragged on her body, and she realized exactly how fast they had been falling. The ship was massive. The lights indicating the emergency panel below flashed from orange to red. Acrid smoke drifted up from whatever door had been forced open below.

Dar's grip steadied them. "It's on your right. Try to land on your feet. Be ready to run."

"Run where?"

"Away." It would have been a drawl if his voice wasn't pinched with panic. He scanned the alphanumerics flashing past them. "We're only a couple corridors from the hangar bays."

Something that foolishly looked like hope lit in her chest. A second later, they tumbled from the forced maintenance shaft port. Nel didn't land on her feet. They slammed into the hard floor in a tangle of limbs. *Up! Up! Run!* She rolled and hauled herself to her feet. Half a dozen gloves pointed at them. Nel barreled into the nearest two as gloves fired wildly, but at least they seemed unwilling to shoot at the impossible snarl of bodies.

A reinforced fist slammed into Nel's cheek. "Son of a bitch!" She hit back, wishing she didn't enjoy the resulting crunch of bone and cartilage as her assailant's nose shattered. Zach was right. She had shit to work out. Through the smoke and blood dribbling into her eyes, she glimpsed a doorway and the open bellies of docked shuttles.

A voice, a woman's, filled with fury and fire and certainty, roared from behind them. Immaculate white flashed, a beacon through the haze of electric fires and roiling atmosphere as the ship walls were compromised. *Lin.* Dar's sister stalked them, long strides eating up the corridor. Running after them. After her. For a second Nel almost waited, almost let Lin catch up, just long enough to grab her hand, grab her throat.

A blast ripped through the space between them. Dar staggered and Nel ducked, dropping back. Panic underscored his usually austere features.

"C'mon, drama king. You're fine." Nel kicked herself free with her new leg and dragged Dar upright. He fell into lurching step beside her. Even through the stiff press of her glove, his grip felt weak. She pushed the thought out of her mind and ran.

A hundred staggering steps brought them into the yawning hangar and she wedged herself behind a pile of cargo. Dar crouched, panting, beside her. With the ship on alert, the entire hangar seemed locked down. Guards patrolled the catwalks above. Tucked between the crates, they were far from invisible, but if they hurried—and Dar got his shit together—they could plan their next move.

"Which bay again?" Nel muttered to him, voice pitched lower than a whisper.

"Eight-one-five-two."

She pressed herself against the hard plastic of the cargo crates and eased herself out until she could glimpse the docking bays. "Fuck. It's gone."

"Are you sure?" Dar glared, obviously skeptical of her ability to identify numbers, let alone their craft.

"Between that big ugly ship and that sporty one that looked like a penis. Yeah. I'm sure."

Dar rolled his eyes, breath heaving. "We just gotta find a ship with an Epsilon system or newer. I can work with something a generation or two earlier if we have to but it's gonna be a bumpy ride. Can you…" He trailed off at Nel's blank stare. "It has to have an 'E' or the letters after it in the call numbers. You do know the alphabet?"

She glared at him, not bothering to answer before inching out to scan their surroundings again. A soft thud of tactical boots sounded from overhead and Nel flinched, glancing up. An IDH guard raised her glove, muttering into her comm. Raising her voice she called down, "Stay where you are, hands at your side!"

At first, Nel thought the woman tripped. She pitched over the railless side of the catwalk, landing with a wet thump at Nel's feet. Her face twisted, mouth gaping, and she scrabbled at the opening of her atmosuit. Wires burst through the fabric from some internal integration, flesh knotting in their wake.

"What the—" Dar rasped, shoving himself farther away against the shelter of the crates.

The woman's face purpled, the sight more gruesome through the glare of her atmo helm. Nel's body flooded with the urge to burn, to flee, but all she could do was stare. The suit ruptured, a synthetic clavicle wrenching itself from its seat, rending arteries and muscle until she collapsed. Lymph and blood dribbled from the frayed electromesh and strangulating wires.

Vomit splattered the ground a few feet away as Dar sputtered and heaved.

Overhead a new klaxon wailed and panic sounded along the catwalks across the hangar.

Fuck the shuttle. They needed an out, and they needed it yesterday. She tore her gaze from the gnarled remains and pointed at the line of narrow ports dotting the hangar walls. "Those."

"They're just escape nodes. They have limited piloting capabilities, just meant to protect you in the event of—"

"Protection. Cool." She grabbed the front of his atmosuit and, in an uneven crouch, stumbled the dozen meters to the edge of the hangar bay. A palm opened the port's iris. She shoved Dar in first, ignoring how weak he felt under her arms, then slid in once he disappeared. The chute deposited them in a small round room. Nel caught a glimpse of what looked like a line of hanging bodies, then the port above sealed, plunging them into darkness.

"Suits. Now," Dar rasped. "Both of ours are compromised."

It said nothing good that her first assumption was remains and not a rack of space suits, but she shoved the intrusive, gory thought from her head and yanked two suits free, tossing one to the corner from where Dar's voice emanated.

Panic flushed her skin to almost feverish as she stripped down to the thin press of electromesh. In the dark, she had to feel the rows of bumps and grooves that demarcated the various hoses and wires. Under her hands they were thick and heavy. The bloated, gasping face of the guard above hijacked her thoughts. When her tech turned on her, would the fact that her only integration was a leg save her? Or just make the inevitable gruesome death take that much longer? Would she bleed out through her femoral?

Dar whispered through the helms' closed circuit once she had clicked hers into place. His words echoed with a wheeze that Nel was trying very hard not to think about. "There's a panel by the chute. I, ah, I can't reach it."

The node wasn't in perfect darkness. A dim pinkish gray square emanated from one wall, and she stumbled over to it. "Two options: launch and another launch but this time in red."

"Not that one. Blue one."

A tap of her finger and the node shuddered, then catapulted away. Nel collapsed against the wall, muscles aching at the force. And then they were still. There were no windows or ports. Only the glint of emergency running lights off their suits, and the faint pulsing light beside the panel that said their life support was on.

"How do we fly this thing?"

"I told you," Dar sighed. "The piloting system is limited. As in 'away from ship' and that's it. We're drifting."

"So we just have to, what? Wait?"

"There's probably hundreds of these things in the sky now. We just have to wait until a retrieval team shows up and hope our life support lasts that long."

Nel felt something bubble up in her chest. Glancing down to make sure it wasn't blood from a glove-blast, she realized it was a giggle. She clamped her jaw shut, stifling her manic laughter.

"What the fuck?" Dar snapped, voice thick with incredulity.

"I just..." She shrugged and dissolved into desperate, sobbing laughter. "This whole thing is just such a shit show. Classic Bently from top to bottom."

"I have to agree with you there. But I fear I share the blame for this one," he let out a weak shudder. "Bently. Those two bodies we saw. What was that?"

She glanced over, as if she could see him, as if even in the dim light she might be able to tell what he was really asking. "What do you think we've been running from this whole time?"

"I know all the reports said integrations were killing people. I just...I thought the electricity was misfiring or something. They were just electrocuted. Not, not—"

"Getting ripped apart? Suffocated? Turned inside out?" There wasn't enough in her clenched stomach to vomit, and she was momentarily grateful for the small blessing. Puking in her space helmet wasn't something she was eager to do again.

"The bodies in *Drugoye*. Were they like that?"

"Worse. Unrecognizable, unless you know what you're looking for."

"And Paul?" The question was so quiet that, were it not for the helm comms, she wouldn't have heard.

"Don't, Dar. It was quick. That's all you need to know." Silence stretched on, and she wondered if she should include some platitude to bolster the lie. The temperature dropped a few degrees on her helm's glass. "I know Harris said she wasn't there but—"

"I saw her too. Think she's the one that got me." He shifted and hissed. A chill descended over her, one that had nothing to do with the decreasing numbers on her readout. She didn't want to think about how long it might take them to be found, about what their rescuers might find when the doors eventually cracked open. She should ask if he was alright, if she could help, but her mind couldn't focus on anything beyond the gurgle in his exhalations.

"You know, I didn't think it would end like this, but it's poetic, if it was her that tagged me."

"It's not gonna end," Nel snarled back.

"Anyone ever tell you that you're a terrible liar?"

"I mostly took off before I had to lie." She tried a faint laugh, but it sounded tinny and fake. "What did your parents expect, raising you in two distinct cultures? I mean. Peace is a nice thought. But shouldn't they worry about the rivalry bit? This is why I never intend to have kids."

"Oo you're gonna have to talk to Lin about that!" he warned. "She's always wanted a whole bunch."

Nel blanched. It was not a conversation she hoped to ever really have. Let alone with a woman who swung between infatuation and betrayal like a pendulum. "Yeah, I'll put that on the list right under 'why did you let them try to destroy my planet' and 'are you the space hitman's Igor?' It'll go great."

"Ask her why she shot me."

"Probably because you're Captain Pompous of goddamned USS Scorn. That's why I usually want to shoot you."

He didn't justify her zinger with a comment. In the wake of conversation, the hiss and pop of their comms expanded. Whispers crept in at the edges, the voices calling for retribution, vengeance, or maybe just to be heard. *If I can hear them, why hasn't it killed me yet?* She shivered. The cold had turned from annoying to nagging to bone-aching. She flexed her fingers in an attempt to bring sensation back. "You know, this is the second time I've almost frozen to death?"

His eyes fluttered open. "Yeah?"

Good. Stay awake, asshole. "On the powerlines. When you lot were chasing me."

"I wasn't chasing anyone. That was all Lin's ridiculous idea. Requisitioning IDH resources to infiltrate every channel of the FBI. She basically took over an entire department meant for damage control just to find you. You must have made an impression."

Nel's brows rose. She knew Lin had bent some rules for her, but an entire department? "When we met I was trashed in a bar and called her all sorts of things. Just furious with everything. First time we hooked up I was a mess, it was grief sex. We were on the roof and her eyes were doing that star thing and all I could think of was surrendering for just a moment." She cleared her throat. "Sorry. Probably gross to hear that about your sister."

"As long as that's all I hear." He snorted. "She always had a thing for emotional messes, you know. It's her type."

"Guess I was a bit too messy." Nel grimaced. "I almost got her court martialed. Or whatever you people call it."

"She got herself almost court martialed. Last I checked you were locked in a holding room. She can make her own bad decisions all on her own. Always has. We probably would have exonerated you. Eventually."

"Like you did with Emilio?"

The ghost of his usual snippiness reared for a moment. "Fuck off."

"Sore spot between you two?"

"More like for me. He's compartmentalized the whole thing. He feels the ends, in this case, justify the means. I just think it's even more evidence of how deep the insidiousness goes with IDH."

"No surprise from me." It wasn't her business, but wasn't dating something friends were supposed to talk about? "You and Emilio. When did that start?"

He was silent. Was he counting? "I guess after Morphose."

She stared at him. "Seriously? That's your overture? I thought I was gonna have to break up a fight, the way you launched at him."

"I had just seen death. And then he was there and he touched my shoulder and all I could think of was just..." He trailed off, frown deepening.

"Feeling alive?" she supplied.

"I guess." He shook his head.

"I didn't even know Emilio was into dudes. How'd you figure that one out?"

His smile was faint but wicked. "He kissed back."

"Do you love him?"

"Fuck. No. Not yet. But..." Dar lifted his shoulder only to wince, breath hissing through his clenched teeth. "I think I could. If I make it out of this."

"I think you both could do worse."

Dar's chuckle was dishwater weak and just as wet. "That's as close to a compliment as I'm gonna get from you."

"And don't start with the melodrama. Someone's going to get us. We're fugitives, prisoners of war, whatever." *It was never really about you.*

"Bently, you see that light by the port?"

"The one that just turned red? Why?" Dread settled like lead in her gut. "What is it?"

"Life support. Got thirty minutes. An hour, maybe, with our suits. If we succeeded, then *The Recursive* is sectors away by now." Silence stretched between them for a moment, and when Dar finally spoke, she realized it was sorrow, not machinations that delayed his answer. "No one's coming for us."

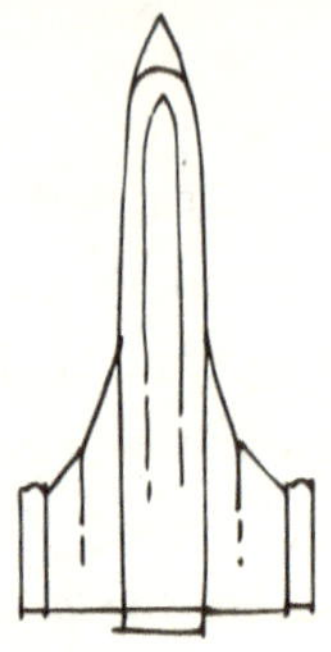

TWENTY-THREE

For once Nel longed for a countdown, a clock, anything to tell her how long they had been floating. How long they might have left. Consciousness waned, every few minutes—*seconds? hours?*—she would shake herself awake to peer across the dim, frigid space to see if Dar still breathed. Her vision had adjusted to the faint emergency lights, but she could only see enough to tell he was ashen, save for his purple lips, which were black with blood. His eyes lidded and his chest barely moved when he inhaled.

Her foot and hands were numb, but phantom warmth crept over her skin with every passing moment. She missed Mikey's voice dragging her down, pulling her onto the fog-shrouded forest path. At least, at this rate, she wouldn't be awake when their air ran out.

The escape node shuddered.

Great, now I'm hallucinating.

A voice crackled through the airlock comm. "Come in, Node 8152. We're picking up life signs, do you copy?"

Nel scrambled upright, crawling to the port and pounding on the comm button. "We're here!" She turned to Dar, crumpled against the far wall. "We made it, man! They'll be here in a second. Promise."

He coughed, head rocking back against the wall.

"Copy that. Stand clear of the door."

She retreated from the door before calling, "Clear!"

A moment later the door crumpled inward, metal and plastic rending and melting. Nel's vision disappeared in a halo of brilliance. By the time she was blinking tracers from her eyes, the rescue team crowded through the doorway, silhouetted by the bright lights of the airlock bay, glass glinting and plasma gloves powering down.

A sob rose from her throat with a bubble of laughter. Nel glanced over at Dar with a grin. "Told you we'd make it."

Her laughter died at the sight revealed by the new light. The floor beneath Dar was slick with blood spilled before he donned his borrowed suit. "Medic," she rasped, then again, louder, glancing between their rescuers and Dar's fluttering eyes. "Medic!"

Nel slumped against the side of the airlock as the rest of the door fell away. She depressed the release on her helm's tinted visor. Its seal popped and she prised it from her face with a gasp. Her breath heaved against the prison of her ribs and she ripped open her suit. The panic still thrummed through her body, but so did fury and sorrow and most of all, relief.

"Take them to detainment. Now," an officer barked.

"He needs a hospital!" Nel interjected, still panting as her lungs compensated for the last few hours.

The officer looked her up and down, then turned back to his second. "That's her. Take him to the infirmary, get him stabilized at least. Put her with the rest."

Nel's relief clotted in her churning stomach. She watched them load Dar's prone form onto a hovering stretcher. The straps that snapped over him looked more like restraints than protection. They may not be suffocating or freezing, but it felt like they were back at square one. *This time with more blast wounds.* "Someone should go with him." Nel made to step forward but Dar shook his head weakly.

"You're terrible in a medical emergency."

It was the truth, and she tried not to let it sting too much as she fell back. "But—"

His response shuddered into nothing, eyes rolling back. His bound body convulsed, blood and clear fluid splattering onto the ground beneath him.

"Shock! Looks like a collapsed lung—" The medics rushed the stretcher away, jogging alongside with needles and bags and a sleek machine Nel hoped could perform a miracle.

"You, follow me."

She blinked and shook the still-fuzzy feeling from her head. The officer was glaring at her. *I'm really not in the mood.* "You want to tell me where we're going?"

His face twisted in a sneer, but she enjoyed the fact that she at least seemed to be successfully annoying. He jerked his head and shot a few muttered orders over his shoulder. Half a dozen guards fell in around her as she finally emerged into the gleaming corridor of their rescue ship. Her heart sank: they were back aboard the *Lahifa.* The walk was short and silent, interrupted only by several groups of guards jogging past in twos and threes. Most looked frazzled.

The officer palmed a door open and motioned for Nel to enter. She sidled past the guard posted just inside and scanned her surroundings. Another door led off to the side beside a large, pristine mirror Nel assumed was a concealed observation window. Those gathered were equal parts civilian and IDH, perhaps those that had seized the opportunity to turn on their commanders. A quick tally of the score of others told her Emilio was nowhere to be seen. Some sat, others stood holding field-triaged injuries against themselves. Yet no one was restrained or wore suit dampeners. Aside from shuddering breath and the occasional muffled moan, it was quiet.

She slunk to a far corner and leaned beside a battered IDH guard and a civilian young man missing a foot. Buzzing rose from her chest and for a moment she thought it was the whispers come to put her out of her continued misery. But this was no vengeful ghost. This was a swarm of hornets, a tsunami of terror.

The boy beside her shuddered and sniffed. Snot ran runnels through soot smudges across his face. He couldn't have been older than Xand, but he wore a hangar tech's uniform. The right leg of his suit was melted and adhered to the crisp red and black skin of his calf. He twisted his leg with a wince to peer at the damage and a bunched tendon bobbed, useless, at the severed end. At least the wound seemed to have cauterized itself. *Is that what mine looked like?* Nel's mouth clenched shut, but when he glanced at her, she tried a smile.

"Lost my left a little while back," she whispered, showing him the battered metal and plastic of her prosthetic.

He stared, then blinked and babbled a few words in a language she didn't recognize, smearing tears away.

"Tech, cut the commentary, eh?" the guard snapped. "She's one of them."

The boy glanced at her, eyes still unreadable, then hunkered down, glowering at his missing limb. The guard didn't spare her a look.

Nel returned to taking stock of her surroundings. It was obviously a medical ward, and while she wasn't restrained, the room distinctly reminded her of a precinct's drunk tank. Her furtive glare settled on the round port of the airlock opposite the door. *Maybe they'll blast us into space.* Nel barely had time to register her dread before the other door beeped and slid open, spilling the scent of antiseptic and a medical symphony of beeps and trills. Emilio limped through, frantic and bruised but surprisingly unescorted. His exhausted face crumbled into relief when he saw her.

She stood and staggered over to him, falling against his shoulder. His head pressed against hers, one hand patting her back. The other, she realized now, was in a sling, pinned between them. She stepped back with a wince. "Sorry. You see him?"

"He's stable. Come on back. We gotta talk." His words lisped over a split and swollen upper lip. Her exhausted body swayed and she was distantly aware that one of the guards by the door was muttering into her comm, watching as Emilio led her through the infirmary door. Medics bobbed about, most of whom Emilio waved away until their limping progress brought them to a quieter spot at the end of a corridor. There seemed to be no triage rooms left, and the shrill alarms and pounding feet were claws against Nel's last nerve. He tapped the pad and ushered her into a private room. It was narrow, but clean and quiet. The lights were dimmed, save for a single bright point beside the extensive panel of medical instruments. The small window provided a reassuring glimpse of their ship, tiny in *Lahifa*'s shadow. Like them, it seemed poised in some strange limbo between imprisonment and freedom, but for now Nel didn't care, as long as their battered home was safe.

"I'm sorry, I can barely breathe through this." He gestured to his nose that, while still straight, was much wider at the bridge than it had been when they left *The Recursive.* Emilio pressed her into a chair and slumped against Dar's cot across from her, panting. "What happened to him?"

"He got hit. Probably by his own fucking sister. We made it to an escape pod thing, but by the time they rescued us he was bad. He collapsed, they were shouting something about a collapsed lung and there was blood, so much blood—" Nel finally screwed up enough courage to look at Dar. The pilot slept, propped on pillows, with his blankets folded carefully over a swath of pristine gauze. His color had vastly improved. Nel stared at his bandaged torso, waiting, daring it almost, to start to bleed through. A squat jar sat on the table hovering at the bedside. It was filled with jagged metal slivers.

"That what they took out of him?" Nel imagined the sharp, twisted edges burrowing deeper and deeper into viscera as they waited in the cold darkness of the escape nodule.

Emilio grimaced, refusing to look at the collected shrapnel. "He keeps things like that. Proof he survived."

"Like a damn serial killer keeping trophies," Nel muttered. She jerked her chin at the privy in the corner and excused herself. The space was blessedly free of a mirror. She relieved herself, then let the water run over her hands, splashing her face until the water ran mostly clear. Hospitals made her nervous, and she didn't know which she hated more—being the patient or standing vigil. Dar's door slid open again and she turned in the privy doorway.

Blast residue and blood splattered Lin Nalawangsa's bone-white uniform. Her black braid was longer, augmented with a gleaming strip of electromesh and wires. Nel had memorized every facet she could recall of Lin, every perfect expression and every infuriating comment. Now, there were hundreds of new lines, new marks, new shadows. Already, the deepest part of Nel, the part she hated the most, pored over every change in an attempt to memorize those, too.

Lin rushed to Dar's bedside, folding to her knees, fingers flexing a few inches above her brother's. She scanned the readouts on the machines but glanced at Emilio, unsatisfied. "He's stable?"

"He is."

Eyes unwavering, she asked, "Is she here?"

Nel considered, just for a moment, pretending not to be there. Letting the twisted wormhole of baggage and feelings and misunderstandings and pain shrivel closed, labeled suddenly Not Her Problem anymore. She could slink back into the privy, hide behind the greasy lankness of her suit-matted hair. It would be that easy. That impossible. She surged from the doorway and raised her arm.

Suit: Aim

Signal zinged up her sciatic along the freeway of her spine and arced to her volar. Electromesh constricted over her thundering heart, warmed her trembling extremities in preparation for flight. *Or fight.* But in all the worlds she had visited, she had never met anything that made her freeze like Lin Nalawangsa. Electricity crackled like they were under high-tension lines.

"Don't shoot," Emilio hissed.

"Not gonna." Her voice had never sounded less certain. Nel's eyes narrowed further. Despite the rebar of her forearms, right raised, left bracing below, her hand shook. She wished Lin wasn't so fucking beautiful.

Lin didn't raise her own glove. She barely blinked. Her black eyes bore into Nel's. Several emotions flashed across her impeccable face. Fury. Relief. Confusion. "You—the explosion on Earth. I thought—"

"You hunted us. Baited us. Watched as we waded through horror after unspeakable horror.

You can only work for monsters so long before you're just as monstrous, Lin," Nel growled. Her voice was thunder, a terrestrial tempest against the sterility of space. "I'd end this whole fucking charade right now if I was cool with war crimes."

Emilio's voice was pinched. "Nel, I know it's hard to see her—"

"Hard? You think it's hard to see her? She's Harris's bulldog. He gives the word, she's gonna blast us out the fucking airlock!"

Lin blinked hard, and when her eyes opened again, they were fixed on Emilio. "We dealing or not?"

"You gave us up?" Nel choked out.

"Does it look like any of us are imprisoned?" Emilio asked, exasperated. "When they hailed us, I saw an opportunity and took it. We needed information, fuel, food, firepower. You two were dead set on suicide-by-megalomaniac, but I wanted us all to actually survive. So I sent her a private encrypted message. It was a hell of a gamble, I'll admit, but I was right."

"About what? Her being a quadruple-crossing nightmare?" Nel snapped.

Emilio groaned and made to grab Nel's wrist.

"Sepulveda." Lin's low voice was a warning and he stilled. She straightened, every movement agonizingly calculated, and took a careful step toward Nel. "You have a right to be angry."

"Angry?" Of course she was angry. Why else did she waver on the edge of thinking "fire" while staring down the one woman who wrecked her world over and over and over again; the only woman to whom Nel had ever surrendered herself, the only woman who, with a smile and a low laugh, could make Nel tap dance into space without a second thought?

Angry was easy.

Angry was familiar.

Lin was three paces away, now two. Furious tears sprouted, hot against Nel's space-chilled cheeks. Her glare ripped across the peach lips, the new scar decorating a blade-sharp cheekbone to the nova of her eyes. A single thought and Nel's world would be simple again. But underneath that single, easy, angry thought was a maelstrom of explosions, betrayal, and several thousand lightyears' worth of distance and longing. Burning ozone rose from the centimeter of air between Nel's shaking, sizzling palm and Lin's starched, blood-splattered breast. "If you're gonna burn, I want to be the one who lights the match."

Lin hesitated, lips working as if to find the right words to fill the chasm between them. "I deserve every ounce of your distrust and condemnation. You've probably given me a dozen chances, even if I didn't know it at the time. But you give me one more? And I'll fix this."

Nel didn't answer, didn't even know how to. All she knew was Lin Nalawangsa was the last person with whom she wanted to negotiate. Were she the same person she had been when they first met, Nel would flip her off and stalk from the room.

"I would burn the universe if I could, Nel Bently." Lin sank to her knees before the archaeologist. A super nova's blaze ringed her eyes like a black hole. "But I'll save it for you."

Several hundred days and a few explosions hadn't erased the mark Lin made on her skin and heart. A single, easy thought, and Nel would be free of the hideous clawing sensation in her chest. But sending her spinning into oblivion wouldn't help.

"Bently, please."

Her petulance frayed at the pain in Emilio's voice. They'd each been through hell and back, and now she was holding her ex-girlfriend at blast-point in Dar's hospital room. She couldn't find the right words, though she knew "sorry" should have been first among them. Her mouth opened but only a wracking, dry sob emerged. With a shuddering breath, she lowered her hand.

Suit: disengage.

"I'll hear her out," she growled. Her vision narrowed with an impending adrenaline crash. "But I'm not trusting a single fucking thing she says, and you and Dar are both idiots if you do."

Emilio gave her an exasperated nod of thanks and turned back to Lin. "I guess we'll talk."

"You hunted us through a fucking asteroid field. You brought an entire armada of warships into the sky above my refugee fleet. You shot at us.

And now you expect us to believe you just what, got a text from Emilio and decided to flip sides?" Nel growled.

Lin faltered, looking exhausted and young and entirely bereft for a moment before the steel of her officer's mask slipped back into place. As she spoke, her gaze moved between each of them, but Nel couldn't shake the feeling that the full weight of Lin's attention never left her. "I should have figured it out sooner. I wish I had. For a thousand reasons. By the time I had my proof I was in too deep to back out. You had disappeared—several thousand people just gone. The only way then, was through.

"I threw myself into the act, clawing my way to the top of Harris's ranks—it's amazing what blowing up your girlfriend does for perceived loyalty. You weren't the only one who was questioning things. I collected rumors, started a few of my own. And all the while, we hunted you. We picked up your trail here and there, some clues real, most not. You guys sure know how to hide," she commended Emilio. "We didn't get our first real lead on you until Tersa—"

"I fucking told Dar that was a stupid idea!" Nel hissed.

"It brought us to Morphose, didn't it?" Emilio remarked.

Lin's head tilted. "Morphose-131? I told Harris we'd get our answers there."

"We didn't find much. A burned-out computer system and, ah…" Nel winced. *How much did she hear, drifting out there on the other side of star systems?* What news trickled from asteroid to ore hauler to security cruisers to independent contractor, filtering up and up to even the highest ranks of Harris's henchpeople. "Jenderal Mansur Nalawangsa."

Lin's eyes went wide. "Is he aboard *The Recursive*?"

"In a manner of speaking," Nel muttered.

"He's dead." Emilio's voice was low but firm.

Lin pinched the bridge of her nose. Her face, so frigid a moment before, crumpled into anguish for a moment. Then, just as quickly, her facade was back in place.

"Look," Nel tried, "we found out some things. About Samsara, about that ship out there that Harris was trying to blame Dar for. About your uncle—"

Lin's fathomless gaze turned back to her for a split second. White heat raced up Nel's body. "He killed them all. I know. It's why IDH was hunting him. Whatever he did, Harris wanted more."

"Aside from his data—which we didn't find, by the way—there's nothing else to be done. We've pored over the footage from *V Drugoye Mesto*. Nel even conducted an autopsy, but unless there's some secret Harris is keeping, Mansur is a literal dead end. You surely have a plan."

Lin's voice scraped over the hard edges of honesty. "My uncle was a brilliant man. And whatever he was doing, it was far bigger than simply sabotaging a planet. Ayah deserves to bury his brother. And he deserves to know why."

Emilio reached out and squeezed Dar's motionless hand. "You're going home."

Lin glanced at their joined hands, processed that new reality with a blink, and nodded.

"So what?" Nel asked, starting to pace. "We find a way to weasel out of this and run? Again? Even I'm getting kind of sick of it."

Lin's pride flashed with a toothy smile. "Run? I told you we weren't the only ones disenchanted. Harris is in solitary. We have enough people and firepower to regroup. IDH has more, hundreds more, but we'll deal with that later. With the exception of a few higher officers who will be dealt with, this fleet is mine. Your ships are welcome among us, should those aboard wish. Think about it all you want," Lin offered, turning on her heel and heading for the door. "Tomorrow this ship leaves for Virya."

Silence expanded around them and Nel glowered at the two men on the infirmary cot. For once she wished Dar was awake. Then at least, she wouldn't be the one who had to make a terrible choice. "There's one thing I haven't figured out yet," she blurted. "I don't know shit about scanners and tracking and trajectories, but I do know about running and holy shit, we were running fast. How the fuck you find us?"

Lin paused in the doorway but did not turn. "Samsara's signal. I hear it all the time. I assumed I was overtired, at first. Then I thought it was the Founders. Even thought it was you haunting me." She looked up then, eyes blazing. "Samsara's ghosts, they spoke to me, Nel. And they led me straight to you."

Nel was cold and shaking in the wake of Lin's gravity. Fury and pain roiled in her chest and she didn't know why her body was still crying. Every thought just spun back to the sliver of sizzling air between Lin's terrible, perfect breast and Nel's vengeful hand. *Lahifa*'s halls echoed with the aftermath of battle as Nel paced outside the infirmary. Cries of death and miracles went on, a hundred personal hells realized and beaten back.

She dismissed the notifications building up on her comm screen. Aside from messages, the entire comm system was disabled, only adding to the chaos overhead. Emilio held a quiet vigil beside Dar's bed. Lin was ruining someone's life elsewhere, surely.

"Samsara's ghosts. They spoke to me, Nel."

With a frustrated snarl, she limped toward the escape node. The ship was large enough that no one recognized her, but she still ducked her head wherever someone passed. Another two corners and she paused before the airlock. The door's hiss and thud were muffled as it slid shut behind her. Blood still stained the floor of the escape node, and other than the hole rended by life-saving plasma gloves, it was dark and isolated. *Good.* She needed stillness. Silence. Solitude. After her stunt in the infirmary room, everyone insisted her suit be disarmed. At least, without a feed to her biometrics and comm, she wouldn't be interrupted. *No matter what happens.*

The ghosts had dogged her since Samsara, from Bakjeeri to Morphose to *V Drugoye Mesto* and with them a nagging thought. Lin's confession had solidified it with terrible, vicious certainty. The signal wasn't the Founders, wasn't IDH, and if her own battered brain and Dar's highest tech were to be believed, it wasn't evidence that Nel had lost her fucking mind. So, ready or not, she needed an answer. Not a string of additional questions dragged forth by each new viscera-stained clue. The truth.

She raked shaking hands through her greasy tufts of hair and pulled a suit from the rack, clipping hoses and wires into place with hesitancy that bordered on reverence. *Three. Two.* With a last glance through the hole torn in the airlock door, Nel settled her stolen helm onto her shoulders and sealed it shut. *One.*

Whispering air and her own hitching breath filled the quiet space within her suit. She needed to calm down. "I—I am calm." She took a long, steadying breath. The voices hadn't made her their victim yet. She had to trust there was a reason. A massive leap of faith, and she would have her answers. *Or be made into this mystery's latest meat puddle.* A shaking finger turned on her personal comm, disconnecting her suit from the ship's quarantined feeds. A warning message popped up.

Suit: Override.

The whispers were waiting.

"I hear you." Nel stepped into the dark center of the tiny room, eyes fluttering shut. Mikey's ghost had spoken to her for months, carrying her broken heart long after she had given up. Maybe it was time to pay it forward. "I hear you."

"Please."

"You're from Samsara?"

The answer did not come as noise, in the sense that she listened to the words in the order in which they were spoken, or even in the sense that they were spoken at all. Her eyes watered, thoughts dying in a memory of sandblasted orange. *Bone dust.*

"Mansur Nalawangsa, he killed you? Is that what you're trying to tell us?"

"He unmade us."

Buzzing filled her skin, followed by a heavy sense of sanctity. It was the same sensation as when she cared for the dead. It was the reverence of holding an artifact removed from her by thousands of years. It was the connection through time, the knowledge that nothing ended. It simply changed.

The voices came from everywhere, filled with the fire of a burning world. They weren't so much in her head as inside her every molecule, resonating through the thick bone of her skull, bouncing from the interior of her occipital down to her sternum and back.

"We are something new. Something borrowed. A lesser sum of greater parts."

The air shimmered, molecules vibrating as they connected with the sheer force of living, sentient sound. Thousands of lives wrapped up in a cacophony. Pain exploded through Nel's head and she lost all control over her body, systems firing with panic. It was a fraction of what it felt like, she was sure. To have your being ripped piece by piece, your essence converted into pure energy. They were not ghosts. Samsara's people had been transformed.

Nel's eyeballs threatened to vibrate out of her skull with the roar of consciousness. Her mind ached, new neurons burrowing through her gray matter to alter her definition of life. Something warm trickled down her face and, judging by the taste of copper, it was blood. Her question stuttered past bloody teeth and searing fury. "What do you want?"

The answer came as a desperate technicolor splash of hunger against the blackness of space.

"Justice."

Check out this sneak peek at the final Nel Bently Book:

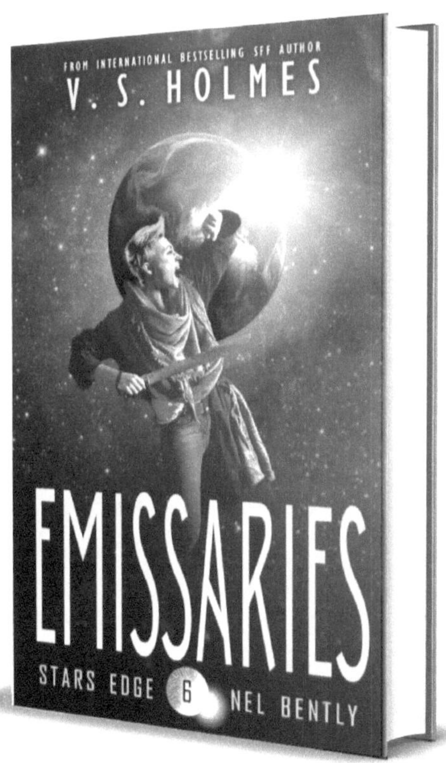

Explore the events leading up to
Travelers through Lin's eyes in:

Disciples

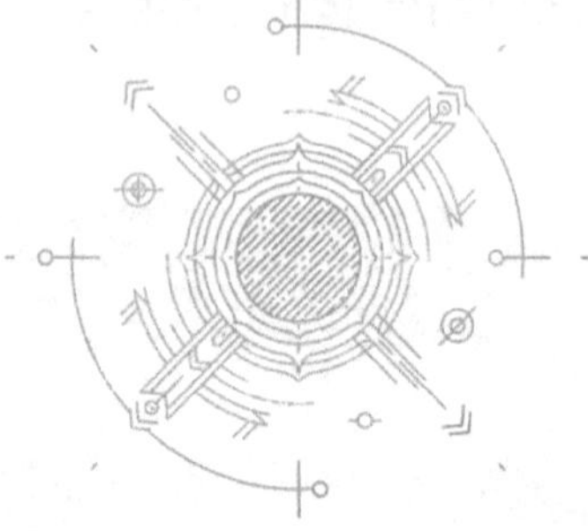

Cryosleep was a temporary death. The lights were dim, a twilight between waking and sleep. Lin blinked and rolled her shoulders, stretched her neck, curled her toes. Viscous stasis fluid drained silently, leaving goosebumps across her beige skin. Nausea shuddered through her. She ignored it. Instead she drifted in the peace of momentary amnesia. The hiss of heated air punctured the stillness. She flexed her fingers and tapped the smooth metal embedded in the flesh of her wrist. "Commence waking sequence in five...." She counted the seconds down silently.

"Good morning, Opsir Nalawangsa." The low voice was male, and just shy of truly human. The lights rose, gradual and faintly yellow.

"Good morning, Phil. Where are we?" She pushed out of her tank, rising in the zero G of her cryo tube. The lights were fully bright now.

"We're in orbit, 437 km from the surface of the planet Earth." There was a pause, and she almost thought the ship's voice held a smile. "Welcome home."

She snorted. "My genes may come from that ball of dirt, Phil, but I certainly don't." The air rolled over her skin, drying as it went. A click and pop echoed from beside the closed door of the cryo tube. She grabbed the vial from the ship's delivery system and held it up.

NALAWANGSA, LIN
IMMUNIZATION LEVEL 2
STABILIZERS
PROTEIN
CARBOHYDRATES
ELECTROLYTES
VITAMINS A, D, B, C
SALINE

She groaned. "What does a woman have to do to get proper grilled fish with her breakfast in bed?"

"When you cure cryo-sick I will personally deliver you a plate of fresh milkfish in bed upon waking."

She rolled her eyes and snapped the vial into the port in her arm. A moment passed then her nausea subsided. Aching in her head ebbed. "How was the trip?"

"Uneventful. You are wanted in Trajectory." Phil's tone often trod the line between a butler's deference and a captain's rebuke.

"Dar?"

"Yes. It appears Komodor Muda Nalawangsa has requested you personally. Shall I tell him you're on your way?" *Probably just to rub in his new rank of Komodor Muda and the fact he's now senior enough to just 'request' me.* "Thanks, Phil. I'll see you there." She unwrapped the plastic from her uniform and slid it on. After seven years of drifting naked in a vat of saline, the stiff electro-fiber felt cumbersome. She flexed her hand, aligning the contacts inside with the conduits tattooed on her skin. A hum. A rush of energy not-quite-her-own. *Paired.* The word wasn't spoken, not heard in the traditional sense, nor was it a thought. It least, not hers. *Increase temperature by 0.5 degrees C.*

Her goosebumps sank back into her skin. She slid the door open and slithered from her cryotube. The lights here were brighter, the snaking lines of green and blue illuminating the stark white of walls and the sharp silver of glass. Her finger brushed the pad in the wall, changing a panel from cycling photos to a mirror. She scraped her hair back and straightened her collar. It was always alarming how little her face changed during years of cryosleep.

"Opsir Nalawangsa—"

"Yeah, Phil, I know. On my way." She shoved through the next door into a corridor. The steep curve told her still-disoriented mind she was on the interior of the ship. A gentle press indicated they were just inside the gravitational field. *Planet-side is starboard.* She kicked off the floor and sailed along the corridor. Other than several bots and the usual techs, the hall was deserted. *Debriefing already started then.* It took days for the ship and crew to recover from a cryo-trip to open space. Longer when they arrived at a planet's orbit. She found the first drop-door to the exterior rings of the ship and pressed the symbol for Trajectory. The ground trembled with the rings' gentle turning. When the doors between the outer rings and a transport shaft were aligned the door slid open. Lin dropped, her grin broad. This was her favorite part. The slight artificial gravity brought by the rotation grew the farther from the core she got, so what started as a gentle drift accelerated into a true free fall.

WARNING: Falling from high places can result in damage or expiration. Engage mag-catch. She ignored the suit for another moment, enjoying the rushing air. Lights flickered past as she hurtled through dozens of levels. She clenched her teeth against biting her tongue. *Suit: Engage mag-catch.* Electromagnets in her suit kicked on with a hum and lurch. By the time she arrived at the door emblazoned with the symbol for Trajectory she was floating. A panel slid across the transport tube and she touched down. Gravity settled over her like a blanket. Even her organs felt heavy. Her palm on the door granted access to the waiting area. Another palm on the next door prompted a cheery robotic voice very unlike Phil's.

"Good morning! Please state your rank, full name, and purpose clearly into the speaker."

Lin leaned forward. "Opsir Muda Udara First Class Lin Nalawangsa, to see Komodor Muda Udara Dar Nalawangsa."

"Accepted, have a lovely day!"

Lin smiled, wondering if the security bot's voice grew irate when you weren't allowed through. The door slid open and she stepped through. Trajectory was as messy and chaotic as the rest of the ship was tidy. The bank of screens to the left showed their past trips, and those of other ships in the fleet. One blinked with a digital scan of Phil's face as he debriefed the crew and discussed issues with other ships' minds. The right was a whirlwind of orbit physics and gravitational maps. Her brother stood within the ring of navigation and communication computers that dominated the center of the room. He snarled something at the image of Phil's head on one of his screens. "I don't really care what the ISS has to say. Our orbit takes precedence. It's much harder for us to navigate then for them."

"Sir," Phil offered, "I think they feel differently. They're expecting a shipment and new crew. Their flightpath has been planned for months, and the weather won't hold forever—"

"I'll show them fucking weather..." His mutter almost drowned in a chorus of beeps that rose from Navigation. "Then put me on the comm with NASA."

"Paging NASA."

Lin saw her opening and stepped up to the raised floor of the Captain's Ring. "You wanted to see me, Dar?"

Dar frowned, but did not look up. He could have been her twin: black, smooth hair, warm beige skin, and deep oval eyes. Their features and parents, however, were the only things they shared.

"I need you to go planet-side."

Lin's stomach lurched. The tingle crawling up her arms had nothing to do with electromagnets or her suit maintaining temperature. "Excuse me?"

Read the rest for free at vsholmes.com

ACKNOWLEDGEMENTS

I very nearly didn't finish this book. Two weeks from its due date to my editor, my entire world came crashing down. It wasn't a single event, but rather the weight of many over the past several years—flight from an unwelcoming state and community, the death of my father, the ongoing pandemic. Looking back, I realize now that I could not write Nel's story when I, too, struggled with similar battles of grief, isolation, and an unseen killer.

Of course, as I stepped back from my writing career, I found countless incredible people who caught me, and gave me the space I needed to find myself, and a new path forward out of this darkness. And those same dear people were there when I, shaky as Nel's first steps with her new leg, returned to this story.

Thank you to the O. E. Tearmann duo for becoming fantastic friends over these years, and reminding me why I write. Thank you to my wonderful editor, Christie Stratos for waiting when I needed you to, and diving into this story with such passion when I returned. Thank you to the lovely queer spec-fic community I've found online for showing me how to lean into the weird, the wonderful, and the darkly seductive with unapologetic determination.

Thank you to Dome (Les Rosenthal) of Sci-fi Saturday Night, for your unflagging love and support all these years. I am sorry that you'll not see the end of Nel's story, but I promise neither she, nor I, would have reached this far without you. Your memory will always be a blessing.

And, as always, thank you to my brilliant partner, Brad. Your love and kindness and resilience are my light in the dark. Even if sometimes you and Nel are uncannily alike.

ABOUT THE AUTHOR

V. S. Holmes is an international bestselling author. They created the BLOOD OF TITANS series and the NEL BENTLY BOOKS. Smoke and Rain, the award-winning first book in their fantasy quartet, became an international bestseller in 2018. Travelers is also included in the Peregrine Moon Lander mission as part of the Writers on the Moon Time Capsule. In addition, they write game content for Stone Blade Entertainment.

As a disabled and non-binary human, they work as an advocate and educator for representation in SFF worlds. When not writing, they work as a contract archaeologist throughout the northeastern U.S. They live with their spouse, a fellow archaeologist, their dog Rory, and own too many books.

www.vsholmes.com